TRIO

TRIO

P.F. KOZAK
DEVYN QUINN
JANE LEDGER

APHRODISIA

KENSINGTON BOOKS
http://www.kensingtonbooks.com

APHRODISIA BOOKS are published by

Kensington Publishing Corp.
850 Third Avenue
New York, NY 10022

All Kensington Titles, Imprints, and Distributed Lines are available at special quantity discounts for bulk purchases for sales promotions, premiums, fund-raising, and educational or institutional use.

Special book excerpts or customized printings can also be created to fit specific needs. For details, write or phone the office of the Kensington special sales manager: Kensington Publishing Corp., 850 Third Avenue, New York, NY 10022, attn: Special Sales Department, Phone: 1-800-221-2647.

Aphrodisia and the A logo Reg. U.S. Pat. & TM Off.

ISBN-13: 978-0-7582-2531-3
ISBN-10: 0-7582-2531-8

First Trade Paperback Printing: June 2008

10 9 8 7 6 5 4 3 2 1

Printed in the United States of America

CONTENTS

HOT PEPPER

P. F. KOZAK

Acknowledgments

Thank you to ML and to IK. Your love and support keep me going. And to my grandfather, who took me to Rip's Bar and Grill when I was six years old, sat me on the bar, and let his coal miner buddies buy me candy. Grandpap, you taught me that sometimes you have to break the rules to give love a voice. *Alla famiglia! Ti amo!*

1

Pepper grabbed her purse and went out the back door, slamming it shut behind her. Her sister had really crossed the line this time. If it wasn't bad enough that she had to come crawling back home and ask for help, Lois wouldn't let her forget how she had disappointed everyone by leaving. This time, she had actually called her a failure, to her face.

She got into her car, which she hoped would start. It needed work. But that took money, which she didn't have. Damned if she would ask her sister for it. She would walk first.

When the motor turned over and started to hum, Pepper breathed a sigh of relief. She didn't know where the hell she would go, but she did know she wouldn't spend another night sleeping on her sister's couch.

Almost out of habit, she headed downtown. Maybe she would run into someone she knew. She smacked the steering wheel with her hand. And what if she did? What would she say? "Oh, and by the way, can I sleep on your couch until I can afford my own place?" Yeah, right.

She drove around for about half an hour, checking out some

of her old haunts. The high school looked the same on the outside. Not having been in it for over ten years, she didn't know if she would recognize anything inside. The public library had already closed for the day, or she would have stopped to check her e-mail.

A new mall had opened on the edge of town. She didn't bother stopping there, either, since what little money she had should stay in her wallet. Then she drove down Elm Street, and saw the sign for Buck's Bar and Grill. Lois told her only a few nights before that Ted owned the place now, since his father passed away. She smiled, knowing she might have just found another sofa.

Pepper parked in the gravel parking lot between two pickup trucks. Obviously, some things never change. Buck's had always been popular with the after-work crowd, the guys stopping for a beer before going home. Later, anyone looking for some company for the evening would drop by, or couples would come in for a drink.

Everything inside looked the same as she remembered, except for the addition of white Christmas lights strung across the room, and the pictures. Paintings she recognized as Ted's hung over the bar, as well as on the walls by the tables. She knew his father would never have allowed the lights, or his artwork, in here. Evidently, Ted really did run the place now.

Lois told her Ted would sometimes tend bar in the evenings, but the guy behind the bar tonight wasn't Ted. She didn't recognize him. Making her way past the men in work clothes and baseball caps, she managed to squeeze in at the end of the bar.

"Excuse me, is Ted here, please?"

The bartender gave her the once-over before he answered. "Yeah, he's in the office. What's your name?"

"Could you tell him Pepper would like to speak to him?"

"Sure will, sweetheart."

He disappeared through a side door for a few minutes. When he came back, Ted followed.

"Pepper? What the hell are you doing here? I thought you were still in Pittsburgh."

"Not anymore. I got laid off and ran out of money. I'm staying with my sister right now."

"Hey, kid. I'm sorry to hear that. Run over there and grab that table in the corner. I'll buy you a beer." Ted went behind the bar. He grabbed two bottles of Iron City and two glasses, and then came back to the table.

"Thanks, Ted. I can use a beer."

"Tell me what happened. I thought you were doing okay in Pittsburgh."

"I was. When my bank offered me the transfer to their headquarters, you know I jumped at it. I had no reason to stay here. I did okay, too. I learned the ropes, they made me a loan officer and sent me to school."

"Lois told me you got a promotion. I didn't know they made you an officer."

"Yeah, well, big f'ing deal. I got promoted, and went to school. My last review was a good one. My supervisor told me I'd probably get promoted again within the next year. Then a bigger bank swallowed us up. They handed me my pink slip and told me not to let the door hit me in the ass. So much for making a better life for myself."

"You couldn't find anything else?"

"No. It's really bad right now. There aren't many jobs to be had, anywhere."

"What are you going to do?"

"Don't know." Pepper poured the rest of her beer into her glass. Screwing up her courage, she plunged in. "I have a favor to ask, actually maybe a couple of favors."

"Tell me what."

"I need a job and a place to stay for a while. I don't suppose you could use a waitress here and maybe have a sofa I can sleep on?" Pepper raised her glass and took a sip. Her hand shook a little. She hoped Ted hadn't noticed.

"What about your sister? She doesn't have room for you?"

"I'm sleeping on her sofa, have been for almost a week. Every day, I hear the lecture of how I should have been a beautician like her. Today, she told me if I weren't so stuck up, I wouldn't be such a failure."

"She said that to you?"

"She sure as hell did. That's when I left and came here. I drove around awhile, and ended up on your doorstep."

"Jesus Christ, Pepper. You'd think after all this time, she would have softened a little."

"Not a chance. You know, once a bitch, always a bitch. I had no place else to go. I thought I could put up with it until I could find a job, and save enough for my own place. But, after today, I'd rather sleep in my car than hear her mouth off to me again."

Ted flagged the bartender to bring them two more beers. "If you want a job here, it's yours. As you can see, business is good. You could fill in on the floor when I need extra help, but I think it would make more sense if you help me with the books. With your banking experience, you'll probably handle the accounting better than I ever could."

"God, thank you, Ted. You've always been a good friend."

Ted nervously tapped his fingers on the table. Pepper remembered he always did that when he felt uncomfortable. He confirmed her suspicion when he said, "We have to talk about the other."

The disappointment welled up in her throat. She tried to swallow it. "It's all right. I understand I can't intrude on your life."

"Pepper, it's not that, not at all. This is more about you than about me."

"I don't understand."

"Butch is staying with me right now, has been for several months."

"He is? What about Sandy?"

"They finally called it quits. Sandy agreed to a no-fault divorce if Butch gave her custody of Stacy. It's over."

"Lois didn't tell me."

"Probably because everyone sides with Sandy. Butch left her."

"Why? I know he loves their kid."

"Yes, but he doesn't love Sandy. He never has."

"He should have thought of that before he knocked her up." She took a good swig of Iron City.

"You're still pissed at him, aren't you?"

"Why the hell shouldn't I be? He fucked up both our lives by getting her pregnant. You know damn well I thought we'd get married."

"Yes, and I also know he still talks about you."

"He does? How do you know that?"

"I live with him, remember?"

"Yeah, you told me that. Shit, if I stay with you, I'll be living with him, too!"

"That's my point. I have the space. My dad left me everything. That big old house is all mine. When Butch asked me if I'd rent him a room, I thought, what the hell, why not?"

"That's how he ended up with you?"

"You know my house is close to his garage. That's good for him, and I like having the company. Can you handle living in the same house with him?"

"Ted, I don't have many options right now. If you have a place for me to sleep, and a shower I can use, I'll deal with it."

"Well, in all fairness, I can't offer that to you until I talk to Butch. He has dibs."

"Yeah, I remember. Dibs is sacred."

"You know, he still does that. He'll call dibs on a piece of cold pizza in the damn refrigerator." Ted took his cell phone out of his pocket. "Let me call him. If he's home, it'll only take him a few minutes to get here."

While Ted called Butch, Pepper went to the ladies' room. She put on some lipstick and checked her hair. She hadn't seen Butch since she left Willows Point. The last time she saw him, he'd come into the bank to make a deposit. He'd heard she planned to move to Pittsburgh, and asked if she wanted to have a good-bye drink with him. She said no. There had been no contact between them since.

When she came back, she saw Ted behind the bar talking to the bartender. She waited for him at their table. He came back carrying another bottle of Iron City and a glass. "I got him. He'll be here in about ten minutes."

"Did you tell him I'm here?"

"I told him you're back in Willows Point. I didn't say anything about your moving in with us." Ted grabbed another chair from the next table and put it between them. "I figure we'll ask him together. Let him say no to your face. I bet he can't."

Pepper pressed her cool glass against her cheek. Her face felt hot. "Ted, before he gets here, I want to know for sure that you're all right with this. I don't know if you're involved with anyone. Will my being around be a problem?"

"I'm not involved with anyone, and your being around won't be a problem."

"What happened to John?"

"It didn't work out. We went different directions."

"When Lois told me you moved back home, I wondered what happened."

"The next promising art student came along and that, as they say, was that."

"I'm sorry, Ted. I didn't know. God, I really didn't mean to lose track of you guys. It just happened."

"This feels like no time has passed since I saw you last." Ted put his hand over hers. "You know, Pepper, Butch isn't the only one who thought of you over the years. I still remember our wild days."

"So do I." Pepper squeezed his hand. "The three of us really had something special in high school. You were the only one who really understood when Butch dumped me."

"He didn't want to. With his parents and Sandy's family pressuring him to do the right thing . . . he caved. He married her because he had to, not because he wanted to."

"Yeah, right. That, and my E-Z Pass, will get me on the Turnpike."

"Look, Pepper, I know he hurt you. I also know one of the reasons you took the job in Pittsburgh was to get away from him. But that's water under the bridge now. You're right. We did have something special together. That's why I think it could work if you moved in with us."

"Do you mind if I ask you something?"

"What?"

"Have you and Butch done anything together since he's moved in?"

"Absolutely nothing."

Pepper scratched Ted's wrist with her fingernails. "So, you've both become monks?"

"More or less."

"That really sucks."

"As I recall, so do you, very well."

"Okay, I'll pay my share of the rent with blow jobs. Is that the deal?"

Ted smiled. "It could work. There aren't many women that can give me a hard-on. You're one of the very few. In fact, you're giving me one now. There's something to be said for that."

Pepper glanced at the locals sitting at the bar. "Do they know you swing both ways?"

"Not really. If I make jokes about big tits a few times a week, they're all satisfied I'm one of them."

"Even with your painting?"

Ted pointed to the far end of the bar. "See that guy down there, the one with the Pirates ball cap?"

"Yeah, what about him?"

"He bought one of my landscapes for his wife's birthday. Says she really likes what I do and surprised her with it."

"No kidding!"

"No kidding. Because I went to school there, I also got an exhibit at Indiana University. I sold about half a dozen from that show, flowers and landscapes mostly. I've even sold a few right here." He gestured to the wall behind them. "All these are for sale, except for that one."

Pepper looked at the painting that wasn't for sale. "Is that the field where you, me, and Butch had our picnics?"

"Same one. That's why it isn't for sale." A few moments of uncomfortable silence followed, as Pepper struggled with the memory. Ted kept the conversation going. "Yeah, between painting and the bar, I've been busy."

Pepper tried her best to keep things light. "Glad things are good for you. How's Butch doing?"

"Butch is doing okay, too, even with the divorce. He's running the garage now. His uncle retired."

"Think he'll fix my car for a blow job?"

"Why don't you ask him? He just came in the door."

Pepper looked toward the door. Butch hadn't yet seen them sitting in the corner. He had his head turned, looking for them at the bar. Her heart thumped in her chest as she stared at his profile. His Roman nose and curly black hair were just as she remembered. He had a suntan, making his olive skin even darker. In his jeans and T-shirt, he still looked every bit the hot Italian stud.

She jumped when Ted put his hand on her arm. "Steady, Pepper, you're shaking."

"Shit!" She took a deep breath and shook her hands, hoping to dry her sweating palms. "Ted, I might need something stronger than a beer."

"You got it, kiddo. I'll get us a bottle." Before going behind the bar, he stopped and spoke to Butch. Pepper saw Ted point back to the corner table and Butch nodded. When Butch turned and came toward her, she put her hands in her lap so he wouldn't see them shaking.

"Hello, Pepper. It's been a long time." He bent over and kissed her cheek.

"Hi, Butch. You're looking good."

"So are you." Butch sat down in the chair next to her. "How've you been?"

"Not too bad. And you?"

"I'm doing all right."

Fortunately, Ted returned at that moment and interrupted the banal conversation. He put a bottle of Jim Beam and three shot glasses on the table. He glanced at Pepper. "Everything okay here?"

"Fine." Pepper hoped that sounded believable. "Could you pour me a shot?"

Butch picked up an empty shot glass. "Me, too."

"Shots all around." Ted opened the bottle of whiskey and poured them each a drink. Pepper concentrated on keeping her hand still and picked up her glass. Ted picked up his and raised it to his companions. "To friends reunited."

Butch raised his and toasted in Italian. *"Cin Cin."*

Pepper offered a weak "Cheers," and then bolted back her shot. She held out her glass for a refill.

Ted poured another one. "Have you had any dinner, Pepper? You don't want this to knock you on your ass."

"No, I haven't eaten anything. I left before Lois finished cooking dinner."

"You'd better eat something, so you don't get shitfaced." Ted flagged down the waitress. "Butch, you want a burger?"

"Sure, and a side of your greasy fries, too."

"Fuck you! You're not paying, so quit complaining."

"Well, hell, if it's on the house, throw in an order of wings, too." His typical Butch wisecrack didn't hide his concern. "What the hell happened, Pepper? Why aren't you in Pittsburgh?"

The urge to cry nearly overcame Pepper. She drank her second shot before she answered. "I lost my job." That's all she could say. The waitress came just then to take their order, giving her a chance to get it together.

After Ted ordered them some food, he told Butch what Pepper had told him, sparing her the ordeal of having to tell her story again. While Butch listened, he focused on Ted, but held Pepper's hand. The familiar feel of his fingers wrapped around hers calmed her. Ted stopped just short of asking Butch about her staying with them.

Ted picked up the bottle and poured Pepper another shot. "I'll let Pepper ask you what she asked me."

"Ask me what?"

With Butch still holding her hand, and with his dark eyes fixed solely on her, Pepper plunged in. "I asked Ted if I can stay with him for awhile, until I get on my feet. He's already said I can work here at the bar, but told me you have dibs on the house."

"You know about me and Sandy? We got divorced?"

"Ted just told me. I didn't know when I asked to stay with him, and I didn't know you had moved in with him."

"What the fuck difference does that make?" Butch turned to Ted. "You got a problem with her staying in your house if I'm there?"

"Not at all. But I thought you might."

"Why?" Butch never had been one to pull any punches. His shoot-from-the-hip style had survived his failed marriage. "Do you think Sandy put me off women?"

"If she had, at least I'd be getting some. We both know that's not the case."

"Then, why do you think I'd have a problem with Pepper staying with us?"

"If you're asking me that, I guess there isn't one. If you both can handle it, then let's try it. Who knows? It just might work."

Butch squeezed Pepper's hand. "Do you think you can handle it, Pearl?"

"Don't you start that already! You know I hate that name. My name is Pepper."

"You can't bullshit me, Pearl. I know that's your real name. Your mama told my mama she named you after Minnie Pearl. I remember when your grandmother gave you a straw hat with flowers and a price tag hanging from it on your sixteenth birthday."

"Fuck you!"

"I also remember that." He tilted his head toward Ted. "I think that's what Rembrandt here is talking about. We have history, Pepper. Can you live with that every day?"

Pepper stuck her chin out defiantly. "I can if you can, Robert."

Ted interrupted. "All right, boys and girls. Play nice."

Butch shot Ted a look that curled Pepper's toes. "You mean the way we used to play?"

"Maybe." He grinned at Pepper. "Chances are good you'll get your car fixed."

"What's her car got to do with it?"

"Her car needs work. Just before you came in, she mentioned asking you if she could arrange a barter. Tell him, Pepper."

"Ted, for Christ's sake!"

"Pepper, what the hell is he talking about? What kind of barter?"

"Since I don't have enough money to get my car fixed, I wondered if you'd work on it for a blow job. It was a joke, for crying out loud!"

Ted laughed. "She also might end up paying me rent the same way. What do you think?"

"I think life just got a whole hell of a lot better!"

Pepper drank her third shot and held up her shot glass. "I want another one."

Ted put the cap back on the bottle. "Not until you eat something." He set the bottle on the floor beside his chair. "I don't want to have to carry you out of here."

"Party pooper."

"If you do move in with us, kiddo, the party is just starting."

"That's the goddamn truth." Butch opened the extra beer and drank it out of the bottle. "Do you have your stuff in your car?"

"No. All I have with me is my purse. Everything else is still at Lois's house."

"How bad was it when you left? Can you go back tonight and get your clothes?"

"I think so. Maybe I'll be lucky and she'll just ignore me."

"I'll go with you."

Ted tapped his fingers on the table. "Butch, I don't think that's a good idea. I'll go."

"Why the hell shouldn't I go? I don't give a shit what Lois thinks of me. My life is none of her goddamned business."

"Lois is already being a bitch to Pepper. If you show up, it'll be even worse."

Pepper agreed. "Butch, Ted's right. Let him help me get my stuff. There's not that much. I sold all my furniture so I could fit everything in my car. Other than my clothes, I only brought back my TV, my stereo, my laptop, and a few boxes of things. Most of it is still packed. I've been living out of my suitcase."

"Damn it, Pepper, it should be me."

"That's what I said ten years ago."

Butch reached into his back pocket and took out his wallet. "Let me show you something." He flipped through his credit cards until he came to the last sleeve. He carefully pulled out a picture he had tucked behind the card and handed it to Pepper.

Pepper stared at an image of herself in a white sundress, her long reddish brown hair framing her face. She remembered the day Ted took the picture. The three of them had gone on a picnic the day after they graduated, in the same field Ted had painted. Ted took his camera. He decided he wanted to paint her in the white sundress. She had posed for him, so he would have the shots to work from. Butch asked him for a copy of his favorite.

"You kept this?"

"Of course I did."

"Why?"

Butch shifted in his chair, then took a sip of beer. "You were beautiful that day." He stared at her for a moment. "You still are."

Pepper's eyes filled with tears. "This was the last time . . ." She couldn't continue.

Butch finished her thought. "It was the last time the three of us were together. I found out a week later that Sandy was pregnant, and all hell broke loose."

Pepper squeezed her eyes shut, trying to keep the tears inside. She remembered being with Butch and Ted that day. They had made sure they went to an isolated spot, where no one would see them. She hadn't worn anything under the sundress. Ted had asked her not to, so she would surprise Butch. The three of them made love on a blanket, surrounded by daisies. It was the happiest day of her life.

She hadn't been with either of them since.

2

Pepper's car wouldn't start. They left it in the parking lot and took Ted's. It was almost eleven o'clock by the time Ted loaded the last of Pepper's things into his backseat.

Lois had been even more unpleasant than usual. Pepper tried to downplay the fact she would be living with Butch as well as Ted, but Lois would have none of it. She reminded Pepper that Butch had walked out on his wife. She told Pepper exactly what she thought of Butch, and of Pepper's decision to move in with two men.

In the car driving back to Ted's house, Pepper apologized. "I'm sorry, Ted. This isn't your problem. You shouldn't have had to go through that."

"Hell, Pepper, what are friends for? Makes me glad I don't have any siblings."

"Before my dad died, things were better. Lois wasn't this bitchy. But something happened to her after that. My mom expected Lois to handle everything my dad used to do. I think she resented that I didn't help her."

"Your mom never wanted you to help, did she?"

"No. I offered to take on some of it, but Mom said she wanted Lois to handle things. I don't think she trusted me with Dad's insurance money. After she had the stroke, she gave Lois full power of attorney."

"I heard there was barely enough left to cover your mom's funeral. Mrs. Kaufmann would have done better to let her younger daughter manage her money."

"How do you know that?"

"The guys who worked on Lois's house are regulars at the bar. I heard about her new kitchen, her new car, and the finished basement. The undertaker told me about the funeral expenses, and how Lois had to scramble to cover the costs."

"Small fucking towns. That's another reason I left. Everybody knows everybody else's business."

"Well, we're about to give them something else to talk about. Does that bother you?"

"Maybe before. But I'm a *menefreghista* now, just like Butch. I don't give a fuck anymore."

"Christ, I can't believe you remembered that word."

"I remember all of his Italian words. Some things you never forget."

"You got that right. It's about damn time the three of us got back together."

When Ted pulled into his driveway, they saw Butch sitting on the back porch waiting for them. He jumped up and came to the car.

"What the fuck took you so long? I was about to come over there."

Ted popped the trunk open. "Lois had a few things to say before we could get Pepper's stuff out of there."

"I'll bet she did. She's always been a real *stronza*. Did she have anything to say about me?"

Pepper handed Butch her suitcase. "My wonderful sister thinks you're the salt of the earth. What makes you think she said anything about you?"

"Maybe because Sandy still goes there to get her hair done."

"Thanks for letting me know that before I walked into the hornets' nest."

"I didn't think of it until just now." Butch set the suitcase on the porch, and then went to help Ted with the stereo. "What did Lois say?"

Ted handed him the speakers. "Before or after she called Pepper a slut for moving in with us?"

"Frigging bitch!"

"Forget it, Butch. It doesn't matter. I'm out of there now."

Pepper took her laptop and an armful of clothes into the house. Ted and Butch carried the rest of her things in. When Pepper saw Butch piling boxes on the sofa, she stopped him.

"Hey, *paisan*, that's my bed. Keep it clear."

"You're not sleeping on the damn couch."

"Butch is right, Pepper. There are three bedrooms. I use the extra one for storage. We'll clear it out tomorrow and make it your room. You can have my room tonight. I have a sofa bed in my studio. I'll sleep there."

"You have a studio? Here?"

"I made over the sunporch into a studio. It gets lots of light, and looks out on the backyard. It's perfect."

"Why do you have a sofa bed in your studio?"

Butch laughed. "Why do you think?"

"It comes in handy from time to time. We may need it when you model for me."

"I never said I would model for you."

"Yes, you did. When I took those pictures, you told me that if I needed you to actually pose, you would."

"That was ten years ago!"

"So?"

Butch picked up Pepper's suitcase. "If she poses, I get to watch." He started up the stairs, and then turned around. "By the way, if you're looking for this, it will be in my room, not his."

Ted turned out the lights. "C'mon, Pepper. Let's go upstairs."

As Pepper followed Ted up the stairs, she remembered doing this before. Ted had the house to himself quite often. His mom had passed away when he was barely thirteen and his dad worked nights at the bar.

One evening, he called Butch and Pepper, and asked them over. She had fooled around with Butch, and with Ted, but never at the same time.

That evening, Ted broke out a bottle from his dad's liquor cabinet. She didn't drink much, but enough to feel relaxed and sexy. Butch sat down on the sofa beside her, and started to tickle her. Ted joined in, sandwiching her between them. Without her realizing exactly how it happened, the tickles became something more.

The feel of their hands on her at the same time made her crazy. Ted fondled her breasts and Butch had his hand under her skirt. When Ted suggested they go to his room, she agreed. She wanted to go upstairs then, just as she did now.

"Ted?"

Ted had almost reached the top stair. He stopped and turned around. "Pepper, are you all right?"

"I'm fine. I want to ask you something before we see Butch."

"What?"

"Do you want it to be the way it was before, with the three of us?"

Ted came back down and stood beside her. "Do you?"

"Yes."

"Well, I think that makes it unanimous."

"Butch does, too?"

"Why wouldn't he? If it makes you feel better, let's ask him."

Ted took her hand, and led her the rest of the way.

Butch had his back to the door, making up the bed, when they came into his room. Pepper laughed. "You're changing the sheets?"

Butch jumped. "Jesus, don't do that! You wanna give me a heart attack?"

Ted grinned. "Butch, Pepper's got another question for you."

"Which is?"

"I just asked Ted if he wants it to be like it was before, with the three of us. He does, and I do, too. What about you?"

"Well, duh! Why the hell do you think I'm changing the bed? I thought that's what we all wanted."

"Just making sure. It's been a while. I mean, we've changed. We're all different, and I think what we do together will be different."

"Probably. Maybe it's like riding a bicycle, and you don't forget how. It's been so damn long, I'm not sure if I remember."

Ted picked up a pillow and stuffed it into a pillowcase. "Which is another good reason for him to change the sheets. I hear his bed thumping almost every night. Can't tell you how many times I've been tempted to come in and lend a hand."

"Damn good thing Pepper showed up, or I might have come knocking on your door." Butch held up his right hand and kissed it. "This is the only lover I've had in quite a while." He wiggled his fingers, then formed a fist and pumped.

Butch's admission surprised Pepper. "It's been that long?"

"It's been that long."

"Damn!"

"Exactly. Remember that old song?" He sang in the clear strong voice that made the school choral director hound him to join the chorus—though he never did. "No one knows what goes on behind closed doors."

"Sure I remember that song. Why?"

"Because, if people knew what my life was like with her, they wouldn't think I'm such a shit for leaving. Now, they'll probably blame you, too, and say we had a thing going all these years."

"I wish we had." Pepper smiled.

"The truth doesn't matter to people, from what I've seen. My own mother won't talk to me. She says Catholics don't get divorced, especially Italian Catholics."

"Well, hell! Like Ted said, we're really going to give them something to talk about now."

"Hey, that's another song cue!" Ted tossed a pillow at Butch.

He tossed it back. "I don't do Bonnie Raitt."

Pepper grinned. "Given the chance, I bet you would."

"I'd rather do you." Without taking his eyes off her, Butch reached down and slowly pumped the ridge in his jeans. "I'm ready."

Ted wrapped his arms around Pepper's waist and pressed his erection into her ass. "So am I."

Pepper's heart thumped in her chest as she said, "I'm ready, too."

"Will you blow me?" Ted's hot breath in her ear gave her gooseflesh.

Pepper nodded yes, and then looked at Butch. "Will you . . ."

Before she could finish the sentence, Butch had unzipped his jeans. "You're damn right, I will." He hesitated. "Shit, Pepper. I don't have any rubbers. I haven't needed them in a long time. I threw out the old ones I had when I moved out, and never got more."

"I have some in my room. I'll get them." Before Ted had a chance to leave, Pepper stopped him.

"It's all right. I'm on the pill. I won't get pregnant."

"That's not the only reason we might need them. Ted, go get some, just in case."

"Butch is right, Pepper. There are some carnal acts that require a condom. If we do any of them tonight, we'll have them handy. I'll be right back."

After Ted left the room, Butch wasted no time asking Pepper the one question she didn't want to answer. "Why didn't you ever get married?"

"I never met anyone I wanted to marry." She refrained from adding *except you*.

"Since you left, you haven't been serious about anyone?"

"I've dated a few guys, but they turned out to be assholes. Who wants to marry an asshole?"

"Then why are you on the pill, if you aren't seeing anyone?"

Just then Ted came back in with a box of condoms. There followed an awkward silence. "I'm sorry, did I interrupt something?"

"Not really. Butch just asked me why I'm on the pill if I'm not involved with anyone."

"Good question. I wouldn't mind knowing that, too."

"You guys are too frigging much! Just because I haven't gotten married doesn't mean I don't fuck." She pointed to the box of condoms in Ted's hand. "Why do you keep condoms in your room if you don't have a boyfriend?"

"You never know when you might need one."

"Exactly! I decided a long time ago I wouldn't get pregnant unless I wanted to. I like knowing I'm protected no matter what."

Ted tossed the box on Butch's nightstand. "That's having responsible sex. Speaking of which, let's have some now. Butch, remember how we used to warm Pepper up?"

"Sure I do. Are you still ticklish?"

"Don't even think about it." Pepper backed away as Butch came closer and bumped into Ted. He grabbed her arms and held her against him.

"Warm her up, Butch."

Pepper hated to be tickled. Both Butch and Ted knew that. She tried to kick Butch, but he dodged her foot and clamped his hands around her waist. When his fingers dug into her sides and started to wiggle, she had the intense urge to wet herself.

She squirmed against Ted with all her strength, but couldn't break free. She gasped, "Stop it! I can't stand it!"

But Butch didn't stop. As he had done so many years before, he tickled her relentlessly. Somewhere in the haze of intense sensation, she felt Ted's erection rubbing against her. She pushed her bum tighter against him, trying to lodge his prick between her ass cheeks.

"Go for her tits, Butch. She's getting hot."

With no preamble, Butch pushed her shirt up. "Hold her still, so I can unhook her bra."

Ted wrapped his arm around her waist and pulled her tightly against his chest. His hard-on poked her as Butch unhooked the front clasp on her bra. Pepper's tits tumbled out. Butch squeezed them roughly, and then pinched her nipples. "Jesus, Pepper, your tits are better than I remember!"

Feeling his hands on her again nearly made her swoon, but no way in hell would she tell him that. She spit back at him, "It's been so long since you've seen a pair, you probably don't remember what the real thing looks like!"

"I fuckin' remember what they look like." He squeezed them again. "It's what they feel like that I forgot."

He buried his face between her tits and licked the deep crevice between them. Pepper moaned. Ted leaned over and whispered in her ear, "Would you like Butch to eat your pussy?" Ted didn't wait for an answer. "Pull down her pants, Butch. Eat her out. That always made her crazy."

"It sure as hell did." Butch unzipped her jeans and tugged them down over her hips. Her panties came down with them. "Oh, yeah, baby! Your pussy is sweet!"

Butch knelt in front of her. Ted continued to hold her as

Butch tickled her labia with his finger. "You're fucking wet, Pepper. You want it as much as we do."

He buried his head between her legs. When the tip of his tongue touched her clitoris, Pepper thought she would pass out. The sensation made her so dizzy, she went limp against Ted. Neither Butch nor Ted slowed down. In fact, Ted bumped harder against her bum as Butch licked and sucked her clit.

Pepper managed to whisper, "Ted?"

He kissed her neck before he whispered back, "What, Pepper?"

"Let's fuck."

"Butch, Pepper says she's ready to fuck. Do you think she's ready?"

Butch raised his head. "Hell, yes! She's soaking wet."

"All right, Pepper. Listen carefully. I'm going to strip and lie down on the bed. You need to take off all your clothes, and then bend over. Butch will fuck you from behind while you blow me, just like we used to do."

Butch pulled off his T-shirt, and then took off his jeans and underwear. "Need some help, Pepper?" While Ted still had his arm around her, Butch pulled Pepper's jeans and panties completely off. She stood in front of him, naked from the waist down. "Let her go, Ted. I've got her."

When Ted released her, Butch pulled her against his chest. Pepper had dreamed of this so many times, and never thought it would happen again. But it was happening. She rubbed against Butch's hard cock, and wrapped her arms around his neck. "I want you to fuck me so bad."

"I'm going to." Then Butch kissed her. She had never felt such intense passion from him before. This wasn't the kiss of an adolescent boy, but of a mature, and hungry, man.

She returned the kiss with equal intensity. Ten years of longing and loneliness bubbled to the surface and boiled over. Pepper raked her fingernails across Butch's back. She didn't care that she probably left visible marks, and may have actually broken the skin.

Butch stepped back, and took a deep breath. "Christ, Pepper, you're hotter now than you were before."

"So are you."

"Are you steady enough to bend over and do Ted?"

"I am if you do me when I bend over."

"You can count on it, sweetheart."

Pepper took off her shirt. When she turned, she saw Ted lying naked on the bed. He had been watching her with Butch, and masturbating. "You've gotten kinky in your old age, haven't you?"

"I'm a painter. Art comes from voyeurism. You didn't know that?"

"I do now." Pepper knelt on the bed, bent over, and gripped the base of his cock. Ted grunted. "I'm sorry. Did I hurt you?"

"Only in a good way. Lick it, Pepper. Make me come."

Pepper felt Butch put his hands on her hips. "One thing you'll soon find out about Teddy boy, here, Pepper. He's turned into an ornery son of a bitch."

"Not that you ever did, *paisan*." Ted slid down closer to the edge of the bed, so Pepper could easily bend over and suck him. "Wait until Pepper sees the porn DVDs you have. We'll see who wins the blue ribbon."

While Butch and Ted insulted one another, Pepper studied Ted's cock. It had swollen bigger than she remembered from before, the veins ropy and purple. The tip had also become reddish purple, with small, clear drops of liquid oozing from the tip.

As she lowered her head to take him into her mouth, she could smell his familiar male musk. She knew his scent. It hadn't changed in all these years.

Butch waited until she had Ted's prick in her mouth before he made his move. "Spread your legs wider, Pepper, and push your ass up in the air."

Pepper opened her legs wider and arched her back. She felt Butch press the tip of his prick against her pussy. With excruciating slowness, he pushed his length into her. She held Ted in her mouth while Butch entered her. It surprised her to hear Ted snarl, "Christ, Butch, fuck her already. I want to watch you pound her."

"Rembrandt, she's gonna' remember this fuck for a long time."

Pepper had a split second to brace herself before Butch's assault started. He held her hips and hammered her. She sucked and licked Ted's cock with the same ferocity. Years of pent-up frustration exploded as the three friends once again loved each other.

Ted finished first. He grabbed her hair and snarled, "Fuck, yes, I'm coming! Swallow it, Pepper, swallow all of it."

And swallow she did. She had to, or she would have choked. Butch continued to bang her while she sucked the last drops of cum from Ted's prick. Once Ted had settled, Pepper raised her head. "Ted, rub my clit, I need to come."

Butch growled, "Yeah, and do her tits, too. Make her come while I fuck her."

Ted crawled out from under Pepper and knelt beside her. He reached under her and fondled her tits with one hand while rubbing her pussy with the other.

Pepper squealed as the two men worked her. Butch thumped her like a bull breeding a heifer. Ted masturbated her with forceful finesse, rubbing her clit hard, but using only two fingers. He remembered to concentrate on the hard center.

The blinding flash came when Ted pinched her nipple. He squeezed it hard between his thumb and forefinger. She started to shake and nearly fell face-first onto the bed. Ted caught her and held her up while her whole body twitched in orgasmic release.

Suddenly Butch yelled, "Jesus Christ! Yes!" If Ted hadn't

been supporting her, the force of Butch's ejaculation would have knocked her down. He banged into her at least half a dozen times before he finally slowed. Even then, he continued to move in and out of her for several more seconds before he stopped.

Ted still held Pepper. He waited until Butch pulled out before he moved. Then he lowered her to the bed, so she could rest. Butch flopped down on the bed beside her. Ted reached down on the floor and grabbed the quilt. He threw it over Butch and Pepper, turned out the light, and then settled in beside them.

3

Butch's clock radio snapped on at seven. Pepper bolted upright when she heard "We Will Rock You" blasting from the speaker on the nightstand. Butch threw the quilt off and jumped out of bed to turn it off.

Ted still seemed to be asleep beside her. "That damn thing scared the piss out of me. How can he still be sleeping?"

"He's never up when I go to work. He says he's not a morning person. Remember how he used to get detention so often for coming to school late?"

"Yeah, I remember."

Butch stood beside the bed, naked. Pepper couldn't help admiring him. He still had a brick-shithouse body, toned and tan. The dark hair on his head also covered his chest. She followed the trail of hair down to his groin. She forced herself not to stare at the erection dangling there. "When do you open the garage?"

"At eight. How about a quickie before I shower?"

"Ted's still asleep."

Butch swatted Ted's foot. "Hey, Rembrandt, wake up. I'm gonna' fuck Pepper. Wanna' watch?"

Ted muttered, "Fuck you, too." He rolled onto his side, and pulled the quilt up around his neck.

"Guess he's not interested this time." Butch crawled back on the bed.

"What are you doing?"

"Aren't we going to fuck?"

"Yes, but here? Shouldn't we go downstairs to the sofa? Ted is asleep."

"So? If the son of a bitch wakes up, he can join us."

"You haven't changed much, have you?"

"Yes and no. Maybe we'll talk about it sometime. Right now, I want some pussy before I go to work."

Butch never had been a poetry-and-flowers sort of lover. When he wanted to fuck, he would just come right out and say so. Pepper liked that about him. She never had to worry about what he might be thinking. He always told her flat out.

Butch rolled on top of her, supporting himself on his forearms. She squeezed his biceps. They were hard as cement. "Damn, Butch, your body is solid muscle. You haven't put on any weight, have you?"

"I sweat it off at the garage, which is where I have to be soon."

Pepper opened her legs wide, bumping Ted with her foot. He didn't stir. Butch reached between her legs and positioned his prick between them. Just before he entered her, he whispered, "Pepper, I've missed you so goddamn much."

The shock of his cock suddenly penetrating her kept her from crying. But the impact of his words shook her deeply. It took years before she finally managed to talk herself out of loving him. Now, he lay on top of her again. They were making love like they had loved before. And he still cared for her. She couldn't believe it.

With each thrust, she tried not to make any sound, but she couldn't help it. Butch didn't even try to be quiet. He grunted with each stroke. She knew he had to leave soon, and couldn't take his time with her. He needed to get off, and she did what she could to help him.

She lifted her legs and bent her knees, so he could ride her deeper. He did. The rhythm shifted, and he pumped himself into her with increasing urgency. When his orgasm hit, his whole body shook with the force of it, rocking the bed. Pepper knew Ted had to be awake. No one could have slept through that.

Butch collapsed on top of her, winded. Pepper stroked his hair, and gave him time to recover. When he had enough breath to speak, he asked, "Can you see what time it is?"

Ted answered. "It's seven-thirty."

"You dickhead! How long have you been awake?"

"Since your clock went off. 'We Will Rock You' seems like it was a good one to start your day."

"You're a fuckin' pervert! I hope you got off on that."

"I have one hell of a woody right now. Maybe Pepper will give me a hand job while you shower."

"Have at it. I gotta go to work." Butch crawled out of bed and grabbed some clean clothes. Then he headed to the bathroom.

Ted rolled over and put his arm around Pepper. "How are you this morning?"

"I'm all right."

"Did you finish just now?"

"No. I need more fooling around before the fucking to get there. There wasn't time."

"I have time."

"You are a pervert, aren't you?"

"No, just kinky. I march to my own drummer. Always did. You know that."

Pepper reached between them and fondled his balls. "I'll do you if you do me. I'm kinky, too."

"Yeah, I know."

Much to Pepper's surprise, not only did Ted slip his fingers between her legs so he could rub her clit, he leaned over and kissed her breasts. Pepper wrapped her fingers around his cock, and slowly started to jack him. Ted stopped her.

"Wait a minute. I want some lube." Pepper gasped as Ted palmed her vulva, coating his hand with a combination of her juice and Butch's semen. Pepper released his prick, so he could make himself slick with the natural cream. "Rub your pussy and make your hand slippery."

Pepper used her fingers to scoop up the residue of her lovemaking with Butch from between her legs. When she again wrapped her fingers around Ted's cock, her hand slid like they had used a stick of butter.

Ted moaned, "Baby, that's good!" He immediately started thrusting into her fist, the way he would using his own hand. Again he leaned down, this time sucking a nipple into his mouth. Pepper's hips lifted from the bed as he slipped two fingers inside her.

They lay side by side, masturbating each other. With sensitivity she had never found with anyone else, he helped her inch toward her orgasm. The nuances of her body movement did not escape him; he adjusted with her. He finger-fucked her harder as she pushed back against his hand. In the same way, she pumped faster as his thrusts became more intense.

When the first waves of her orgasm rippled though her body, she gripped his cock hard. Ted gasped. His cock felt alive in her hand as the muscles violently contracted. Then her own climax obliterated her sense of his. She squeezed his cock again as tremors moved through her. Ted groaned, and Pepper felt hot liquid squirt onto her hand.

Pepper had her eyes closed, and hadn't noticed Butch standing in the door. When she heard his voice, she jumped, almost like when her mother had caught them making out on the back porch swing.

"You two should think about doing porn. That was hotter than my movies." He picked up his watch from the dresser. "Rembrandt, I'll let you change the sheets this time. See you both later." He left for the garage.

Pepper sat up, and wrapped the sheet around herself. "Do you think he's pissed?"

"About what?"

"About our being together like that."

"Why the hell would he be pissed? I said I wanted you to jack me off. Trust me, Pepper. If he had a problem with that, he would have said so right then and there."

"You're sure?"

"I'm sure. What's the matter? We've done this before. Does it bother you now?" Ted propped himself up on his elbow.

"No, it's not that. I just feel funny that I didn't know he was watching. I had my eyes shut. I don't know how much he saw."

"He saw you come. That's all you need to know. He'll be thinking about that all day. He'll probably have to whack off in the men's room before he comes home tonight."

"What time does he get home?"

"Usually between four and five."

"When do you leave for the bar?"

"Same time, between four and five."

"Do you guys ever see each other?"

"Sure we do. Butch doesn't work every day, and neither do I."

"Speaking of work, do you want me to start at the bar today? You can get me going on the accounting. Maybe I can help you with ordering and paying the bills, or if you need someone on the floor, I can do that today."

"Whoa, Pepper, slow down! Buck's isn't going anywhere. We'll get you started in a few days. You need to settle in here. We'll clean out the room down the hall, and see what condition the bed is in. There are so many boxes on it, I haven't seen the mattress in a couple of years."

"Ted, I don't want to sponge off you. I want to work, and pay my own way."

He traced his finger up her back. The tingles made her shiver. "Sweetheart, there are any number of ways for you to earn your keep. Working at the bar is only one of them."

Pepper eyed Ted's groin, where another erection had started to form. "What, you really want me to blow you for my rent? I don't mind blowing you, but I'll still pay my fair share, thank you very much."

Ted grinned. "That's good to know, but that wasn't what I was talking about."

Pepper blushed, but held her ground nonetheless. "Then explain to me what you mean."

"I want to hire you as a model."

"You don't have to pay me for that."

"You've never modeled, have you?"

"Just those times you took pictures of me."

Ted unfurled the sheet Pepper had wrapped around herself. "Lie down on the bed, like you did for Butch."

Pepper looked at what was now a full-blown erection, and licked her lips. "Are we going to fuck?"

"No, you're going to pose."

"What are you talking about?"

"I'm trying to show you why models get paid." Ted pushed her back on the bed. "Open your legs a little more, and turn your head to the side." Pepper did as he asked. "Now put your right hand on your breast and your left hand between your legs, like you're masturbating."

Pepper looked at him. "You're kidding, aren't you?"

"You moved. That's not allowed. And I'm not kidding. Assume the position like I told you to."

Pepper did. "Now what?"

"Now I'm going to take a shower. I'll be back in about fifteen minutes. You're on your honor not to move."

Pepper didn't move anything but her lips. "Ted, what the fuck?"

"You're modeling. Instead of painting you right now, I'm going to shower. But when I do paint you, you'll have to hold the position I put you in for longer than fifteen minutes. This is your job interview."

"How much do I get paid for this?"

"See, you're already understanding why this is a job. It's frigging hard work to model. I've done enough of it to know."

Pepper almost turned her head to look at Ted, but stopped herself. "You've modeled?"

"In art school. I posed nude for art classes. It gave me some extra cash, and got me laid more than once. If you play your cards right, it might do the same for you."

"Does that mean you'll finally sleep with me?"

"Don't know yet. Considering you gave me a hard-on at the bar, another one last night and two this morning, I would say the odds are in your favor."

"Well, that's worth marking on the calendar."

Ted picked his clothes up. Before he went to the bathroom he offered Pepper some advice. "I'll give you a tip. Distract yourself. Think about something that will take your mind off how much your nose tickles. 'A hundred bottles of beer on the wall' always worked for me."

Pepper held the position, even after Ted had left the room. She knew that he meant what he said, even if he had joked about it. If he wanted her to model for him, she would. She would show him she could do it, even if her nose did itch. Actually, the intense itch between her legs bothered her more than her nose.

She couldn't see the clock, so she had no way of gauging how much time had passed. So, Pepper did what Ted said to do—she tried to distract herself. She thought of all the fun times she had shared with Butch and Ted. She also thought of all the other times with them, how they had fooled around together, and learned the ropes together.

Butch always wanted to fuck. Pepper loved fucking, but she had to show Butch how a woman needs more than a dick in her pussy. Ted seemed to know that instinctively, and would often be the one to warm her up for the main course with Butch. Then, Ted would jack off watching Butch do her. Pepper didn't mind. In fact, knowing Ted liked watching made her so hot.

Ted liked guys. She used to sneak him copies of *Playgirl*. They would drool over the naked men together, get hot, and then fool around. If they were alone, they would either sixty-nine or masturbate each other. Ted loved to be jerked off, almost as much as he liked to be blown.

None of the men she'd slept with over the years came close to satisfying her like she had been satisfied with Ted and Butch. In this case, three was definitely not a crowd. The only thing missing was that Ted had never fucked her or Butch. Maybe that would change now that they were together again.

Pepper thought she heard Ted come back in the room, but he didn't say anything. She didn't know if she should move or not.

"Ted, are you there?"

"I'm right here."

"Can I move?"

"No."

"Why can't I move yet?"

"I'm doing a sketch of you lying there. It will give you an idea of what I have in mind. How are you doing?"

"My neck's stiff."

"Yeah, I'm getting another stiffy, too."

"Very funny."

"Do you know, Pepper, you have bumps and curves in all the right places?"

"Thank you, I think."

"Before you move, pay attention to your body. Notice where you are the most uncomfortable. We'll adjust your position for the actual painting."

"You're going to paint me like this?"

"If you'll let me."

"But it looks like I'm masturbating."

"Exactly. It'll be even more erotic if your fingers are separating your labia and you actually pinch a nipple."

"Ted! Who the hell is going to see this?"

"Don't worry. I won't hang it in the bar."

Pepper broke the pose and sat up. "You're damn right you won't hang it in the bar!"

"Pepper, I wasn't finished!"

"Well, I am!" Pepper grabbed the sheet and tried to untangle it, so she could wrap herself in it again. "I don't want a picture of me diddling myself where anyone in town can see it."

"Pepper, no one will see my paintings of you, except Butch—maybe. These are for me."

"What do you mean, paintings? How many are you going to do?"

"That depends. Let me show you something." Ted brought his sketch pad over and sat down on the bed. "This is what I just sketched."

Pepper took the pad and stared at it. "That's me."

"You bet it is. Aren't you beautiful?"

Pepper followed the lines of the unfinished pencil sketch. She clearly saw the outline of her torso, the curve of her breasts, the beginning of her hand between her legs. "Where's my head?"

"This is what's called a study. If I draw you first, then I'll know what I want to do when I start to paint."

Pepper traced the lines with her finger. "It looks like something you'd see in a museum."

"Have you ever heard of Andrew Wyeth?"

"Sure I have. He's an artist from Pennsylvania, right?"

"That's right. He's from Chadds Ford. He's one of my favorite artists. His stuff and Edward Hopper's made me want to paint."

"I didn't know that."

"In college, I took this art course where we studied his Helga paintings. Christ, Pepper, I fell in love with them. The more I looked at what he did with Helga, the more I wanted to do the same thing with you." Ted touched Pepper's hair. "Your hair is the color of apple cider, like hers." Touching the tip of her nose, he added, "She had freckles, too."

"Ted, I don't understand what you want to do."

"Why don't you shower and get dressed? Meet me in the kitchen. We'll have some breakfast, and we'll talk about this. I have a book I want to show you."

"What about my room?"

"We'll clean it out after we eat. Put on some old clothes. We'll be carrying stuff to the attic and the basement. Oh, the towels are in the cabinet underneath the bathroom sink."

Ted took his sketch pad and went downstairs. Pepper wasted no time digging an old pair of jeans and a T-shirt out of her suitcase. She showered and dressed as fast as she could. Her curiosity about what Ted wanted to do with her made her nervous and excited at the same time. She wanted to know what he had in mind.

Pepper ran down the stairs and through the dining room and practically burst into the kitchen.

Ted stood at the stove, frying eggs. He saw her fly though the door. "Jesus, Pepper, where's the fire?"

"I want to do more than see them." He tried to grope her.

Pepper dodged his hand. "Oh, no, *paisan*. You can look, but that's all. Ted's in charge. He told me to blow you and that's what I'm going to do."

She took off her shirt and panties. Pepper knew Butch wanted to touch her. That turned her on almost as much as seeing his thick cock dangling in front of her face. She slid forward and perched on the edge of the couch. "Come closer."

Butch took two small steps toward her. His erection bumped her chin. She opened her mouth and easily caught his prick between her lips. Then she covered it with her mouth.

Butch moaned, "Fuck, that's good! Suck it, Pepper."

He bunched her hair in his fists, pulling it just enough to make her scalp tingle. Without meaning to, he held her head still. If she moved, her hair pulled too much, and it hurt. He slowly slid his prick in and out of her mouth. Pepper sustained the suction while Butch controlled the movement. He gently fucked her mouth until Ted returned.

Pepper saw Ted standing behind Butch. He had also taken off all his clothes. After he sat down beside her, he leaned over and whispered in her ear, "Open your legs so I can rub your clit."

Pepper opened her knees. When Ted's fingers connected with her flesh, Pepper jumped. Her teeth scraped Butch's cock, and he groaned. She adjusted her position and continued to hold him in her mouth.

Her pelvis tilted forward and almost imperceptibly rocked as Ted massaged her clit. It had never been this good before. Their combined experience and maturity promised to take them places where none of them had ever been.

Sooner than she would have liked, Ted stopped her. "It's time to get down to business. Butch, kneel on the sofa and bend over the arm. Pepper, I want you to help me behind him."

"Sorry. I'm excited."

"About what?"

"About everything! I'm back with you and Butch, I have a job and a place to live, and now you want me to model. Yesterday at this time, I had jack shit!"

"I've been there; so has Butch."

"We're all in the same boat, aren't we?"

"I suppose we are. None of our lives have turned out the way we thought they would."

"That's the damn truth. Maybe we're finally getting back on track."

"Maybe we are."

"Can I ask you something?"

"Sure. Go for it."

"You said you and Butch haven't done anything since he's moved in. Have you at all since he got married?"

"No. He's not into it, Pepper. He doesn't give a shit what I do, but he's made it clear he prefers women."

"Even though Sandy hasn't put out for him in a long time?"

"Yup. The damnedest thing is, he stayed faithful to her. No one believes that, but it's the truth. When they'd fight, he'd come have a beer with me and talk. Sometimes he'd stay the night here at the house. But nothing ever happened between us." Ted served the scrambled eggs. "Grab the toast. It just popped."

Pepper put the toast on their plates. "Did you want anything to happen?"

"Sure, I did." He put the frying pan back on the stove and sat down. "In case you're wondering, I still do."

"Does he know that?"

"Pepper, why are you asking me all these questions?"

"You really want to know?"

"Of course I do. You're giving me the third degree. I want to know why."

Pepper pushed her eggs around on her plate, trying to find the courage to tell him what was on her mind. She finally blurted it out. "You've been in bed with Butch and me lots of times, but you've never actually slept with either of us. Maybe it's time you did."

Ted sipped his coffee and then calmly replied, "Maybe you're right."

Surprised by his acquiescence, all Pepper could manage to say was, "Really?"

"Really." Ted picked up a sketch pad and a book from the empty chair beside him. "This is what I want to show you."

The large art book had a woman with braided rust-colored hair on the cover. Pepper glimpsed *Andrew Wyeth: The Helga Pictures* on the spine just before Ted opened it. He had a page marked.

"These are the pictures you told me about upstairs, aren't they?"

"These are the ones. Look at these sketches he did."

Pepper took the book. On facing pages were three pencil drawings of a nude woman in different poses. One of the drawings looked very much like the one Ted had started that morning. "This is what you had me do, except the hands are different."

Ted smiled. "You're catching on, kiddo. Now look at the painting he did."

Ted flipped the page over. Pepper saw the title *Black Velvet* over the painting. A nude woman lay stretched out, her head turned to the side, with a black velvet choker around her neck. She had one hand just above her breast and the other on her stomach. Her legs were crossed at the ankle.

"It's beautiful, Ted. She looks so real, like he took her picture with a camera."

"I know. The flesh tones and her skin texture are the most natural I've ever seen. I've worked real hard trying to do the same thing." He picked up the sketch pad. "Now, look at these."

Ted flipped the pages one at a time, giving Pepper a chance to see the drawings he had made. She couldn't believe what he had done. The first few pages were copies of the Helga drawings. As the drawings progressed, they gradually became more sensual and erotic, until finally they morphed into a new image.

"My God, Ted, that's me!"

"Yes, Pepper, that's you. It's what I did from memory and from the old photographs I have of you."

Pepper took the tablet, and again looked at each page. The progression of the changes looked like an animated movie. "Do you remember the flip books we used to have when we were kids? If I could flip the pages of your drawings, it would come alive. Helga would change into me."

"Pepper, Helga did change into you. I have more of these. As I studied the Helga paintings, I could see my own version of them in my head. Always, something about the posture or the facial expression would change. I finally realized I kept seeing, and drawing, you."

4

Pepper stared at the pages of drawings. By the end of the sketch pad, the pictures of her became more explicit. One showed her kneeling, with her hand between her legs. Another had her bent over a chair, with her legs spread wide. All of them were sensual, and quite erotic.

"Ted, I don't know what to say."

"Say you'll model for me. Say you'll be my Helga."

"You want to paint these, don't you?"

"Some of them. These are more studies. Think of it as my practicing to really paint you."

"Does Butch know you have these drawings?"

"I've never shown them to him. It was tough enough that he had to leave you and marry Sandy. This would have been rubbing salt into the wound."

"Will you show him now?"

"If you want me to. Maybe I should also show him the sketches I've made of him."

Pepper grinned. "You've done some of Butch?"

"Almost as many as I've done of you."

"He'll have a frigging stroke when he finds out."

"Not if you tell him how hot he is, and how much you like them."

"Theodore, you're working all the angles with this one!"

"I've had ten years to plan it. Are you in?"

Pepper closed the sketch pad. "I'm in. It's too damn good to say no."

"That's my Pepper. You never could say no."

"Fuck you, Rembrandt."

"Ditto, Pearl."

Pepper threw a lump of scrambled eggs at Ted. They hit his chest and rolled onto the floor. "Don't shoot yourself in the foot. If you want me on your side, you'll remember that my name is Pepper."

"And you are hot, Pepper."

Ted and Pepper finished breakfast, cleaned up the kitchen, and then went back upstairs to work on clearing her room. When Ted opened the door, Pepper nearly fainted. There were boxes everywhere. Books and magazines were piled on top of the boxes and on the floor. A couple of old easels leaned against one wall, and a stack of unused canvases were stacked against another.

"Don't you ever throw anything out?"

"I'm a pack rat. Whenever I try to throw out anything, I look at it and figure there's still a use for it. I suppose I went overboard."

"I suppose you did." Pepper picked up an old *TV Guide* lying on top of a box. It had a picture of Xena, Warrior Princess on the cover. "Why on earth would you keep this? You were never a Xena fan."

"Look at the date."

When she saw the date, she didn't know if she should laugh or cry. "This isn't the same one, is it?"

"Of course it is. Why do you think I kept it?"

Pepper remembered the week before they graduated, Ted had a few friends over to the house, including her and Butch. Several times that night Butch grabbed the *TV Guide* and disappeared into the bathroom. Pepper didn't think much of it, until Ted took her aside and showed it to her later.

"Are the pages still stained?"

Ted opened the magazine to the article, with more Xena pictures. Dried semen spotted the pages. Ted started to laugh. "Look at this." He pointed to a yellowed stain, and then to another spot close to it. "As you can see, this one's fresh. I think he must have found it when he put some of his stuff in here. I know I didn't leave this on top of that box."

"He's jerking off to pictures in a ten-year-old *TV Guide*?"

Ted tossed the magazine onto the bed. "I guess so. Just think what he'll do when I show him my sketches of you. I'll have to laminate the damn things so he doesn't cream on them."

"Well, we'd better get to work. Somewhere under all this stuff is my new bedroom."

Pepper and Ted worked nonstop until lunchtime. Pepper convinced Ted that he should throw out some things, but most of it ended up in the attic. By the time they decided to break for lunch, they had cleared the bed and most of the floor.

Ted bent over the bed and pulled back the old flowered sheet. "Well, the mattress looks pretty worn." He pulled the sheet completely off, exposing the whole mattress. "Don't know if it's a keeper. We may have to get another one. Want to try it?"

Pepper patted Ted's ass, then slid her finger down the seam of his jeans. "What do you have in mind?"

Ted grinned. "Still hot to trot, Pepper?"

"Always."

"How many lovers did you have in Pittsburgh?"

"A few. If I wanted company, I could usually find some."

"I bet you could."

"How many lovers have you had?"

"Plenty in art school. Since moving back home, not so much."

"Did John know about the guys you slept with?"

"I couldn't tell him. He got jealous if I looked at another guy, let alone went to bed with him."

"I never understood why you moved in with him to begin with. What was he, fifteen years older than you?"

"Actually, seventeen. I met him sophomore year. I was twenty, he was thirty-seven."

"Damn, Ted. That makes no sense. What on earth did you see in him?"

"After I signed up for his class, he took a personal interest in me. He liked my work and helped me with my technique. We were friends, and then lovers. When I ran low on money and had to find a cheaper place to live, he offered me a room in his house. I took it."

"But he dumped you, didn't he?"

"About a year after I graduated, things fell apart. He moved on to greener, and younger, pastures."

"It feels pretty damn awful, doesn't it, I mean to get dumped?"

"I sure got a taste of how you must've felt when Butch married Sandy."

"What did you do when you had to move out of his house?"

"I'd saved some money for grad school. I took some of it and got a cheap apartment. Between modeling and waiting tables, I managed a couple grad courses before my dad got sick. That's when I had to come back. He didn't have anyone else."

"I wish I'd known you'd broken up with John and moved back home. I only found out the other night that your dad had passed away."

"I thought of you a lot after I came back. You were already in Pittsburgh. I thought about trying to find you, but I figured you had your own life. I didn't want to bounce back into it and open old wounds."

"I wish you had come looking for me." Pepper moved closer to Ted and put her arms around his neck. "God, how I've missed you. I love Butch, you know that. But I've never been able to talk to anyone like I can talk to you."

"The same here. I'd say you're like a sister to me, except for this." Ted put his hands on Pepper's ass and pulled her pelvis against his. "Just when I'm totally convinced I'm gay, you walk back into my life and make me hard without even trying."

Pepper leaned forward and lightly kissed his lips. "Just think what I could do if I tried."

"Are you coming on to me, Pearl Kaufmann?"

"No more than I did the night of our junior prom, Theodore Duncan." Butch broke his collarbone when he fell playing baseball and couldn't go. Ted filled in at the last minute—there were practically no tuxes left to rent.

"You came on to me big-time that night. You wanted it bad."

"So did you, but you wouldn't fuck me. At least you let me blow you."

"Best damn backseat head I've ever gotten."

"I want to do more than blow you."

"I know you do." Ted brushed Pepper's hair away from her face and rubbed her forehead. "You've got a big dust smudge on your face."

"You're changing the subject."

Ted ran his finger down her cheek and then across her lips. Pepper opened her mouth and sucked his finger. Ted pulled it out, dragging it over her lower lip. "My hands are dirty."

"We're both dirty, in more ways than one."

"What the hell is it about you? I'm gay. I shouldn't be feeling what I'm feeling now."

"Says who?" Pepper reached between them and caressed his erection. "You march to your own drummer, remember?"

"You're the only woman I've ever had anything like this with." Ted paused, and Pepper felt him tense.

"What's wrong, Ted?"

He glanced at the floor, and then looked directly into her eyes. "Pepper, I'm a virgin. I've never fucked a woman, only men."

She held his stare. "I thought that might be the case."

"No way in hell am I going to fuck for the first time in front of Mr. Italian Stallion. I do have some pride."

Pepper turned and patted the bed. "Well, you asked me to try out the mattress. Let's do it together."

"Shouldn't we at least shower, and get some condoms?"

"And give you a chance to change your mind? No way!"

"You aren't afraid of having sex with a gay man?"

"No, not if you're not afraid to sleep with a straight woman. I've been tested, and I'm clean, in case that's a problem."

Ted smirked. "Isn't that my line?"

"C'mon. I know you. You would have told me already if you had a problem."

"You're right. I would have, and I don't. I'm clean, too."

"Well then, let's get naked." She grinned at him like a seductive wood sprite.

"Are you going to tell Butch?"

"Probably. Do you care?"

Ted slid his hand under Pepper's dusty T-shirt and squeezed her breast. "No. Actually, I don't."

Pepper took Ted's hand and kissed his fingers. "This is so cool. I've never deflowered a virgin before."

"Butch took yours, didn't he?"

"Yeah, and it hurt. He's always been hung like a frigging horse."

Ted smiled. "I know."

Pepper pushed Ted back onto the bed. "This won't hurt one bit. I promise." Then she kicked off her shoes.

Ted laughed. "I've heard that before. It did, but I didn't care."

She straddled Ted, and pulled her T-shirt over her head. Ted immediately focused on her breasts. "You know, you like tits a little too much for a gay guy."

Ted reached up and pinched her nipple. Pepper's breath caught. "I like your tits. That's for damn sure."

"I want to see your pecs. Take off your shirt."

"This is a side of you I've never seen. This is fucking hot, you in charge."

Pepper helped him pull his shirt over his head. "Hey, I'm taking your virginity, right? That makes me the seducer." Pepper pinched Ted's nipple. He moaned. "You liked that, didn't you?"

"Jesus Pepper, my prick's gonna break if you don't do something soon."

"We're going to do something I've wanted to do ever since I've known you." Pepper scrambled off the bed and quickly took off her jeans and panties. "Now, your pants come off."

Pepper took off Ted's shoes and then unzipped his jeans. She pulled his pants and undershorts off in one long tug.

Ted closed his eyes as Pepper straddled him again. "Shit, I can't believe I'm doing this."

"Relax, Ted. You might just enjoy it."

"That's what I'm afraid of. Then I'll really be fucked up."

Pepper gingerly took Ted's prick and pointed it toward her pussy. She slid closer to it, so the tip touched her labia. Then she rubbed the head of Ted's cock against her clit.

Ted arched his back, and raised his pelvis off the bed. "Jesus Christ, Pepper! What the fuck are you doing?"

"Getting us both ready. A virgin should never know exactly when it will happen." With the confidence of a hooker deflowering a teenage boy, Pepper lifted up just enough to feel Ted's prick slip toward her cunt. Then she bore down on him with all of her weight.

Ted groaned and grabbed her ass when his prick popped

into her cunt. Pepper slowly rocked back and forth, giving him time to adjust to the sensation. He thrust upward, completely burying himself inside her. Grunting more than speaking, he managed to say, "Pepper, I can't stand it! I have to hump."

"Roll me over and fuck me!"

Using his brawn in a way Pepper had never known Ted to do, he lifted her and then flopped her over onto her back, almost knocking the wind out of her. He didn't seem to notice how hard she hit. With his cock still inside her, he lifted himself up and pushed his prick back in.

Pepper gasped, "Fuck, that's so good! Do it again."

And Ted did do it again, and again. He humped her with such force, Pepper had no choice but to hang on and let him ride her.

His orgasm hit without warning, surprising him as much as it did her. Pepper grabbed his ass cheeks and held him tightly against her as he shook. As many times as she had blown him, she had never once heard him groan as loudly as he did when he came inside her. Dusty sweat dripped off of his face onto her chest. She had never seen anything so beautiful in her life.

He collapsed on top of her. Pepper didn't care that his weight made it hard to breathe. She held him, stroking his hair and rubbing his back. When he finally raised his head and looked at her, she whispered, "You're not a virgin anymore."

"Thanks to you. If you worked for one of those escort services, you could make a frigging fortune."

"If you hadn't given me a job, that might have been my only other option." Pepper grinned. "I just slept with the boss. Do I get a raise?"

Ted rolled over onto the bed. "You aren't on the payroll yet, you can't get a raise. But you just gave a damn good interview. There may be some extra fringe benefits in the works."

Pepper put her leg over Ted's and whispered into his ear. "Like what?"

"Like you, me, and Butch making this work."

Pepper raised herself up on her side. "What are you talking about?"

"Making this arrangement permanent."

"Get outta here! We can't do that!"

"Why the hell not?"

"I'm staying here until I get on my feet. I never said I would move in forever."

"Butch said the same thing. He's still here."

"What makes you think Butch would want to stay here as a threesome?"

Ted put his arm around Pepper's waist. "If I tell you something, you have to swear to me that you won't let Butch know I told you."

"What, for heaven's sake?"

"Swear to me, Pepper. I mean it."

"All right, I swear. I won't tell him."

"Remember that picture of you Butch has in his wallet, the one he showed you last night?"

"Yeah, what about it?"

"That picture is one of the reasons Butch walked out on Sandy."

"Excuse me? That makes no sense."

"He's had that picture in his wallet all these years, kept it hidden behind his credit cards. Sandy found it, and accused him of having an affair with you."

"Ted, that isn't true. You know that."

"She wanted him to get rid of the picture. He wouldn't do it. Not too long after that blowout, he walked."

"What about his kid?"

Ted gently smoothed Pepper's hair. "He doesn't want Stacy growing up watching her parents argue every day. This wasn't the first time Sandy's busted his balls for shit he's never done."

"He can still see Stacy, can't he?"

"He's got visiting rights. Sandy didn't fight him on what he asked for."

"But what about our living together? Won't that be a problem when Sandy gets wind of it?"

"Don't know. I hope not."

"You still haven't said why Butch would be okay with the three of us living together permanently."

"He's told me more than once that it doesn't feel right that you aren't with us. We talked about how those years were the happiest we've ever had."

"For me, too. I didn't know either of you felt that way."

"Look at us now, Pepper. We're buck naked on a bare mattress, not giving a damn that we're dirty and sweaty, talking about shit that matters."

"Cool, isn't it?"

"Very cool. Butch should be here."

"Does he ever come home early?"

"Once in a while. Depends on the workload. There are a couple of guys that work for him that lock up if he takes off early."

"Can we call him and find out what's up today?"

"Sure we can. Let's jump in the shower and rinse the dust off first."

"Together?"

"That will be another first for me, with a woman."

"It's about time, don't you think?"

"Maybe it is."

Ted had a hand-held showerhead. The spray could be set to fine mist or pulsate. In the shower with him, Pepper felt like they were playing with the garden hose. First Pepper rinsed him off, and then Ted rinsed her.

When he twisted the nozzle on the showerhead until the pulsating massager kicked in, Pepper wasn't sure what he meant to do. She quickly found out.

"You didn't get off when we fucked, did you?"

"No. That's okay. I did this morning."

"Well, don't you want to now?"

Before she could answer, he pointed the pulsating stream between her legs. When the warm water hit her pussy, Pepper grabbed Ted's arm to keep her balance.

"God, that feels good."

"It's supposed to. Lean against me so you don't slip. Let me make you come."

Ted slowly moved the pulsating spray the length of her vulva, and then back again. Pepper's hips rolled like those of an exotic dancer. The water pounding against her clit became her single point of focus.

It didn't take long before the pulsing water took her over the top. Pepper gasped and lurched forward as her clit throbbed with sensation. Ted made sure she didn't fall.

Once Pepper steadied herself, Ted twisted the showerhead back to fine mist and turned down the hot water. He then pointed the spray at his own groin. The cool water wilted his growing erection.

"Why did you do that? I would've blown you."

"Sweetheart, I'm two for two today. If Butch does come home early, I want some juice left, just in case."

Pepper swatted his bare ass. "Something tells me that won't be a problem."

5

Ted dialed Butch's cell, then handed the phone to Pepper. "For crying out loud, Ted! I don't know what to say to him. You find out if he can come home."

"No fucking way, Pepper. He needs to know *you* want him here. Not the same coming from me."

Pepper put the phone to her ear just as Butch answered. "Hello, Ted? Is something up?"

"Hey, Butch. It isn't Ted. It's me, Pepper."

Butch chuckled. "Yeah. I'd know your voice anywhere."

"I wondered when you're coming home today. Ted said sometimes you're able to leave early."

"I had your car towed in. I'm checking it out now."

"Do you know what's wrong with it?"

"Looks like you need a new starter. And it definitely needs to be tuned."

"How much will it cost to fix it?"

"We're doing a barter, aren't we? We'll work out a payment plan."

"Between you and Ted today, I don't know if I'm coming or going."

"Coming mostly, I expect."

"Very funny." Pepper couldn't help but smile.

"I can probably get outta here in about half an hour or so. Is that good?"

"That's very good. We'll see you soon."

Pepper turned off the cell and gave it back to Ted. "He's coming home early."

"You know you're flushed?"

Pepper put her hands on her cheeks. They felt hot. "I can't help it. He does that to me."

"He's working on your car?"

"He had it towed from the parking lot. I'm just glad it can be fixed."

"He's a good mechanic. He'll have it humming before he gives it back to you."

"He's already got me humming. Just hearing his voice on the phone made me horny."

"You probably did the same thing to him."

Pepper stared right into Ted's eyes for a moment. "Do you really think we can talk him into making this last longer than a month or two?"

"Pepper, I don't think he will need much convincing. Let's see what he says."

"What about you?"

"What do you mean, what about me?"

"You're still more into guys than girls. Will this be enough for you?"

"That depends."

"On what?"

"A few things, like can we live in the same house and not drive each other crazy? Can we still have our own lives and see other people if we want? Will Butch let me do him like I did you this morning?"

"That last one's a big if."

"There's one more. If you and Butch decide to get married, you'll probably want to live alone."

"Whoa, Ted! We're a long ways from that one."

"Maybe. We'll see." Ted took back his phone and pocketed it.

"Has Butch ever said anything about doing it with you?"

"Once. He admitted he'd thought about it a few times, but that's as far it went."

"Well, that's something, anyway. You'll have to give me a chance to soften him up."

"Actually, making him hard might be a better idea."

"I'll do my best. How about giving me some pointers on easing him into the idea?"

"You could tell him I want to buttfuck, and he has dibs on who's top or bottom."

"Has he ever been with a guy? I know he hasn't been alone with you, but has he with anyone?"

"Don't know. Why don't you ask him?"

"Maybe I will."

Ted and Pepper had a ham sandwich and some coffee while waiting for Butch to come home. At about two-thirty, he came in the back door. The clean work clothes he had put on that morning were now smeared with oil and smelled of gasoline.

Pepper got up to put her plate in the sink. "Damn, *paisan*, nobody better strike a match around you."

"Yeah, well, some of this is from your car."

"Doesn't matter. You still stink."

Butch grabbed her arm and swung her around. Holding her tightly against his dirty clothes, he kissed her. He pushed his tongue into her mouth, and rubbed the hard line of his prick against her leg.

Years of longing for her first love churned in Pepper's belly. She still wanted him as much as she had ten years ago, and she still wanted the intimacy they had shared with Ted. She wanted them to be three.

Ted interrupted. "Excuse me, you two. Should I leave so you can fuck on the kitchen floor?"

Pepper pulled back from the kiss. "I'm not fucking his sorry ass until he takes a shower." She turned her head and winked at Ted. "Of course, I wouldn't mind watching you fuck his sorry ass on the kitchen floor."

Butch squeezed her buttocks. "When did you get so kinky?"

Ted took advantage of the opening Pepper gave him. "What, didn't you know? Our Miss Pepper picked up a few things in Pittsburgh. Fortunately, none of them are contagious. Tell him, Pepper."

Pepper rubbed Butch's chest with her palms. "Ted's right. I learned a few things in the big city. If you're a good boy, maybe I'll share some of them."

"You fucked a lot?"

"Enough to keep me happy. Now, I've got both of you to pick up the slack."

"Rembrandt only fucks men, remember?"

"Not anymore."

Butch let Pepper go and stepped back. First he looked at her, and then he stared at Ted. "What the fuck happened here today?"

Pepper threaded her arm through Butch's. "Ted got laid."

"Sure as hell did. Now I know what all the fuss is about." Ted grinned. "Christ, I wish I had a camera. The expression on your face is priceless!"

"Is this why you wanted me to come home, to tell me this?"

"Partly. There's more to it than that." Pepper led him to the table. "Sit down. Let me get you a cup of coffee." After she got

Butch a cup, she refilled hers and Ted's. "Do you want a sandwich?"

"I'd love a sandwich. Mrs. Lorenzo's son never turns down food. It's how she brought us up."

While Pepper made Butch a ham sandwich, Ted got the ball rolling. "We have something to run by you. Pepper, what do you think? Should I just throw it at the wall and see if it sticks?"

"What, you talkin' about spaghetti?"

They tried to ignore him. "Go for it."

"Pepper just meant to stay here until she can afford her own place, maybe a month or two at the most. I asked her today if she'd want to move in with us for a longer time."

Butch sipped his coffee, and glanced at Pepper. "How long?"

Ted answered for her. "As long as we can stand to live together, however long that is."

Pepper handed Butch a plate. "Did I remember right?" The club sandwich she had made for him had three slices of bread, with lettuce, tomato, double meat, and cheese. Both layers were slathered with mustard.

"Goddamn, Pepper. No one's made me one of these in years. Thank you."

"You're welcome."

Before he took a bite, he asked her, "Are you sure about this? I mean living here like Ted said, with both of us."

Pepper sat down across the table. "I am if you are. But before we go ahead with this, I want to make sure it won't cause a problem with you seeing your kid. I couldn't live with that."

"It won't."

"How can you be sure? Won't Sandy go ballistic when she finds out you're living with me?"

"She might." He took a bite of sandwich and chewed with a contented grin on his face.

"Butch! Then how do you know she won't try to yank your visitation rights?"

"Because Sandy has a new friend, so I'm told. She won't want to draw attention to her personal life, so I expect she'll lay off mine."

Ted seemed surprised. "You didn't tell me that. Who is she seeing?"

Butch bit into his sandwich again. He smiled at Ted while he chewed. "You fucking won't believe it when I tell you."

"C'mon, man. Who is it?"

"Glenda Howell."

"You've got to be kidding!" Ted looked genuinely surprised.

"Nope. They've been seen at dinner, holding hands. Glenda's car has been parked in what used to be my driveway every night for the last few weeks."

"Shit, Butch. This is real dish."

"I know. Ain't it great?"

Totally bewildered, Pepper spoke up. "Will someone please explain this to me? Who is Glenda Howell?"

While Butch ate, Ted explained. "Glenda Howell is the lawyer who represented Sandy in the divorce. She moved here a few years ago and set up a private practice."

"I don't understand. Why is she seeing Sandy?"

Bits of his sandwich nearly fell out of his mouth when Butch laughed. "Pepper, she's a fucking lesbian! The whole town knows that."

"Oh, my God! Sandy's having an affair with her lesbian lawyer?"

"You got it. Will Sandy want that brought out in court? I don't think so."

Ted snickered. "So, that's why she wouldn't sleep with you. You turned her gay."

"Fuck you, Rembrandt."

"On the floor or upstairs, *paisan*?"

Pepper felt the edge in Ted's question. Trying to keep things friendly, she made a joke. "Nobody fucks anybody until he showers. Gasoline isn't my favorite aftershave, thank you."

"Well, you'll have to save one for me. I have to go to the bar soon, and won't be home until at least nine o'clock."

"Ted, I should be going with you. You have to train me."

"Bullshit, Pepper. You're staying here with me tonight."

"Butch is right. You need to get settled before you start at the bar. We'll work out a schedule in the next few days."

"All right. But I'm telling you both, you're not going to keep me. I'll pay my own way."

"Hey, Ted, I sure as hell didn't say I would keep her. Did you?"

"Nope. But I am open to an occasional barter."

Butch grinned. "Which reminds me. You can make your first payment tonight."

"Jesus, between the two of you, I might not be able to walk tomorrow." Pepper kicked Butch under the table. "Not that I mind."

Butch picked up his plate and coffee cup. "Since I don't want to offend, I'm going to take a shower. Pepper, hold that thought until I get back." Taking his food with him, he went upstairs.

Ted and Pepper cleaned up the kitchen. Pepper glanced at the kitchen door several times while drying the dishes. Ted noticed.

"Darlin', you have to give the man time to clean up. It will be a few minutes."

"Damn it, Ted! I can't help it. I don't know why he gets to me so much. He always has."

"Me, too. If ever there was one hot Italian stud, he's it."

"Sounds like Sandy came close to gelding our Italian stallion."

"I know he's been horny. But he hasn't done anything about it, not with me or with anyone else. He hasn't had sex for a long time, until you showed up yesterday."

"Well, that's going to change."

"It's already changing. And I'm counting on you to bring him around to my side of the fence." Ted grabbed a dishtowel to dry his hands.

"Do you care how it happens? I mean who does what?"

"I don't care how it happens. I want to touch him and smell him and feel him close to me just like you do. He can call the shots, if that makes a difference."

"You know I'll do what I can. When do we show him the sketches?"

"One step at a time. Let's get him used to the idea that we can live together first." Ted finished drying his hands and picked up his car keys from the counter. "I've got plenty to do at the bar. You two are overdue for an evening alone."

Pepper hugged him. "Thanks, Ted. You're a good friend."

"After today, don't I make a good lover?"

"You've always been a good lover. Today, you were a good fuck."

"Fair enough. Distinction noted."

"Hey, Rembrandt, isn't it against the rules to turn straight?"

Pepper had her back to the door and jumped when she heard Butch. Rather than letting her go, Ted hugged her tighter. "*Paisan*, I don't play by the rules. You know that." Then Ted kissed her, not a friendly kiss, but a lover's kiss. He kissed her deeply and passionately. Pepper responded to the unexpected heat, and returned the kiss in kind. She could feel Ted's stiffening organ against her leg.

Ted broke the kiss, leaving Pepper surprised and breathless. "Have fun tonight. I'll see you both later." He turned, and went out the back door to his car.

Pepper wanted to turn around, but all the emotion churning

in her stomach stopped her. Suddenly, she didn't know if she could handle it, any of it. She especially didn't know if she could handle being alone with Butch for the first time in ten years.

"Pepper . . ." She felt Butch's hands on her shoulders. "What's wrong?"

Pepper tried to force a laugh, but it came out closer to a choking sob. "I don't know. I think I'm nervous."

"For fuck's sake, nervous about what?" Butch turned her around to face him.

She looked up into his freshly washed and shaved face. He had combed his wet hair straight back. With his olive complexion and thick eyebrows, he looked as if he should be on *The Sopranos.*

"Pepper, for Christ's sake, talk to me."

"I'm sorry. I just never thought we would be alone again. Now that we are, I don't know what to say."

"Well, I sure as hell do. It's something I've waited ten years to say." Butch leaned over and kissed her forehead. "Pepper, I'm sorry. I know I fucked up. I've lived with that every day since Sandy got pregnant."

Pepper squeezed her eyes shut, fighting to hold in the tears. "How long, Butch? I've always wanted to know. How long had you been fucking her before you knocked her up?"

"You wouldn't believe me if I told you."

"Try me."

"Can we go sit on the couch to talk about this?" Without waiting for an answer, Butch led Pepper into the living room. Pepper sat down. Butch went straight to the liquor cabinet. "Do you want a shot?"

"It's too early."

"Says who?" He took a bottle of Jim Beam out of the cabinet and poured them each a double shot. "It's good to live with a guy who owns a bar. The cabinet is always well stocked."

"It was with his dad, too." Pepper took the glass, actually

glad he had ignored her temperance. "We drained more than a few bottles from it."

"If Ted ever caught shit for it, he never told us." Butch sat down beside Pepper. "Do you really want to know the whole story?"

"You can spare me the grisly details. I just want to know why her . . ." Pepper paused and took a swallow of whiskey before she could finish. "I want to know why her, and not me."

"I know how fucking lame this will sound, but it was an accident."

"It usually is. Did your rubber break that night?"

"I wasn't wearing one. I was drunk."

Pepper couldn't hold it in any longer. "You fucking son of a bitch! How could you have let it happen?" She slammed her glass down on the coffee table. "We were so careful. Every time, you wore a rubber. I lied about my age and got on the pill. All that so I wouldn't get pregnant. If I hadn't done anything, it would've been me, not her, and Stacy would be ours."

"Don't you fucking think I know that? I only laid her once, at a party the week you went to New York with the chorus. One lousy fuck and she got pregnant."

Pepper tried to brush the tears from her cheeks, but they were instantly replaced by more. Her nose also started to run. "You got a hanky?"

"No, but you can use this." Butch put his glass down and stood up. He pulled his T-shirt over his head and handed it to her.

"I can't blow my nose on your shirt."

"Go ahead. It's better than spitting on me."

In spite of herself, Pepper had to laugh. She wiped her face and blew her nose. The shirt smelled like him. She wiped her nose again, just to smell it some more.

"Was it really a lousy fuck?"

"Yes, it was really a lousy fuck."

"And you weren't seeing her while you, me, and Ted were hanging together?"

"No way in hell! I didn't even like her. Her whining always got on my nerves. It still does."

"Then why did you fuck her?"

"I wanted some. You weren't around. I got drunk enough not to care who I fucked."

"You could've fucked Ted."

"C'mon, Pepper. You know I don't do guys."

"Not ever?"

"Not once." Butch gave her a peculiar look. "You don't think because I moved in with him we're fucking, do you?"

"No. Ted already told me you two never have. He said it's been a long time for both of you."

"I don't fuck around. Living with what I did cured me of that. Once burned, twice shy."

"You fucked around with me last night, and again this morning."

"That's different."

"Why's it different?"

"Because I love you. I always have. I still do."

For a moment, Pepper couldn't think straight. Butch's words staggered her. When she looked at him, and saw his eyes glassy with tears, she understood more than he could ever explain to her. She saw the regret, the loneliness, the pain. She saw a man still paying for the mistake of a teenage boy.

"Why didn't you ever tell me?"

"I wanted to tell you before you moved to Pittsburgh. Remember, I asked you to have a drink with me?"

"I said no because it hurt too much. I couldn't stand the thought of saying goodbye to you face-to-face."

"Yeah, I know. I figured that out when I saw your reaction. So I left you at the bank, went out, and got drunk. I slept in my car that night. I couldn't face going home."

Pepper shook her head. "God almighty, how did this all get so fucked up?"

"Because I couldn't say no to some pussy."

"How long has it been since you've had any?"

Before he answered, Butch picked up his glass and belted back what was left in it. "Sandy hasn't slept with me in four years. Before that, I got some on our anniversary, Valentine's Day, and my birthday. If she felt generous, maybe I got one for Christmas or New Year's. Never both."

"God, Butch. That's awful."

"Yeah, I know." He picked up Pepper's glass and finished it off. Then he went back to get the bottle again. Pepper stopped him.

"Don't get drunk."

"Why the fuck not?" He picked up the bottle of Jim Beam.

Pepper took the bottle out of his hand and put it back in the cabinet. "Because you don't have to anymore. It's over."

"Is it?"

"Yes, *paisan*, it is." Pepper wrapped her arms around Butch's neck. "You're going to get laid so much now you'll beg for a night off."

"Is that a fact?"

"That is indeed a fact. And something else. Ted really wants to fuck you. He says you have dibs on being the top or the bottom."

"No way."

"Yes, way." Pepper leaned down and kissed Butch's chest. "Know what else?"

"What?"

"I would really get off watching you and Ted do it. That would be so hot!"

"How much would you get off?"

"Enough to make myself come. You and Ted could watch me do myself while you fuck."

Butch squeezed her ass. "Goddamn, Pepper. You're going to make me cream in my shorts."

"Oh, no, *paisan*. There's a much better place to cream if you're going to cream."

Pepper stepped back and pulled her shirt over her head. Then she took off her jeans. Butch had unzipped and stood stroking himself through his underwear.

"It's unfucking believable, but you're hotter now than you were before."

"So are you, Robert Lorenzo. What are you waiting for? Get naked already."

Butch wasted no time. He skimmed off his clothes, and then picked Pepper up. "Think Ted will mind if we fuck on his couch?"

"Just don't leave any stains. He would hate cum stains on his furniture."

Butch put Pepper on the couch, and then grabbed his shirt off the floor. "Lift your ass." Pepper raised up, and Butch slid his shirt under her. "Now, if we leak, we won't stain the couch."

With no prelude, he climbed on top of her. Pepper wanted to be fucked as much as Butch wanted to fuck her. There would be time to fool around later. Now, she only wanted one thing, to feel him inside of her.

When his cock slid into her, she clutched at his back and gasped. Before Pepper had time to adjust to his size, he lifted his pelvis and banged into her again. He humped her with the intensity of a man so hungry for sex that nothing else mattered.

As much as she could, Pepper relaxed into his rhythm and let him ride her. She wanted him to fuck her for as long as he wanted. His weight on her and the force of his pounding made her feel like she had finally come home. She belonged here with Butch, and with Ted. They belonged together.

6

Ted came in at about nine-fifteen. Butch and Pepper were sitting on the couch, in the dark. Ted didn't see them when he walked through the room on his way upstairs.

"Hey, Rembrandt. We've been waiting for you."

"Jesus Christ!" Ted spun around, nearly tripping on the carpet. "You scared the living crap out of me."

"Sorry, didn't know you were so jumpy."

"Why are you sitting here in the dark, or shouldn't I ask?"

Pepper giggled. "You can ask. But I think you already know."

"Did you save any for me?"

Pepper patted the spot next to her. "Come and sit with us. We need to talk."

Ted sat down and put his arm around Pepper. "Talking wasn't what I had in mind."

"Keep your dick in your pants for a few minutes, Rembrandt. We'll get to it."

"Easy for you to say. How many did you have tonight?"

"Not nearly enough to make up for all the ones I've missed."

"Same here. Pepper, you have your work cut out for you."

Pepper lifted Ted's hand and kissed it. "Maybe I won't have to do all the work."

"What's that supposed to mean?"

Butch leaned forward so he could see Ted. "Pepper told me she would get off watching us do it. Don't think I could get it up alone with you, but if Pepper is into it, it might be different."

"Well, now, this is moving in the right direction."

Pepper chimed in. "Butch told me he's never done anything with a guy, except what the three of us have done together. I think he's nervous."

Not wanting to sound like a wuss, Butch added, "Well, hell, the only thing I've ever had up my ass is my doctor's index finger. Ted's prick isn't exactly small."

Pepper cooed, "I know."

"Ah, c'mon, Butch. Once you've been buttfucked, you'll be hooked. Trust me, you'll love it."

"I thought you said I'd have dibs on who gives it and who takes it."

"Hey, man, whatever you want." Ted stroked the erection that bulged in his jeans. "I sure as hell have enough left to give one tonight. Do you?"

Butch laughed. "I've had frigging blue balls for years. Damn right I have enough juice for one more."

"Then it's your call, buddy."

Butch reached under Pepper's shirt and caressed her breast. "Whaddya say we let Pepper decide? What would get you hot, sweetheart?"

"No contest. I want Ted to do you."

Butch sat back on the sofa. "You don't want to think about that?"

"Don't have to. If I could buttfuck you, I would. Since I

can't, Ted will do it for me." Pepper squeezed Ted's hand. "And I want it to be a good one."

"I promise, it will be." Ted stood and unzipped. Butch didn't move from his spot on the sofa. "Hey, man, you heard the lady. Strip."

"Jesus Christ! What are you going to do, dry hump me?"

Ted smirked. "What's the matter, *paisan*? You don't think I know what I'm doing?"

"With as many times as you've taken it up the ass, you could probably write a frigging book about it."

"What do you think, Pepper, should I go easy on him?"

Pepper ran her index finger down Butch's bare chest to his jeans. "Maybe the first time. He's an ass virgin, after all." She played with the tab on his zipper for a few seconds before pulling it down. When his erection popped out of his fly, Pepper feigned surprise. "My, my, looks like someone we know and love is excited."

"That's good. Blow him while I run upstairs to get some lube and a condom. I'll be right back."

Pepper shoved Butch's shoulder. "Stand up."

"Why?"

"I'm going to blow you like Ted said." Pepper lightly touched the tip of his penis with her finger. "You don't want to be blown?"

"Fuck, yes." Butch stood and pushed his jeans down below his hips.

"Take them off, *paisan*." Pepper waited while Butch got naked.

"What about you?"

"What do you mean?"

"Let me see your tits."

Pepper knew Butch would get even hotter if she teased him. She raised her T-shirt and flashed him. "You mean you want to see these?"

Butch immediately reacted. "Wait a damn minute! Pepper said she would get herself off where I could see her."

"Once I'm in, she can do whatever she wants. I thought you might like her to loosen you up rather than me."

"Doing what?"

"Bend over and you'll find out."

With obvious reluctance, Butch knelt on the sofa and leaned over the arm. "By the way, I'm empty. I went earlier this evening."

"Unless you haven't gone in a couple of days, it isn't a problem."

Butch muttered, "Maybe not for you."

"Relax, man. This won't hurt, much."

"Ted, stop busting his chops. He's new at this."

Ted chuckled. "Can't help it. I've waited a long time to butt-fuck our Italian stallion. I have to get a few licks in."

"Pepper already did. Are you going to keep me bent over like this all damn night?"

Ted slapped Butch's ass. "Maybe."

"Fuck this!" Butch started to get up. Pepper stopped him.

"All right! Enough. Either we're going to do this, or we're not. Ted, stop fucking around and show me what to do."

Ted leaned back. "Well, Miss Pepper! Didn't know you were a closet dominatrix. I'll tuck that one away for future reference."

Butch fidgeted. "Pepper, I wouldn't be frigging doing this if you hadn't asked me to. Tell Rembrandt he'd better stick it in PDQ, or I'm outta here."

"I think he heard you, Butch."

"Before I 'stick it in,' I want Pepper to help you relax." Ted picked up a tube of lubricant. "Pepper, are you squeamish about sticking your finger in Butch's asshole?"

"Nope. I think I might like it."

"Hold out your hand."

Ted squirted a clear gel across her fingertips. "Smear that on your fingers. We'll start slow. Use your pinky first. Be careful of your fingernails."

"I keep them short, but I'll be careful." Pepper had no qualms at all about stretching Butch. In fact, it made her feel included in a way she hadn't expected. She carefully probed between Butch's ass cheeks until she found his anus. Her pinky slipped in easily.

Butch grunted and then gripped her finger with his sphincter muscles. "He's tightening up, Ted. What do I do?"

"Nothing. Give him a few seconds to get used to it. When you feel him relax, put in your index finger, wait a minute or two, and then put in two fingers."

Pepper did as Ted told her. When she swapped her index finger for her pinky, Butch forcefully pushed backward. Pepper held her ground, bracing herself with her other hand against his ass cheeks.

"How's he doing?"

"His asshole is tight as a nut on a bolt."

"Butch, try to relax."

"I'm fucking working on it, all right?" The tension in his voice couldn't be missed.

"Pepper, switch with me. I'll do the finger stretching, you massage his cheeks. That usually works."

Pepper pulled her finger out. Butch's T-shirt lay crumpled on the floor. She picked it up and wiped her hand. "You may have to throw this shirt out. It's really gross." She tucked the shirt under Butch, to protect the sofa.

Butch lowered his head between his forearms in utter frustration. "Jesus fucking Christ! I have my ass in the air about to get plugged, and you're worried about my frigging shirt and cum on the couch?"

Pepper stifled a giggle, knowing that would make matters

worse. Instead, she leaned over and kissed his bum. "Now, now, Mr. Lorenzo. You're supposed to be relaxing, remember?"

"Yeah, right. I'm relaxed."

"Not yet, but you will be."

Before massaging his buttocks, Pepper kissed his neck and then slowly worked her way down his spine. Butch shivered when she licked his tailbone. She glanced at Ted. He gave her a thumbs-up. While she licked and kissed Butch's rump, Ted slicked up his hand. He pushed his middle finger into Butch's ass. Butch lurched and groaned.

Ted finger-fucked Butch's asshole, slowly moving his finger in and out. Pepper took her cue from Ted and kneaded the hard flesh of his butt with the same rhythm. She could actually see Butch's back muscles soften as he relaxed. She knew Ted noticed as well, because he took the opportunity to push in a second finger.

"Okay, buddy, I have two fingers in. How're you doing?"

"I'd be doing better if Pepper would come around where I can see her."

"Go ahead, Pepper. I can take it from here."

Pepper shifted her position to the end of the sofa. Butch raised his head and stared right at her chest. "Christ, your tits are good."

"Wanna suck on one?"

Not waiting for an answer, she stuffed a nipple into Butch's mouth. His tongue lapped at her like a nursing calf. He flinched again, and Pepper realized Ted now had three fingers in. Butch continued to suck her tit, and didn't complain.

"He's about ready, Pepper. Pull that chair over and sit in front of him. Make sure he has a clear view of your pussy while you get yourself off."

Butch lifted his head, releasing Pepper's nipple. "Rembrandt, you read my mind."

Pepper pulled the chair around. She saw Ted pull out his fingers and put on a condom. He squirted lubricant on his dick and on Butch's ass. "You've got plenty of lube, *paisan*. You're open. It should slip right in."

"It damn well better slip . . . aaaaah." Before Butch could finish his sentence, Ted rammed his prick into his ass. The sound Butch made actually scared Pepper.

"Christ, Ted, don't hurt him!"

"He's all right, Pepper." Ted had one foot on the floor and one on the sofa. His cock was buried in Butch's ass. "He needs time to get used to it."

Through clenched teeth, Butch hissed, "You son of a bitch! I didn't expect it."

"That's the point, *paisan*. You would have tensed up again if I'd told you." Ted pointed to the chair. "Pepper, you're on. Give us a show."

Pepper hesitated a moment. "Butch, are you sure you're all right?"

"I'm friggin' fine. Show me your pussy."

Pepper sat down and put a leg over each arm of the chair. Sitting spread-eagled, she slipped her fingers into her wet flesh. When she touched herself, she suddenly realized how hard her clit had become. She rubbed the hardened bump, and sighed.

As Pepper masturbated, Ted slowly pulled his prick halfway out, and pushed it back in. Butch remained focused on Pepper. Ted humped again, this time a bit faster. Butch pushed backward, but didn't appear to be in any pain.

"How does that feel, Butch?"

"Like my balls are going to bust if I don't come soon."

"Once you come from a buttfuck, you'll never want it any other way."

Staring directly at Pepper's wet pussy, Butch snorted, "Don't count on it, Rembrandt."

"I'm really going to fuck you now. You wanted some warning. That's all you're going to get." With that, Ted humped Butch with the same ferocity he had Pepper that morning. Again, Butch made a guttural sound, but never took his eyes off Pepper,

She rubbed herself with increasing intensity, her clit on fire with lust. Watching the two men she loved fucking took her higher than any porn movie ever could. She glanced at Ted and realized he also had his eyes glued on her.

The heat between the three friends continued to build. It would be a photo finish to see who would climax first. The prize went to Ted. Pepper saw him grimace and bang Butch's ass with all his strength. That was enough to push Pepper over the top. She squealed and raised her ass off the chair, her pussy wide open right under Butch's face.

Suddenly Butch gasped for air. He raised his torso up with such force, he would have thrown Pepper off his back. Ted had the strength to hold him. With astonishing agility, Ted reached under Butch and grabbed his cock. As Butch spurted, Ted pumped him, milking him dry.

Butch collapsed over the arm of the sofa, taking Ted down with him. They stayed sandwiched together back to front for several seconds before Ted had his wind back. He raised himself up, pulling his prick out of Butch. Then he flopped back onto the other side of the sofa.

Pepper lowered her legs. Butch remained bent over the end of the sofa. He had his eyes closed. Pepper knelt in front of him and smoothed back his hair.

"Are you all right?"

He opened his eyes and smiled. "Yeah, I'm fine, now that you're here."

"Did it hurt?"

"Not exactly. Don't tell him I said this, but I kinda liked it."

Ted swatted Butch's ass. "I heard that, *paisan.*"

"Next time, I plug you, Rembrandt."

"You're on. I hope you give as good as you got."

"Better. My dick's bigger than yours."

"Not by much, stud puppet."

Pepper leaned forward and kissed the tip of Butch's nose. "Don't forget to leave enough for me."

"Sweetheart, give us a few minutes. Maybe we'll have one more before we go to sleep."

Ted stood up. "Not me, my friends. I'm ready for bed. You had me up at seven o'clock this morning. I need my beauty sleep."

Butch sat up. "What about you, Pepper? You sleeping in your own room tonight?"

"It isn't ready yet. I have to scrub everything before I make up the bed. It's really dusty in there."

Butch smiled. "Good. Then you'll sleep with me again tonight. Ted, you want to join us?"

"No, thanks. You'll probably hump like rabbits most of the night." He picked up his clothes, and then turned back to Pepper. "Get me up when Butch leaves. I want to do more sketches of you tomorrow."

"You have sketches of Pepper?"

"A few. I'll show them to you sometime." With that, Ted went upstairs to bed.

Pepper picked up Butch's soiled shirt and tossed it on the floor. Then she sat down beside him. "It's late. We should go to bed. You have to get up early tomorrow."

"Not so fast. I want to ask you something."

"What?"

"Do you think we can pull this off? I mean the three of us living together and fucking our brains out?"

"Yeah, I do. If Ted ever gets another boyfriend, that might change things. But for now, I think it could work."

"Know something frigging weird? So do I."

"Do you want to try it?"

"I think I do. I know you and Ted do."

"It was his idea. It's good of him to share his house with us."

"When I asked if I could move in, he looked like a kid on Christmas morning. Told me I could stay here as long as I wanted. I think he's lonely."

"I do, too. He never did have a lot of friends. Everyone thought he was weird but us."

"He's too damn smart for this place. Never did understand why he wanted to come back."

"It's home, Butch. I'm back, too."

"But you lost your job. Otherwise, you wouldn't be here."

Pepper took a moment before she answered. The thought she had unnerved her. "Maybe that's true. But if I had found out that you got divorced, I would have come home in a heartbeat."

"Why?"

"Why do you think?" She picked up a sofa pillow from the floor and put it back in its place.

"Tell me. I want to hear it from you."

"Because I'm still in love with you."

"Even after I hurt you so much?"

"Why do you think I'm still single? I never did find anyone else I felt this way about."

"We're damn lucky we're getting a second chance."

"I know. Lots of people don't."

"When I left Sandy, I wondered if I would get to see you again. Never in a million years did I think you'd move in with Ted and me."

"Like I heard someone say in a movie once, 'The gods are good.'"

"Hey, you're talking to a former altar boy at Sacred Heart. *God* is good."

"Yeah, yeah, sure, sure. By the way, have you been excommunicated yet?"

"According to my mother, I have."

"She's really not speaking to you?"

"Nope. My dad stops by the garage to shoot the shit, but my mom won't talk to me." Butch chuckled. "Dad never liked Sandy. Actually asked me once how I put up with that cunt after she bitched me out over something stupid in front of him."

"C'mon, he used that language with you?"

Butch grinned. "Yeah. I think he might have had a couple of beers on the way home from work. Then Sandy really pissed him off."

Pepper laughed. "She must have. I can't even picture your dad being that mad."

"Hell, Sandy never liked going to my family's house. She pissed off my parents more than once when she wouldn't stay for dinner." Butch made a fist and lightly punched the palm of his other hand. "You know, I don't know how the hell I ended up being the bad guy in this mess."

"This must be hard for you, with your mom." Pepper knew Butch had always been close to his mother. "Can't your dad do anything?"

"He says to give her some time with it. Dad doesn't hold it against me. My mom, well, she's very Catholic."

"There's nothing religious about disowning your own son. I don't care what church you go to."

"Look, my mom's my mom. Maybe she'll get over it." He touched her cheek. "I don't want to fight about her, or about how Catholic she is. Won't get us anywhere."

"I suppose you're right. But it isn't fair that everyone's blaming you."

"Ted's not, and you're not. That's all that matters to me."

Pepper picked up her T-shirt and panties. "We should go to bed."

Not bothering to pick up his clothes, Butch took Pepper's hand. "Let's go upstairs. We'll see how tired we are once we're in bed."

7

After Butch left for the garage, Pepper went to wake up Ted. She had fallen asleep the night before while Butch felt her up. They had done the nasty again this morning, and then showered together. Before Butch left for work, he gave her a long, wet, and wonderful good-bye kiss.

Pepper knocked on Ted's door. No response. She knocked again, a little louder. Still nothing. When she cracked the door open, she saw Ted sprawled across his bed, without a stitch on, sound asleep.

Not knowing quite what to do, she went in and stood beside the bed. Ted had an erection, a mouthwatering one. She figured she knew one way to wake him up.

Being careful not to jostle him, Pepper leaned over the bed and gingerly lifted his erect prick. Ted didn't stir. After admiring his endowment for a moment, she carefully encircled it with her mouth.

Ted shifted and murmured, "Oh, yeah, that's good." He still seemed to be asleep. She continued to gently lick him. Suddenly, he jolted awake and shouted, "What the fuck!"

Pepper lifted her head and sweetly said, "Good morning, Theodore."

"Pepper! I thought I was dreaming."

Pepper pumped his prick with her hand. "Not a bad dream, I hope?"

Ted lay back as Pepper continued to jack him. "Oh, no, sweet Pepper, definitely not a bad dream."

"I didn't know how to wake you up. I thought blowing you might do the trick. It worked."

"Blow me some more. No one gives head like you do."

Happy to oblige, Pepper crawled onto the bed. "I haven't had any breakfast yet. At least I'll get some protein."

Pepper enjoyed giving blow jobs. She always had. Ted had taught her early on the gay way, as he called it. The guys she had dated in Pittsburgh always asked how she had learned to give head like a pro. She refrained from telling them her gay boyfriend had given her personal lessons.

Ted writhed on the bed as she sucked with increasing forcefulness. She knew he liked it rougher than Butch, and told her more than once to show no mercy. She didn't. He tried to pull back against the suction, and she wouldn't let him. With the same sucking motion she used when drinking a thick milkshake, she pulled on his prick.

Suddenly her mouth filled with liquid and she automatically swallowed. Ted moaned and spurted again, and she swallowed that, too. The third time didn't produce much liquid. Then he settled down.

Pepper crawled up beside him, and put her head next to his on the pillow. "Are you awake yet?"

"I'm awake, and your breath smells like cum."

"S'pose I should go use some mouthwash, huh?"

"Not before I taste it." Ted pulled Pepper on top of him, and kissed her. He licked her teeth, and then pushed his tongue further into her mouth. Pepper humped his bare leg.

Ted pushed her onto the bed and rolled on top of her. "Horny today, are we?"

Pepper ran her fingers through Ted's hair. "I didn't get off again this morning. Butch had to leave."

Ted teased her. "I don't know, Pepper. You may be too much woman for the two of us to handle."

"Then, I'll do what I did in Pittsburgh. I'll pick up somebody."

"Is that really what you did?"

"Sometimes. I dated a few guys from the bank, too."

"Was it enough?"

"No."

"So, what did you do?"

"Played with myself, mostly. You know, her right hand is a girl's best friend."

"A guy's, too. That's what Butch and I've been doing."

"Pretty shitty, huh?"

"Yup. Nice to know there's a break in the clouds."

"You can say that again."

Ted sat up on the edge of the bed. "I'm going to shower. We'll eat, and then get to work."

Pepper lifted herself up on her elbows. "Aren't you going to get me off?"

"Nope."

"Why not?"

"Because I want to draw you while you're horny, maybe even while you masturbate. I want to see how the lines of your body change when you get hot."

"Geez Louise! I thought I could count on you."

"You can. I want to teach Butch how to get you off. It's about goddamn time. If he wants to fuck in the morning, he can set his alarm to get up earlier, so he has time."

Pepper scooted off the bed. "I like how you think, Theodore. I'll go get us some breakfast going while you shower."

By the time Ted came into the kitchen for breakfast, Pepper had the food on the table. "Shit, Pepper. You made pancakes?"

"Sure, why not? You had everything I needed."

"Butch will be sorry he missed this."

"He said he usually grabs something at the diner across the street from the garage."

"Not the same as you making pancakes. This is great!"

"Geez, doesn't take much to make you happy, does it?" Pepper sat down across from him.

"Not anymore. I feel like my family has come home."

"Me, too. Butch sort of said the same thing."

"What did he say?"

"He said he wants to try it. I think he likes living with you."

Ted swallowed a mouthful of pancakes. "I like having him here. I thought of getting a cat for company, but having someone to talk to is better."

"You're allergic to cats."

"Yeah, that's one in Butch's favor. That and his brick-shithouse body."

Pepper giggled. "Are you as gay around him as you are around me?"

"Sometimes. I try not to lay it on too thick. Don't want him getting homophobic on me."

"We'll see how he reacts now—I mean, after last night."

Ted squirted more syrup onto his stack of pancakes. "Damn, Pepper. These are good." Just before stuffing another forkful into his mouth, he asked, "You think Butch will want to butt-fuck with me again?"

"He told me again this morning he's looking forward to shoving it up your ass the way you did his. I think he meant it."

Ted looked up at the ceiling. "Thank you, God!"

Pepper grinned. "It's not polite to pray with your mouth full."

Ted swallowed. "Sorry."

"I guess Butch figures he can only go to hell once. According to his mother, he's already going for divorcing Sandy. So he might as well do what the fuck he wants from now on."

"A good philosophy to have. I've been living that way all my life."

"Butch thinks you're too smart to be in Willows Point. He can't understand why you stayed here. Why did you stay after your dad died?"

"Because running my dad's bar gave me a job and a flexible schedule so I can paint. I also got the house."

"Which is great for Butch and me. Thanks for letting us stay here."

"If you ask me, it's a pretty sweet setup. I'm my own boss. Why would I leave?"

"Because you're different than most people around here."

"So are you." He gazed at her intently.

"That's one of the reasons why I left."

"Tell me something. In Pittsburgh, were you any better off than you were here? I mean, did you have more friends, go to parties, make more money, that sort of stuff?"

"No, no, and no. Most of the guys I met didn't do a hell of a lot for me, and I didn't go out much, except to bars. I did make more money, but it cost more to live there."

"Then why did you stay there?"

"I didn't want to come back here, not with..." Pepper stopped. She still had trouble saying it out loud.

"Not with what?"

"Not with Butch being married to Sandy, and figuring you were still with John. Why the fuck would I want to come back?"

"We're why you never got involved with anyone, aren't we?"

"Yes and no. It took a long time to look around for someone else. When I did look, I couldn't find anyone I wanted to be with."

"Sounds like that's more yes than no."

"Maybe it is. It seems like a miracle that I ended up back here with the two of you. I never dreamed it could happen."

"Neither did I. That's a big reason why I think we can make this work. We want to be together."

"There'll be lots of gossip about us."

"There already is, with Butch's divorce and my questionable sexual preference. Now, you're the frosting on the cake."

Pepper held up her coffee cup to make a toast. "Here's to the three of us being in love."

Ted clinked her cup with his. "Nicely put, Pepper. I think we have been for a long time."

After they finished breakfast and cleaned up, Ted took Pepper into his studio. Pepper wasn't prepared for what she saw.

"My God, Ted. This is amazing!"

"It's pretty damn cool, isn't it?"

"When you said you converted the sunporch into a studio, I didn't know you meant you built a completely new room."

"You remember, the porch was long, but not very deep. I got to thinking, if I knocked out the wall facing the backyard, I could expand the room."

Pepper stood in front of the new wall. The sun streamed in the large windows that ran the length of it. "The little windows with the screens your dad had in here weren't anything like these. Where did you find such big windows?"

"I ordered them. This side of the house faces east and gets plenty of morning sun." Ted pointed to the far end of the porch, where the window shades were down. "I put the same windows down there. That side gets the best afternoon light."

"Doesn't it get hot in here, with all the sunlight?"

"Nope. I had central air put in the house after my dad died. If it gets too warm or too cold, I just have to adjust the thermostat."

"How can you afford all of this? It had to cost plenty."

"I've never told anyone this, not even Butch. But my dad

left me a chunk of change when he died. With his insurance policy, his bank account, and the bar, I don't have to worry."

Pepper walked around the studio. Ted had several finished paintings hanging on the wall. She looked at each one like she was walking through a museum.

The diversity surprised her. Along with the landscapes he had at the bar, he had portraits, nudes, and still lifes. All of them were realistic, resembling photographs. There were other paintings propped against the wall, and one unfinished work of an old-fashioned gas pump on an easel.

Canisters of paintbrushes sat on a table beside half-used tubes of oil paint and jars of powdered tempera. Several different sizes of palettes were stacked by the paint. Two other palettes were smeared with color.

Ted had angled a sketching table with special lighting in the corner, and put a laptop with a digital camera on a stand beside it. When Pepper saw the open sketch pad on the table, she stopped and stared at the picture of a nude man.

"Christ, Ted, that's Butch!"

"There are a lot more."

"Can I see them?"

"I'll show them to you later. I want to sketch you while the light is good in here."

"Aren't you afraid Butch might see this?"

"I told him when he moved in that coming in here is by invitation only. The same goes for you, Miss Pepper. This is my private sanctuary."

"I guess I should be honored you let me come in."

"You're one of the very few."

"You know Butch expects to watch you draw me. He asked me to call him later and let him know how long you'll be working. He hopes to do only a half day today."

Ted took Pepper's hand. "Let's sit for a minute. I want to tell you what I'm thinking." He led Pepper to the sofa, and moved some picture frames so they could sit down. "I want Butch to watch me sketch you. He's never seen me work."

"How did you get that sketch of him?"

"From some old photographs, and from memory."

"That's amazing! It really looks like him."

"It should. I've been drawing him for years, just like I have been you."

"Why us, Ted?

"I've never stopped loving either of you."

"I thought it was just me, I mean, that I couldn't stop loving you and Butch."

Ted squeezed Pepper's hand. "After we all stopped seeing each other, did you ever cry yourself to sleep?"

Pepper's eyes glassed over remembering how much she'd cried. She looked at Ted and nodded. "Yeah, I did."

"So did I. Don't know if Butch cried, that's not his style. But I do know he's spent years beating himself up over what happened."

"He told me. He apologized for fucking up last night."

"I remember the night Butch came into the bar to tell me he'd left Sandy. I honestly thought somebody had died, he looked so bad. He wanted to know if he could stay with me. It took everything I had not to plant a big, wet kiss on him when I said yes."

"Why didn't you tell me?"

"That's a hard one, Pepper. I hadn't heard from you in a long time, and figured you had built a new life for yourself. I didn't want to upset the applecart."

"I tried to build a new life. It didn't fly."

"I'm sure Butch would've tried to track you down, now that his divorce is final. As it turned out, he didn't have to."

"Yeah, Lois thinks I'm like a bad penny. I keep turning up."

"Screw Lois. You don't have to ask her for anything. Butch and I'll make sure you're all right. You have a home, with us."

"We are a family, aren't we?"

"It seems all we have these days is each other. I'd say that's a family, wouldn't you?"

Pepper wiped her eyes and smiled. "Yeah, I would."

"I never got around to telling you how I'm using you as bait."

"You're what?"

"Using you as bait. I want to reel Butch in."

"I don't know what the fuck you're talking about, Theodore."

"You got him to buttfuck. Now I want you to get him to pose, both by himself and with you."

"You're out of your frigging mind. He won't do that." She pictured Butch's response to such a request.

"I think he will, if you ask him."

"Ted, you've definitely gone over the high side with this one. I'll pose for you, but the chances of Butch taking off all his clothes and standing naked while you draw him are slim to none."

"Not if he's feeling you up while he's doing it."

"What?"

"Okay, let me lay it out for you. I want to sketch both of you nude, separately and together. Then I want to do a painting of you and Butch making love."

Pepper laughed. "You aren't serious?"

"Who says? I've wanted to do a work like this ever since I can remember. You and Butch as models? Perfect."

Pepper stood and walked over to the window. She focused on the birdbath in the backyard. "Look, there's a cardinal. Isn't it beautiful?"

Ted reached over to a stack of paintings leaning against the wall by the sofa. He pulled out a small canvas. "Here, take a look at this."

He handed her an oil painting of the cardinal she had just seen, perched on the edge of the birdbath. "God, Ted, this is really good." Pepper looked at the bird and again at the painting. "It's the same one, isn't it?"

"Yup. It must have a nest somewhere close by. It comes for some birdseed and a bath every day about this time."

Still holding the painting, Pepper walked the length of the studio, and back to where Ted still sat on the sofa. She took it all in—the paints, the pencils, the sketch pads, the canvases. She stopped in front of him. "You really are an artist, aren't you?"

"I really am. And I want to paint the two people I love."

Pepper put the painting down and went back to the sketch of Butch. "Are you going to show him this?"

"Yes. But I want you to back me up when I do."

Pepper lightly traced the lines of the drawing with her finger. "He's beautiful, isn't he?"

"There's a reason Michelangelo's art is so great. He used Italian men as models."

"I can't promise I can convince him, but I'll try."

Ted jumped up and wrapped his arms around her. "Thank you, sweet Pepper. I knew you'd help me."

"Shouldn't we get started? I don't want you to lose the light."

Ted kissed her hair. "Take off all your clothes."

Pepper glanced at all the windows. "Can anybody see in here?"

"No. I made sure of that. The backyard is plenty big, and I reinforced the fence my dad built around it. I sure as hell don't want nosy neighbors watching me paint."

While Pepper undressed, Ted opened the sofa bed. He already had white sheets on it. "How long has it been since you've opened that bed?"

"About a month. I changed the sheets afterward. They're clean."

"That's not why I wanted to know."

"Why did you ask?"

"I wondered if you've slept with anyone in here."

"A few times. Didn't like how it felt to me, so I stopped doing it."

Pepper crawled onto the bed. "Then why did you change the bed a month ago?"

"Because I had to jerk off after working on that drawing of Butch. I messed up the bed."

"I'm surprised you haven't come on to him. Sounds like you've been ready to jump his bones since he moved in."

"I have. But he hasn't been in great shape. I didn't want to make it harder for him."

"From what I've seen, you couldn't make it much harder. He's been like a poker."

"Which is what he needed to do, poke-her, get it?"

Pepper laughed. "Yeah, I got it all right. And it felt great!" She stretched out on the bed as if making a snow angel. "So, what do you want me to do?"

"Relax!"

"I would be more relaxed if you were here beside me."

Ted pointed to the sketching table. "I'm going to be sitting on my stool, making love to you with my pencil on the sketch pad."

"Can I have a pencil to diddle with?"

"No, I want you to diddle with your middle finger."

"God, Ted, I don't know if I can do this."

Ted flipped the page over with Butch's drawing, and then picked up a pencil. "Sure you can. Relax and focus. I want to see what position your body naturally takes when you mastur- bate. I've imagined it. Now, I want to see it."

"Can I close my eyes?"

"Absolutely. Fantasize about Butch, if that helps. Forget I'm here. Just do your thing."

Pepper took him at his word. She closed her eyes and thought of Butch being there with her. Ted said he would show him how to give her an orgasm. She imagined that now, pretending the finger between her legs belonged to Butch.

The more she thought about Butch rubbing her, the hotter she got. Her hand went to her breast and she squeezed her own flesh. When she pinched her nipple, a soft sound bubbled up in her throat. She pinched harder. The sparks went straight to her clit.

Pepper tickled the skin around her vagina before dipping a finger inside. She wanted to be fucked so bad. Her finger moved faster, trying to reach the core of her body as only a man's cock could.

She rubbed, and squeezed, and fucked herself, completely forgetting Ted sat there watching. She only thought of Butch, and of his hands on her. At the moment of her orgasm, Pepper shouted Butch's name.

8

Pepper sat on the bed wearing only a painter's smock that Ted had given her. He'd handed her his cell phone before he ran upstairs to the bathroom. She dialed Butch's number.

"Hello. Don't tell me, Pepper?"

"Who else?"

"I figured. What's up?"

"When can you come home?"

"I've cleared the decks to leave soon. The other guys here will cover for me."

"Good. Ted wants to show you how he works."

"I know how he works after last night."

Pepper giggled. "Not that. I mean how he draws me."

"Did you work with him this morning?"

"I sure did. You won't believe some of the pictures he drew."

Butch lowered his voice. "I can't really talk right now. I'll be home in about fifteen minutes."

"There are people around?"

"You got it. See you soon." Butch hung up.

While waiting for Ted to come back, Pepper wandered over

to look at the sketch pad again. Ted had drawn her in amazing detail. After she had an orgasm, he asked her to hold the position with one hand on her breast and the other between her legs. After her posing lesson the day before, she understood what he wanted her to do.

When he finished, he let her see what he'd done. There were several small drawings of her torso in different positions, and one bigger drawing of her whole body. It startled her to see how much the likeness resembled her, and how quickly he had drawn the different positions.

It embarrassed her, too. The drawings clearly showed her masturbating. Ted had captured the heat in her body, and her lack of inhibition when she climaxed. Even with her self-consciousness about being the model, Pepper recognized the artistry in Ted's work. His talent couldn't be denied.

Pepper didn't hear Ted come back into the studio. Only when he wrapped his arms around her shoulders did she realize he was there. "What do you think?"

"How long have you been behind me?"

"A couple minutes. You've been looking at my drawings like an art critic would."

"I can't believe that's me."

"It is. Aren't you beautiful?"

Pepper turned around. Ted continued to hold her. "You made me beautiful. There's more in those pictures than just me."

"What do you mean?"

"When you showed me the pictures of Helga in that Wyeth book, I got a feeling from them. I knew the man who drew them loved her. I get the same feeling when I look at those drawings of me."

"Well, it's true. I do love you."

"But you're gay, aren't you?"

"I've always thought I was. You know I've always been into

guys. But I think now it doesn't matter if it's a guy or a girl. What matters is what I feel for the person."

"Like what you feel for Butch and me?"

"Exactly. I'm hot for both of you. I didn't plan that. It just happened."

"I'm hot for both of you, too. A girl isn't supposed to fall in love with two guys."

"And a gay guy isn't supposed to want to fuck a woman. But here we are. It's the three of us. It's like we've come full circle, and hooked up again."

"Speaking of the three of us, Butch will be here in a few minutes. I don't know who was there, but he couldn't talk."

"He's careful at the garage. Lots of people in town would love to know what he's up to. They listen a little too closely when he's on the phone."

"That stinks on ice."

"I know. He's learned to live with it. After a while, you get used to it. It's like you're some kind of celebrity or something when people gossip about you."

"I'll try to remember that when I hear people whisper when I walk by."

"I'm telling you, Pepper. You have to let it roll off. If I didn't, I couldn't live in this town."

"Do the guys at the bar ever rag on you?"

"No. Believe it or not, they defend me. It's their wives who gossip and spread rumors."

"Probably at Lois's beauty parlor. What a bunch of hens. I never could stand to go in there."

"What? You wouldn't like to do Sandy's hair?"

"I'd love to shave the bitch's head. Does that work?" Ted laughed.

"Works for me." Butch stood in the door. "Am I allowed to come in?"

"Hey, *paisan*! Welcome home." Ted went over to escort him into the studio. "How's your asshole today?"

"Wasn't too bad, until I had to take a crap. Then, I remembered the Golden Rule. You know, do unto others . . ."

"Looking forward to it, buddy."

Butch did a once-over of the room. "So, this is the off-limits studio?"

His remark surprised Pepper. "You've never been in here?"

"Rembrandt never invited me. Didn't he tell you? You only get in here with an invitation."

"He told me." Pepper opened the smock and flashed Butch. "I got an invitation."

"Yeah, I bet you did."

Pepper closed the smock and tied the sash. "Wanna see what he drew?"

"Sure I do."

Pepper glanced at Ted and saw him give her a nod of approval. Pepper took Butch's hand and led him to the sketching table. "Look at this."

Butch sat down on the stool and looked at the drawings. Pepper stepped back, to give him time to take it all in. Ted gave her a thumbs-up.

Almost inaudibly, Butch muttered, "Jesus Christ." Then he did what Pepper had done to the sketch of him. He lightly traced each drawing with his finger, studying the lines with the movement of his hand. Neither Ted nor Pepper interrupted. They waited for Butch to turn around.

When he finally turned toward them, all is said was, "That's Pepper."

"Aren't they good?" Pepper went over to the stool. She wedged herself between Butch's knees and then wrapped her arms around his neck. "We live with a real artist."

Butch put his hands on her hips. "You're fucking hot in those pictures. Did you really do all of that?"

"I really did."

Ted spoke up behind her. "Tell him what you thought about, Pepper."

Pepper looked directly into Butch's eyes when she said, "I thought about you. I imagined you making me come, and Ted drew it."

"Lord have mercy!"

Ted laughed. "Your Catholic roots are showing, *paisan*."

"That's not all that's showing." Butch rubbed his prick against Pepper's leg. "Those pictures gave me one hell of a woody."

Pepper looked over her shoulder at Ted. "What time do you have to be at the bar today?"

"I own the damn place. I don't have to show up at all if I don't want to."

"Want to draw Butch and me making out?"

"Ask me twice."

Pepper turned back to Butch. "Get naked and let's fool around."

Butch glanced at Ted before answering. "I don't know, Pepper. Sounds kind of weird to me."

"It's not weird. Artists draw things. Ted wants to draw us together. Sounds like fun to me."

Ted volunteered, "Robert, I think Miss Pearl will make it worth your while."

Pepper ignored Ted calling her Pearl. She could see Butch digesting the idea, and kept quiet so he could concentrate. She wanted to laugh at his bewilderment when he said, "Last night, you talked me into letting Rembrandt stick his dick up my ass. Today, you want me to let him draw us getting it on. What's next? Videotaping live sex acts for the Internet?"

Ted defused that one. "I promise, when I tape you, it will be to sketch the freeze-frames. I swear, none of it will be posted on the Internet."

"Well, then, that makes it okay, doesn't it?" Even with his ambivalence, he added, "Should I shower first?"

Not missing a beat, Ted asked, "What do you think, Pepper? Does he stink?"

Pepper leaned over and sniffed Butch's neck. Then she lifted his shirt and sniffed his chest. Before pronouncing her verdict, she lifted his arm and sniffed his armpit. "He doesn't stink at all. In fact, he smells kinda good."

Butch tried to grope her tit. Pepper jumped back. "Oh, no, *paisan*. Strip and get on the bed. We're making out for Ted, re-member?"

Without saying a word, Butch stood up and took off all his clothes. Pepper took off the smock and crawled onto the bed. Butch joined her. Ted flipped the page on his sketch pad and again picked up a pencil.

Pepper whispered into Butch's ear, "Don't think about Ted. Think about what we're doing. Ted will do what he needs to do."

"Do I get to fuck you?"

"Maybe. But we have to fool around first, so Ted can see what we look like together."

Butch licked her cheek. "How fucking perverted can we get?"

"We're grown-ups now. We can be as fucking perverted as we want."

Butch yelled at Ted. "Hey, Rembrandt, can I go down on her?"

"Do it, man. I'm with you."

Pepper tried not to think about Ted drawing them, but still tensed up when Butch crawled between her legs. She closed her eyes and took a deep breath. Ted had seen Butch go down on her before. He knew what to expect. She had no reason to be nervous.

Butch nuzzled her inner thighs. Her focus shifted from Ted

to the sensation of Butch licking her leg. When his tongue connected with her clit, Pepper sighed, and melted into the bed.

He licked her slowly, even lazily. Each tickle of his tongue made her clit throb more. She pushed her pelvis against his face, reflexively wanting to be penetrated. Pepper thought she heard clicking noises, but was too far gone to care. Butch wasn't. He stopped and lifted his head.

"What the fuck are you doing?"

Ted lowered his digital camera. "Taking some pictures."

"What for?"

"What do you think? I need to study them."

"Yeah, while jacking off." Butch climbed off the bed. "I don't do porn. I'm outta here."

Pepper pulled herself together and grabbed his arm. "Butch, wait."

"Pepper, I'd do fucking anything for you. But this is too much. Pictures? C'mon."

"He needs them."

"What the fuck does he need pictures for? He paints, right?"

"Yes, and he wants to paint us."

"What?"

"Ted wants to paint us." Pepper got up, took Butch's hand, and led him back to the sketching table. "Look at this." She flipped the pages back on the sketch pad. "That's you."

Butch stared at the picture, and then looked at Ted. "How the fuck did you do this? I never posed for you."

Pepper answered before Ted could. "He did it from pictures, and from memory. That's why he needs pictures. He studies them to be able to draw us."

"She's right, *paisan*. Wanna see what else I've done from pictures?" Ted reached behind the sofa and pulled out a couple of sketch pads, one clearly marked "Pepper" and the other marked "Butch". He handed them both to Butch. "Go ahead. Have a look."

Butch sat down on the bed, and laid the large tablet beside him. Pepper looked over his shoulder. He flipped though Pepper's first. Page after page of drawings showed Pepper sitting and standing, laughing and crying, clothed and nude. Butch paused on one page and gently touched it. "That's the picture in my wallet. God, how many times did I look at it?"

"Me, too, buddy. I scanned my copy into the computer and enlarged it to make that drawing."

"How long have you been doing this, I mean making drawings of her?"

"I started before we all broke up. Over the years, I kept coming back to it."

Pepper pointed to the other tablet. "Look at that one, and prepare yourself, he's been drawing you, too."

Butch opened the other pad. Pepper had her hand on his shoulder and felt him twitch when he saw the first drawing. "That's me in my football uniform."

"I drew it from the picture in the yearbook."

"And this is me standing by my first car, the one I rebuilt the engine in." He glanced at Ted. "My uncle told me I could have it if I could make it run. He taught me how to be a mechanic using that damn car."

Pepper laughed. "Remember, we fucked in the backseat to celebrate when you got it going."

Again, Butch looked at Ted. "You did this from a picture?"

"I liked the expression on your face. You looked like you'd just won the damn lottery."

"I felt like I did. I kept it going for about four years before I junked it."

Butch continued to flip the pages. As he did with Pepper, Ted had drawn Butch in various poses and emotions. The last few pages became progressively more erotic.

Pepper giggled. "Love the caption you gave this one." Ted

had scrawled the word *HUMMER* beside a drawing of Butch. In it, Butch had a full erection.

"It stands for High Utility Maximum Mobility Easy Rider. It fits, doesn't it?"

Pepper leaned over and looked down at Butch's cock. "Barely, if I'm wet enough."

Butch flipped the page over. "I hope you two are enjoying yourselves."

Pepper crawled onto the bed and knelt behind Butch. "I would be enjoying myself more if we could go back to what we were doing."

"You don't care that Rembrandt is taking pictures of us?"

"No, I don't mind. I trust him. Don't you?"

Butch stared at Ted for several seconds before he answered. "I've trusted him for years. He's my best friend. Came through for me in spades when I really needed it." Then he looked down at a drawing of himself jerking off. "What kind of picture do you want to paint?"

"I want to paint you and Pepper making love."

"What are you going to do with it?"

"I'm thinking I'll hang it over the king-size bed I'm going to buy for Pepper's room."

In unison, Butch and Pepper said, "What?"

"We need a bed big enough for the three of us when we want to sleep together. We can throw out that old bed that's in there. I'll get a bigger one to replace it."

Butch unexpectedly grabbed Pepper and threw her down on the bed. "I'm moving in with you." Then he tickled her.

Pepper thrashed on the bed, trying to escape the assault. She couldn't. Butch kept tickling her, and Ted's camera clicked away. This time, Butch didn't seem to mind. In fact, he deliberately pinned one of Pepper's legs to the bed, forcing her legs wide open.

"Get some good ones, Rembrandt. I want my own album."

Ted walked around the bed, snapping pictures from all angles. When Pepper gasped, "Stop, I'm going to pee myself," Butch finally eased up.

Butch rolled over onto his back, and his erection flopped onto his belly. Ted snapped a few more shots of him, and then put the camera down. "Mind if I join you?"

Butch pointed to the window by the bed. "You can if you lower the damn blinds."

Ted obliged, but also took a shot. "What? You afraid someone will see your sorry ass in bed with me?"

"What the fuck? By tomorrow, my naked ass will probably be on the Internet, with you and with Pepper."

"Not a chance, unless you put it there."

Pepper had her breath back. "I have to pee. Don't do anything until I get back." She bounced off the bed and ran upstairs to the bathroom. It took a bit longer when she realized she had to do more than pee. After she cleaned up, she headed back to the studio. On the way down, she grabbed some condoms and the tube of lubricant, just in case.

When she came back into the studio, she couldn't believe her eyes. Ted had stripped, and knelt on the bed blowing Butch. "Hey, I told you not to do anything until I got back."

Butch opened his eyes. "Rembrandt wanted to give me some head. Not as good as yours, but not too bad."

Pepper jutted out her lower lip and feigned pouting. "I feel left out."

Ted raised his head and looked at Butch. "She feels left out. Don't you think we should do something about that?"

"Damn right we should. Come here, sweetheart."

Both Butch and Ted looked at her like a couple of lecherous wolves. She shivered. "What are you going to do?"

"What do you have in your hand?" Ted craned to see.

Pepper tossed the condoms and the tube of lube on the bed. "I brought this, just in case you guys decide to buttfuck again."

Ted smiled an absolutely evil smile. "Have you ever been buttfucked?"

His question made Pepper nervous. "Hell, no. Doesn't it hurt?"

Ted turned to Butch. "Tell her the truth, *paisan*. Does it hurt?"

Butch smiled. "Oh, baby, it hurts so good."

"Well, there it is, Pepper. How about we do a sandwich?"

Much to Pepper's surprise, the suggestion seemed to appeal to Butch. "Rembrandt, that's not a bad idea. I want to loosen her up."

"Whoa! Back off, buckos! I haven't said I would."

Using a sweet, sympathetic voice, Ted coaxed her. "Sweet Pepper, we'll be careful, won't we, Butch?"

"Sure we will." Rather than sounding concerned, Butch sounded like a letch persuading her to get into the backseat with him and his friend. For some reason, that turned her on.

"You guys better not hurt me."

Ted took her hand and pulled her toward the bed. "We'll make sure you're ready before we do anything."

"Yeah, right." Pepper wasn't convinced.

Butch took her other hand. "Sweetheart, we'll have you so hot, you'll be begging us for it."

"Didn't you say you don't do porn? Could have fooled me." Even with her protests, Pepper could already feel her clit throbbing. Turning herself over to her two lovers did make her hot, and she probably would end up begging for it.

"Since no one is taking any pictures, I don't think you could call this porn. What would you call it, Ted?"

"One hell of a good time, buddy."

Butch chuckled, obviously enjoying this edgy threesome.

"Bend over, Pepper. Ted, hand me the lube." Butch slicked up his hand.

Pepper got down on all fours. "Be careful."

"Don't worry, I'll go easier on you than Ted did on me. By the way, are you empty?"

"I just went. I should be."

"Good."

Pepper braced herself. Ted noticed her tensing. "Missy, you have to relax. You know what we did with Butch last night."

"Okay, you're right." Pepper took a deep breath and exhaled through her mouth. Butch chose that moment to push his finger into her ass. Pepper yelped.

"Did I hurt you?"

"No, just surprised me. I'm all right."

"Remember, relax and enjoy the ride." Butch slowly finger-fucked her, while Ted played with her tits. "How's that, Pepper?"

Pepper pushed back on his finger. "I want it deeper."

"You can tell you're used to being fucked. That's my middle finger. I can't go any deeper."

Ted pinched her nipple. Pepper moaned. "She's ready for another finger. Try her and see how she does."

Pepper felt her anus stretch. Her vaginal muscles contracted and then relaxed. She moaned, "Oh, God! I want to be fucked!"

"Yeah, Pepper. I felt that, sweetheart."

Ted looked up. "What happened?"

"Her pussy grabbed at my hand. I felt it the whole way up my arm."

"Go for three, Butch." Pepper pushed back when Butch inserted his third finger. He kept his hand still while she rocked back and forth.

"I'll be damned! She's humping my hand."

Ted leaned over and whispered in her ear, "You're a natural, sweet Pepper." Then he lifted her chin and kissed her, pushing his tongue deep into her mouth. Pepper sucked his tongue like she had his cock that morning. Ted pulled back. "She's ready, *paisan*. You have dibs."

"I should take her pussy and you do her ass. You know what you're doing back there. I'll experiment with you, not her."

"Now, there's a pickup line I've never heard." Ted retrieved a condom. "Toss me the lube."

Pepper had never wanted it so bad in her whole life. In a hoarse whisper, she asked Ted, "How do we do this?"

"You straddle Butch and mount him. Stick your ass up in the air. I'll take care of the rest."

Butch pulled his fingers out, and then propped himself against the back of the couch. "Turn around, Pepper, and sit on my lap."

Ted helped Pepper swivel around. "That's it, love. Put a knee on each side of his beefy thighs."

"Ever consider directing porn movies? You'd be good at it."

"I'll remember you said that when I tape you and Pepper doing it."

Pepper snapped, "If one of you doesn't fuck me soon, I'm going to fuck myself."

Butch lewdly shook his dick in front of her. "Here it is, mama. You want it, come and get it."

Pepper didn't care about Butch's rudeness. She wanted his prick inside of her. "Ted, are you ready?"

"I'm ready, Pepper. Mount the son of a bitch."

Pepper grabbed Butch's prick and held it up. Then she lifted herself up and slowly lowered herself back down. Butch's erection filled her cunt.

Butch grimaced. "Jesus, that's good. Ted, fuck her ass."

"I'm on it." Ted pushed Pepper forward, and her tits rubbed against Butch's chin. She felt Ted pulling her ass cheeks apart.

When he pushed the head of his cock into her anus, she raised up. Pepper came back down on Butch's prick just as Ted lunged forward.

She had never felt anything like this. Both men were inside her. She thought her belly would explode, it felt so full. But at the same time, it felt good, even wonderful. Ted leaned over and licked her neck. Butch fondled her tits. She had never been so gloriously happy in her life. The two men she loved wanted her as much as she wanted them.

Ted slowly pulled out and pushed himself back in. "Pepper, is that all right?"

She nodded yes, unable to speak. Then she heard Butch. "Sweetheart, move with Ted. Lift up when he pulls out, and come back down when he pushes in."

Pepper managed to say, "Okay."

It took a couple of tries to get the rhythm, but once they had it they moved together. Like a finely tuned clock, Butch thrust upward as Pepper came down as Ted pushed in. Then they reversed the movement and did it again. For several minutes they did this erotic dance, moving together, and feeling together.

Pepper's climax took her by surprise. She gasped for air and went rigid, trapping both men inside her. She bore down on Butch, while Ted managed to continue thrusting. Suddenly Butch yelled, "Jesus Christ!" and raised his hips off the bed, taking Pepper with him. With one final thrust, Ted also cut loose.

The three lovers had consummated their union.

9

Pepper saw Butch getting out of his truck. After pulling into the driveway behind him, she opened her window and yelled, "Did Ted call you, too?"

"A few minutes ago. Told me to get home pronto. Do you know what's going on?"

"No. He called me at the bar and said the same thing. It sounded important." Pepper jumped out of the car and caught up with Butch. "I hope nothing's wrong."

"Me, too." They ran up the back stairs and into the kitchen. There was no sign of Ted. Butch shouted, "Hey, Rembrandt, where the hell are you? Is everything all right?"

They heard his voice from the direction of his studio. "Everything's fine. I'll be right there."

When Ted came in, they could see he had been working. He had paint on his hands, and a big smudge on his flushed face. He was also breathless. "You two got here fast. I thought I had a few more minutes."

Pepper grabbed the dishcloth. "You sounded like the roof

caved in. Of course we got here fast." She rubbed the smear of paint on his cheek. "What the hell is going on?"

"I finished it."

"What?"

"The painting of you and Butch! I finished it."

Butch got a glass of water and handed it to Ted. "Here, drink this. You're red as a beet. Don't want you to pass out on us."

"Thanks." Ted sat down and drank the water.

Pepper knelt beside the chair. "It's wonderful that it's finished, but for heaven's sake, couldn't that have waited until we got home from work?"

"There's more."

Butch couldn't contain his impatience. "For Christ's sake, Ted, what the fuck is going on?"

"I got a call today, from the Carnegie Museum in Pittsburgh. They want me to exhibit some of my stuff in a contemporary American exhibit they're doing." Ted stopped talking, unable to continue.

Pepper took the now-empty glass. "Butch, get him some more water. Put some ice in it."

Butch quickly refilled the glass and gave it back to Pepper. "Ted, sip this and breathe slowly. You're going to hyperventilate."

Ted took a minute to compose himself. "I'm sorry. This is just so fucking unbelievable."

Butch grabbed a chair and put it beside Ted's, straddling it to sit down. "What's so unbelievable? You're a good artist. You deserve to be in an exhibit."

Ted put the cold glass against his forehead. "Pepper, remember what I told you about how much I love Andrew Wyeth and Edward Hopper?"

"Sure I do."

"Well, their paintings will be in the exhibit. So will paintings by N. C. Wyeth and Thomas Eakins, and a bunch of others. My pictures will be in a section for new artists called 'American Realism—Continuing The Line.'"

Pepper clapped her hands. "Ted, this is incredible!"

"It's fucking unbelievable."

Butch laughed. "Yeah, you said that already."

Ted shook his head in wonderment. "My paintings will be hanging in the same gallery with Wyeth's and Hopper's. I can't believe it!"

Something occurred to Pepper. "Do you know if the museum sent a couple of guys to the bar a few weeks ago to see your stuff?"

"The person I talked to sounded like he'd seen my work. It makes sense that they saw it at the bar."

"I remember two guys in business suits came in and asked to see Theodore Duncan's work. I told them to look around, that you'd painted every picture in the room. They looked at all of them."

"Why didn't you tell me?"

"Because they didn't ask to buy one. Lots of people come in to look at your pictures. I remember these guys because I'd never seen them before."

"How the hell did they know about you in Pittsburgh?" Butch eyed Pepper.

"Don't look at me! I didn't tell anyone." Pepper shot the question back at Ted. "How *did* they know about you?"

"You're gonna love this part. The museum asked some professors at Carnegie Mellon if they knew any local artists with a style like Wyeth's. John teaches there now. He told them about my work, and how to find me. The guy on the phone told me the museum decided my paintings will fit in."

Butch reacted first to the mention of John's name. "Well, that's a fucking bolt from the blue."

"That's the damn truth." John's part in this made Pepper uncomfortable. "Have you been in touch with John?"

"Not a word. The people from the museum told me about John's referral."

Butch picked up on Pepper's concern. "Do you want to see him again on account of this?"

"Jesus Christ, no! That's the last thing I want."

Pepper's voice cracked a bit when she asked, "Are you sure?"

Ted took her hand and squeezed it. "Pepper, the last four months with you two have been the happiest of my life. I have what I want right here in my own backyard."

Butch patted him on the back. "Thank you, Dorothy."

Ted smiled. "Better watch that. You're starting to sound gay."

"That's what happens when you take it up the ass as often as I have."

"Now, now. Be nice." Pepper stood up. "I want to see the painting."

"Before you do, there's one more thing. They have to decide what to show. So, they asked me for photographs of my stuff, including my most current work. Since this painting is the only thing I've done in the last four months, I want to send them a picture of it."

"What the fuck for?" Butch stood up beside Pepper. "You said that painting would go in Pepper's room, over the bed."

"That painting will stay in this house, just like I said. But I want them to see it. It's the best thing I've ever done."

Pepper slipped her arm through Butch's. "What if they want to show it?"

Ted's fingers fluttered over his glass like a flutist's. "Yeah, what if?"

"Rembrandt, I don't want my bare ass hanging in a gallery in Pittsburgh."

Ted caught Pepper's eye. She could see his conflict, as much

as she could feel her own. "I want to see it, Ted. I can't say yes
or no until I do."

"Yeah, okay. C'mon, then."

Ted put his glass on the table. Butch and Pepper followed
him into his studio. Whenever they posed, Ted always turned
the easel so they couldn't see it. He asked them not to look at
the painting until he had finished it. Both Butch and Pepper
had honored his request.

The canvas sat on the easel, still turned so they couldn't see
it. Ted walked around to his spot in front of the painting. Butch
and Pepper waited by the sofa, wanting to be sure they had
Ted's blessing.

Much to their surprise, Ted headed back to the door. "Take
your time and look it over. I'll be back in a few minutes." He
left them alone.

Butch stared at the door for a moment. "I think Rembrandt
is about to puke."

Pepper thought so, too. "He didn't look too good, did he?"

"Fucking artists!"

Pepper held Butch's hand. "Are you as nervous about seeing
it as I am?"

"I don't know about nervous, but I'm sure as hell not choked
up about anyone besides us seeing it."

"Me, neither. That's why I'm nervous."

Butch went toward the easel, pulling Pepper along behind
him. "Let's see what he did."

Pepper closed her eyes. "Oh, God! I can't look. How em-
barrassing is it?"

Butch didn't say anything. Pepper opened her eyes. Butch
stood silently staring at the picture. She turned to see it for herself, and her breath caught.

The tempera painting reminded Pepper of the pictures in
Ted's Andrew Wyeth book. The skin and hair almost looked
like a photograph, they seemed so real. Pepper looked at her

arm and then at the picture. It perfectly matched her freckled fair skin and copper colored hair, as it did Butch's olive skin and his disheveled black hair.

But that's not what left Pepper speechless. Even with their naked bodies intertwined, Butch and Pepper's faces held the focus of the painting.

Butch had his hand on her breast and his leg over her stomach. Ted managed to capture the sense of movement as Butch rolled on top of her. Butch's leg covered her pelvis, with only a bit of entangled pubic hair visible, her rusty brown with his jet black. Their genitals were hidden from view.

What she couldn't pull her eyes away from was how Butch looked at her. The expression on his face mingled tenderness with passion, love with lust, and joy with pain. She had her arms wrapped around his shoulders, accepting him with absolute adoration. Between them, she could feel their history, the grief of their separation, and the gift of their reunion.

Pepper glanced at Butch. He seemed as entranced by the feeling of it as she. Not wanting to sway his opinion with hers, she asked, "What do you think?"

Butch ran his fingers through his hair. "I don't know. I've never seen anything like it."

"Neither have I." Pepper pointed to Ted's signature. "Look." In tiny letters in the corner, in perfect calligraphy Ted wrote his name, *Theodore Duncan*.

"How long do you suppose it took him to write it like that?"

"Don't know. But I've never seen his name like that on any other painting, have you?"

"Nope." Butch asked the question she didn't know how to answer. "What do you think of it?"

She closed her eyes and tried to focus, not knowing how to make the words come out right. "That's us."

"No kidding!"

"I don't know how to say it. If it weren't us, I'd say it's the most beautiful painting of lovers I'd ever seen."

"But?"

"But fuck, Butch, it's us! I mean, anyone who knows us and sees this painting will know it's us."

"And they'll also know you're in love." Ted stood in the doorway, now looking quite pale. He suddenly leaned against the doorframe, as though he might go down.

"Rembrandt, you'd better sit. You look like shit." Butch went over to help him.

"I just lost my breakfast."

"Figured as much." Butch led him to the couch. "Christ, I've never seen you so fucked up. You need to get a grip."

Pepper put a pillow behind Ted's head and then sat down next to him. "Butch, grab the waste can in case he gets sick again." She rubbed Ted's stomach in a circular motion. "How do you feel?"

"Gross."

Butch put the can next to Ted, and then sat on the arm of the couch. "That's some picture you made."

Ted tried to turn his head to look at Butch, and immediately stopped. "I'm going to toss."

Pepper grabbed the garbage can just as Ted leaned forward. She held it for him as he vomited again.

"Butch, run and get him a can of ginger ale. And bring a towel."

Ted retched into the can for a couple of minutes before he settled down. When Butch came back, he brought the soda, some paper towels, and a wet dish towel. He handed Pepper the paper towels and ginger ale, then folded the towel and put it on Ted's forehead. "How is he?"

Pepper wiped Ted's face, and then popped the top on the soda can. She handed it to Ted. "He's all right. He just needs to calm down."

"Says you!" Ted sipped the soda. "This is the most incredible day of my life. I have a right to be a wreck!"

Butch laughed. "He's coming around."

Ted again turned his head toward Butch. This time, he managed it. "What did you think of it?"

"Of what?"

"Don't fuck with me, *paisan*. Do you like it?"

Butch looked at Pepper. "Ladies first."

"Pepper? C'mon, somebody say something. This is killing me."

"Ted, it's beautiful." Pepper looked down at her hands before she finished her thought. "But everyone will know it's us."

"Pepper, I'm not going to hang it in the bar. It belongs in this house. All I want is to let the museum show it for a while, if it makes the cut."

"I say let him do it."

Both Ted and Pepper stared at Butch. Pepper was incredulous. "What did you say?" He might as well have said he wanted to study ballet.

"I said we should let him do it. It's the most beautiful painting I've ever seen. How can we say no?"

"Because people know me in Pittsburgh! What if someone recognizes me?"

"What if they do? And honestly, Pepper, did you hang out with people who go to museums?"

"How the hell would I know if they go to museums?" Pepper knew she sounded shrill. She couldn't help it. "That's you and me fucking, Butch. Doesn't it bother you if people see it?"

"Before Ted showed it to us, I would've said yes. But now . . ." Butch stood and went back to look at the painting. "This sounds weird, but it kinda looks like it should be in a church or something. It makes me feel good inside, like going to church used to."

"Hey, man, you never heard anyone say, 'God is love?'"

"Yeah, I've heard it. This is the first time I've seen it."

Pepper came over beside Butch. "If I could stop thinking about it being me, I'd agree with you. I thought it would be hot, and it is. But it's holy, too, like the statue of David."

Ted grinned. "I told you, Michelangelo used Italian men as models."

Pepper studied Butch's body in the painting. "You're so beautiful in it."

"So are you." Butch turned Pepper to face him. "Maybe we should forget that it's us and let everyone see how good Rembrandt is."

Ted chimed in with, "Listen to him, Pepper. For once in his life, he's making sense."

Without taking his eyes off Pepper, Butch retorted, "Rembrandt, I'd watch my step if I were you. I'm on your side."

Ted muttered, "Who would've thought?"

Butch brushed Pepper's hair back. "Whaddya say, Pearl? Do we cut Theodore some slack?"

Pepper kicked him. "Don't call me Pearl!"

"For God's sake, Butch, don't piss her off!" Ted got up. He came over and wrapped his arms around her waist. "Pepper, remember what you said after I showed you Wyeth's pictures of Helga, about how they made you feel?"

"I remember."

Butch looked over Pepper's shoulder at Ted. "What did she say?"

"She said she got a feeling from them, like the man who drew them loved Helga." Ted hugged her tightly against him. "What do you see when you look at my picture of you and Butch?"

Pepper turned her head and again looked at the easel. "The same feeling, except it's for both of us."

"You got it, darlin'. That's exactly what I'd hoped you'd see. There is love in that picture, not just of two, but of three."

Pepper couldn't deny what Ted said. He had somehow captured the love they shared, and she couldn't refuse someone she loved. "All right, you win. If the museum wants to show it, I won't pitch a fit."

"I knew you'd come around." He hugged her again and kissed the top of her head. "Oh, and by the way, you just got a promotion."

Pepper turned around. "What are you talking about?"

"You've helped me out so much at the bar lately, I'm promoting you to manager."

"You're what?" Again, Pepper was incredulous.

"I need more time for this." Ted made a sweeping motion with his arm, taking in the whole studio. "Along with keeping the books, you've been doing my work at the bar. I haven't done payroll, ordering, or scheduling in weeks, trying to finish this painting."

"Well, you're right about that. Speaking of which, I need to hire another part-time waitress. We need more coverage for happy hour."

"See that, you're already running the damn place. Let's make it official."

Pepper grinned. "Do I get a raise?"

"If you sleep with the boss, you might."

"That can be arranged."

"I thought so." Ted gave Pepper a bear hug. "I know I've said this before, but I have to say it again. I'm glad you're back."

Pepper's eyes welled up as she whispered, "I'm glad I'm back with both of you."

Once both Butch and Pepper agreed to let Ted tell the museum about his new painting, he rallied. He finished his ginger ale. Then he took pictures of his paintings, including his latest work. He wanted to give the museum plenty of choices.

Pepper talked him into including the cardinal. To humor

Butch, he agreed to include the drawing of him and his first car. Butch didn't care that the museum only wanted paintings. He thought the drawing deserved consideration with everything else.

They celebrated with pizza and beer for dinner. Ted ate four pieces, and showed no signs of his earlier nervous stomach. While nursing yet another beer, Ted suggested the celebration should continue upstairs.

Butch had also cracked another beer. "Why the fuck do we have to go upstairs? Let's get it on right here."

Ted challenged Butch. "You have a short memory. That's why we got the big bed for Pepper's room. Who the hell wants to do it in the kitchen when we've got a king-size bed waiting?"

Pepper agreed. "For Christ's sake, Butch, we eat here." She got up and took the empty pizza boxes to the trash can on the back porch.

Butch yelled after her. "What's your point, Pepper? We eat in your bed all the fucking time. We eat you out, you suck us. It's a happy meal you won't get at Mickey D's."

Ted laughed. "Do you know you're fucking crude?" He followed Pepper outside with the empty beer bottles.

Butch yelled again. "Yeah. I know. That's why you both love me so much."

Pepper came back in, while Ted stayed outside bagging the recyclable trash. She rinsed out the dishcloth, and then wiped the table. "How many beers have you had, *paisan*?"

"Lost count. I think this is number four."

She came around to his side of the table to finish cleaning it. "Maybe you've had enough?"

"Sweetheart, since you've come back, I can't get enough." He grabbed her and pulled her down on his lap. He whispered in her ear, "Let's you and me do Rembrandt right here on the table. My asshole needs a break. He did me real good night before last."

Pepper giggled. "He did it on purpose. Said you were overdue for a good one."

"Yeah, well, so is he. Are you in?"

"I'm in, if he fucks me while you do him. Good?"

"Fucking wonderful. Grab the lube before he comes back."

Pepper jumped up and threw the dishcloth in the sink. She ran into the pantry to get the tube she stashed there.

Ted came back in and washed his hands. "Where's Pepper?"

"In the pantry. She'll be right back." Butch reached into his back pocket and pulled out his wallet.

"So are we going upstairs?"

"For the second round." Butch took a condom out of his wallet and tossed it onto the table. "The first round will be right here."

Pepper came out of the pantry. "We don't have any Crisco. Will this do?" She held up a spray can of butter-flavored Pam.

Butch burst out laughing, while Ted stared at her in disbelief. Once she got the reaction she wanted, she held up the other hand. "Just kidding! Here's the lube."

"Good one, Pepper! You nearly gave Rembrandt a heart attack."

"Thank you. Did you tell Ted he's it?"

"Not yet." Butch stood up and unzipped his pants. "Teddy boy, you're it." Over the last several months, they had taken up tag-team buttfucking. Much like calling dibs, whoever got tagged as "it" by the other two on any given night took it up the ass.

Ted narrowed his eyes and crossed his arms. He gave both Butch and Pepper the eye. "Well, now. This is a surprise. I thought we'd do Pepper tonight."

"Nope. I have a hankering for some ass. Pepper's in if you fuck her while I fuck you."

Pepper watched Ted carefully, to make sure he didn't object. When he unzipped his jeans, she knew he'd accepted being "it."

"All right, boys, how do we do this? We've never done it in the kitchen before."

Butch assumed the role as leader of this session. "I want to see your tits while I take Rembrandt. Take off your clothes and lay down on the table."

Ted nodded. "He's right, Pepper. If you're on your back, I can do you while Butch plugs me."

"This sounds like fun, guys. I can see what's going on with you two if I'm on my back."

Butch exposed his cock. "That's the idea, sweetheart. Everyone gets some." He opened the lubricant. "Let's get you loosened up, Ted."

Rather than just lowering his jeans like Butch did, Ted took everything off. "Damn good thing I have the fence around the house. Our neighbors would get a show tonight."

Once Pepper had taken her clothes off, she laid down on the table. "While Butch is warming you up, why don't you warm me up?" She propped her feet on a chair.

"Not a bad idea." Ted pulled out a second chair, so Pepper could put a foot on each one. He set them far enough apart that Pepper had to stretch her legs wide open.

"Damn, Ted! I'm not a gymnast. I never could do a full split."

"Maybe not, but the view is pretty damn good from here."

"Yeah, mamma. Wet pussy, my favorite." Butch shoved at Ted's shoulder. "Bend over, unless you want to go cold turkey."

"Not with your big fucking dick, *paisan*. Work it."

Ted bent over and licked Pepper while Butch loosened up his ass. Pepper's pelvis undulated on the table as Ted sucked her clit and she watched Butch finger-fuck Ted. Within minutes, the three lovers had generated enough steam to fog the windows.

"Rembrandt, your ass is like rubber. You're ready." Butch picked up the condom from the table.

Ted raised his head. "So is Pepper."

Butch stared at her tits while he put the condom on. "Next round, I'm doing her." He came around and deep-throat kissed her while Ted rubbed her clit. Pepper moaned into his mouth.

Ted pushed him back. "Hey, man, you're doing me, remember?"

Butch stood up. "Yeah, I remember. But Christ, her tits are good."

"Yeah, they are." Ted inched Pepper forward, so her ass was right at the edge of the table. "Is that comfortable for you?"

"It's fine. Fuck me already."

Ted obliged. He positioned himself between her legs and leaned forward. Pepper lifted her hips off the table when his prick popped inside. Ted moaned. "Fuck, that's good."

"Then you'll really like this." Butch rammed his dick into Ted's ass, pushing Ted's dick deeper into Pepper. Ted groaned loudly.

"Oh, yeah, do me, *paisan*. Stuff that prick of yours in my asshole."

"You got it."

As usual, Butch wasn't gentle. He never was when he fucked either of them. Pepper could feel the strength of each thrust as Butch pounded Ted. In turn, Ted nailed her. Pepper had learned to relax into the rhythm of her lovers. When they did three, one of the men would usually lead. This time Butch did.

Pepper loved the feel of her two lovers moving at the same time. The sensual dance they did as three became more erotic everyday. They understood each other, and naturally moved in synchronized rhythm. This time, they danced to Butch's beat, a wild, passionate tango of soulful harmony.

Butch finished first, and then Ted. Even in the throes of his own climax, Ted rubbed her clit with such intensity that Pepper joined the men's orgasms with her own.

Just as they lived together, they loved together. They belonged together as three.

NO STRINGS
ATTACHED

DEVYN QUINN

Prologue

Gold Rush Casino
Reno, Nevada

Angelino DiMarco stretched out on his expensive leather couch like a panther under a scorching desert sun. Scotch on the rocks in one tanned hand, immaculate white shirt unbuttoned to the waist, he was the image of idle wealth. Lara knew he was trouble when she saw the icy glint in his eyes.

DiMarco smiled, a baring of teeth more akin to the grin of hungry piranha than a display of actual affection. "So you got something for me?"

Shaking her head, Lara returned the show of teeth. "You know I haven't got the money, Angie. You ain't the only one Donnie fucked over. I worked to earn most of the money he gambled away."

"Is that so?"

She shrugged. "Yeah."

Focused on her tits, DiMarco grinned in a way that said he wasn't feeling sorry for her at all. His gaze didn't just strip away her clothing, it tore it to shreds and tossed the remains. "That's too bad for you, babe."

Throat tightening with embarrassment, Lara flushed hot all over. She was dressed in a midriff-baring baby tee; the material clung to her ample breasts, outlining her nipples. The pink tips were on prominent display through the sheer fabric. A faded denim skirt hugged her rear, showing her legs to their best advantage in thigh-high leather boots. She might as well have been naked.

DiMarco swirled the amber liquid in his glass. "We gotta do something about that."

Lara took a shallow breath and eyed the swarthy Italian. His words didn't hold a single note of reassurance. "W-we do?"

DiMarco sipped and ogled. Lean and sinewy, his tan was an expensive fake, his muscles sculpted in a private gym. A man with money to burn, he clearly hadn't seen a hard day's work in his whole life. The office around him stank with stale cigarette smoke, alcohol, and the sweat of sex, lots of sex.

"Don't play stupid. Donnie skipped town owing me over a hundred thousand." DiMarco's keen gaze seemed to slice her to the skin. "Since you were married to him, you get to stand up and take the screwing he tried to give me." He downed the last of his drink. Ice clinked when he set the glass aside. "You get what I'm saying, sugar?"

Stomach twisting into knots, Lara gave a single nod. "Yeah, I get what you're saying." *Payback*. DiMarco wanted it. In full. No doubt about it. She was screwed with a capital *S*.

She closed her eyes for a moment in sheer frustration. *Shit. Shit. Shit.* How did she always manage to get herself caught between the rocks and the hard places in life?

DiMarco's voice broke into her thoughts, all low and smooth. "I'm willing to give you a chance to make things right. I think you and I can come to some sort of an, ah, arrangement where your physical assets are concerned."

The ground beneath her feet crumbled away. In other words he wanted to fuck her.

No surprise there. DiMarco had sniffed around her like a coonhound since the day he'd laid eyes on her. With Donnie out of work and not a dime between them, she'd had to go back to stripping to make the rent.

She risked a quick glance over her shoulder, toward the sole avenue of escape. Playing cards around a table, DiMarco's bodyguards were situated perilously close to the door. There were two brawny men, neither looking very bright or alert. Not quite into their game, both smirked like cats eating canaries. They'd obviously watched their boss fuck a lot of women.

And judging by the glint in their eyes, they expected a turn as well.

Using her body to get out of this jam wasn't something she wanted to do. Still it was preferable to the possible alternative: a trip to the desert to feed the coyotes.

Gritting her teeth, Lara lifted her chin. "I guess I'll do whatever you want."

DiMarco nodded his approval. "Good girl." Brown gaze smoldering with anticipation, he got up. "You and I understand each other fine." His wolfish grin widened. He sauntered over. "Let's see what we have here. Turn around."

"Why?" The question popped out.

Wrong thing to say.

DiMarco's hand shot out, catching her by the chin.

Lara bit back a cry of pain.

DiMarco's grip tightened. "You'll do what I say when I say." He let her go. "Now turn the fuck around."

Revolted by how eager she was to obey, Lara forced herself to stay calm. "Whatever you want, boss." Prickles going up and down her spine, she slowly pivoted on one spike heel.

DiMarco stepped behind her, giving her rear a hard squeeze. "Bend over and put your hands on my desk."

She bent, spreading her fingers along the smooth mahogany. The solidity of the wood under her hands helped steady her stance. The heels under her feet wobbled. Her knees were trembling so hard she could barely make her legs support her weight.

He grunted. "I bet that asshole of yours is virgin." One booted foot went between hers, urging her to spread. Wider.

Clenching her eyes tight, Lara sucked in a sharp breath. She tensed, waiting. *It's only sex*. Like it or not, her body was the only commodity she had of value. Might as well start using her physical assets to get ahead. She'd had enough hard knocks to last a lifetime.

Big hands followed, cupping her ass cheeks. "I think you and I can do some business here." His fingers dug in painfully, tightening like a vise. A burning iron stabbed from the place he touched straight to the center of her gut. Her nipples tingled in response. Her hands clenched the wood; her breathing grew shallow.

Using just the tips of his fingers, DiMarco eased up her skirt. The flat of his palm unexpectedly connected with her ass. Hard. "Sexy."

Lara gritted her teeth. "Damn, that hurt."

"It was supposed to." He chuckled, sounding obscene and amused at the same time. "Good, tight ass. No flab, no droop. You keep yourself in nice shape."

"Thanks." She winced when he pinched again. "I think."

DiMarco swept her T-shirt up to her neck. "Nice tats." He ran his hands over her exposed skin, fingers tracing the lines. "I like it." Warm palms slid down her sides. "Very dark and sensual."

"Thanks." Etched in ink from shoulders to ass was a female Grim Reaper in all her dark glory. Skulls littered the ground around the Reaper's feet. The head of a recent victim dangled from one hand. Lara's arms, ass, abdomen, and ankles were also decorated with a wickedly Gothic motif. With her long spiky black shag and heavily lined silvery-gray eyes, she knew her personal style was a tad on the extreme side.

DiMarco reached around to cup her breasts. Capturing the tips, he pinched.

A hot tingle brought the blood rushing to Lara's nipples. A soft gasp escaped. Electric heat traveled straight to her core. Acutely aware of her pulsing clit, she couldn't hold back a shiver.

Fingers clenching at her thighs, DiMarco pressed his hips against hers. Only clothing separated their bodies. "You like that?" He laughed softly from behind. "The way you strut that stage tells me you're a woman who enjoys a good fuck."

Closing her eyes, Lara felt her inner muscles coil in violent reaction. Her skin covered in a fine sheen of sweat, her whole body vibrated with need. The silky dampness of her panties clung. A mental image jolted her—of DiMarco naked in bed with her, their limbs entwined and his cock sheathed deep inside her.

Yeah, she liked sex. Definitely and completely.

DiMarco's exploring hands traveled down her flat abdomen. One palm slid over her Venus mound, cupping her intimately. He wiggled a finger into her panties, parting her labia and stabbing into her warmth. "I knew you'd be wet."

Lara gasped. "Oh, God!" Racing electric shocks went all the way to her toes. Carnal appetite spontaneously combusted, then blazed with an all-consuming heat. The delicious sensations his touch incited ran riot over her senses, delivering an unwelcome jab to her libido. Unable to stop herself, she gyrated her hips with a smooth and silent urgency. She couldn't stop the needs of her traitorous body, hijacking her control.

"You're one hot bitch." DiMarco's fingertip waltzed slow circles around her clit. "You want more, don't you?"

Lara ran her tongue over dry lips, trying to distract her thoughts. No good. His touch was becoming more than she could bear, and the idea that she might enjoy being sexually dominated bothered her. Yet the same time something deep inside her psyche took pleasure in entertaining the forbidden thought.

"Please, Angie, not like this," she finally managed to gasp out.

To her relief his hand slipped away. She heard him step back. "Turn around."

Thank heavens. Knees trembling, Lara slowly pivoted around to face him.

Smiling, DiMarco lifted his wet fingers to his mouth. Licked. "Mmm. I always knew you were hot to trot, babe. I'll make a shitload selling off this sweet ass of yours.

It took a moment for his words to sink in. When they did, dismay filled her. "I thought we . . ." Her words trailed away.

He laughed and tweaked a nipple. "You thought I wanted you?"

She nodded stupidly. "Yeah, I did."

DiMarco gave a vigorous shake of his head. "Nah. You're just a piece of meat to me. Donnie didn't know what to do with you, but I do. You're tight, virgin quality. Selling that hungry twat of yours for a couple of years will pay me back just fine." He tweaked her nipple again and winked. "I never dip a wick in my ladies. Business, you know. Just business. All I want from you is cold hard cash, babe."

Lara froze. Hearing his words, shame incinerated her. "I'm not a whore," she spluttered, shocked. What the hell had she been thinking? She felt dirty, used and deceived by her own desperation.

DiMarco's brows shot up with unholy amusement. "You're already stripping to the skin on stage," he pointed out. "Spreading your legs is just the next step." He reached out, stroking her cheek with damp fingers. "That body of yours is all sin. The way that nice tight pussy of yours responds to a man's touch is like a firecracker going off."

Squelching the violent desire to kick him in the nuts, Lara tugged down her T-shirt and skirt. She clenched her fists until her fingernails dug painfully into her palms. "I won't do it! Hell will freeze before I whore myself for an asshole like you."

The second Lara said the words, she knew she was in trouble. The shit had just gone from hip-deep to neck-deep and was about to close over her head.

DiMarco clamped his mouth into a thin line, anger tightening his jaw. "What did you say?"

She clarified. "I said eat shit, Angie! I won't do it." The words popped out before she thought about the consequences.

"Bitch!" Without warning DiMarco struck her backhanded.

Senses going haywire, Lara reeled back against the desk. Fiery lights danced in front of her eyes, blurring her vision. Cold shock flooded her veins. Her lip split, giving her a taste of her own blood.

Her hand automatically rose, palm pressing against her swelling cheek. "Please, Angie," she hastened to say. "Don't . . ."

DiMarco towered in front of her, looking ten feet tall and bulletproof. He fumbled for his belt buckle. "I think laying this across your ass will help you remember your place a bit better."

Heart tripping in her chest, she eyed the belt. "I didn't mean any disrespect."

DiMarco ignored her. He folded his belt and smacked it against his palm. The crack of leather against flesh sounded ominously like a gunshot. "You better listen real well, baby doll. I want every goddamned cent that no-good bastard owes me. I don't give a shit how you get the cash. Robbing a bank or sucking a dick, it makes no difference. Just get the money."

As if that miracle would occur.

Lara felt limp and lifeless. Hopeless. No place to run. No place to hide. She'd just hit shit creek and there was no paddle in sight.

Suddenly aware no miracle escape would present itself, she realized she was about to pay.

Painfully.

1

Deminonde Ranch
Fitzgerald, Nevada

The dressing room the dancers shared looked exactly like an orgy was about to take place. A lot of naked, writhing flesh. Women in various states of nudity hustled to get their costumes and makeup on.

Leaning toward her own brightly lit mirror, Lara winced as she painted a crimson shade of lipstick over her mouth. Di-Marco had given her one hell of a fat lip.

"This is bullshit," she muttered under her breath. Why should she be responsible for Donnie's debt anyway? She wasn't even married to him anymore. The divorce had gone through without a hitch last week. Two years of her life down the drain. Punishing her wasn't right. Christ, it was hard enough figuring out how to salvage the remnants of her messed-up life.

Ignoring the half-nude women, one of the night managers strode into the dressing room. Big, bald, and bad to the bone, he didn't even look at the swarm around him. He'd seen enough tits and bare asses to last a lifetime. "Time to hustle those bodies, girls," he announced. "Get out there and show some pussy and get the guys all horny. We got a full house tonight."

Glancing over her shoulder, Lara drew a deep breath. Time to paste on her smile and get ready to strip to the skin. The last thing she wanted to do, but it was necessary if she expected to eat and pay the rent.

Recapping her lipstick, she tossed it aside. She stood up, expertly balancing on five-inch stiletto heels, complete with ankle cuffs. A black leather-and-chains halter top and black leather skirt completed her outfit. The snaps on the halter and skirt made it easy for her to tear them away. A pair of garters, fishnet hose, and skimpy thong panties completed her outfit. A badass bitch goddess ready to devour a few horny bastards and spit out their bones.

She headed toward the exit behind the other girls. Jim eyed her with approval. He grabbed her arm as she passed, pulling her back. The other women left without a backward glance. "I need to see you a minute."

Lara bristled. "Get your fucking hands off me, okay? I'm not in the mood to be manhandled anymore tonight."

Jim's hand immediately dropped away. "Hey, don't bite my head off. Miss Helen wants to see you in her office."

That stopped her dead. "She does?" Miss Helen was Helen DiMarco, Angelino's sister and Madame of the Demimonde. A stylish woman in her late forties, she gave the place its public face and made sure the line from classy to trash was never crossed.

Jim nodded. "As soon as possible."

Lara moistened her lips. *Oh, shit.* Miss Helen did the hiring and firing. Getting her ass canned would deliver the coup de grace on an already terrible day. "What does she want?"

He shrugged. "She didn't say. Just hustle ass."

Lara hustled.

When she opened the door to Helen DiMarco's office, the woman herself was settled behind her desk. All business and no nonsense, she pulled no punches. "I heard my brother got a little hands-on with you at the casino," she said by way of a greeting.

Emotion tightened Lara's throat. "Yeah. He's ragging my ass about the money Donnie owes him." She pointed to her fat lip. "That son of a bitch busted me in the fucking mouth. He's damn serious about getting his money."

Helen DiMarco frowned. "That's not right. We don't do business that way. I'll talk to him about manhandling you girls. Bruised merchandise doesn't sell."

Lara plopped down on the nearest chair. "Like he gives a shit," she announced, her tone flat with disillusionment. "All Angie wants is his money. If I had it, I'd pay it back just to shut him up." She leaned forward, burying her face in her hands. There might have been a light at the end of the tunnel, but it sure as hell felt like the oncoming train. If it weren't for bad luck, she wouldn't have any at all.

Leaning backing her chair, Miss Helen slid off her glasses. She tapped one earpiece against the string of pearls around her neck. "So let me help you get it."

The words filleted through. Suspicion rose. Lara lifted her head, frowning. "Did Angie put you up to this?"

Miss Helen raised one hand in a gesture meant to placate. "Don't get your feathers in a ruffle, honey." She slipped her glasses back on and glanced at a folder on her desk. "I've got a little proposition that might help you settle up with Angie."

Lara pulled a face. "Sucking dick, right?"

Miss Helen chuckled. "Oh, definitely."

"Any girl can do that."

Miss Helen tapped her folder. "My clients aren't asking for *any* girl. They want you."

A puff of disgust escaped. "A lot of guys want to fuck me. Doesn't mean I want to fuck them back. Why can't they pick one of the working girls? I might strip, but that doesn't mean I give it away to anyone who wants a piece."

"I did explain that not all the girls working here were available. However my clients prevailed on me to speak with you, present their case so to speak. Since they spend a hell of a lot of money at our establishments, I am doing that."

"Wait, are you seriously suggesting that I have sex with these guys?" she asked, the steel in her voice leaving no doubt as to her feelings on the subject. "You know I don't whore myself." *Though you were willing to give it up to get out of hot water with Angie,* came the damning thought.

That truth, however ugly, revealed a lot. She had to admit that, yeah, she'd use sex if necessary to get her way. What woman wouldn't? *What woman didn't?*

"Were I to make an introduction, how far you proceeded would be entirely up to you," Helen DiMarco said, hinting. "As would any compensation you might require for your time."

Ah. The key word. *Compensation.* "And you think I might be interested in what these guys have to offer a girl?"

A subtle nod. "What you get, you'd keep. The customer pays for the amenities of our extensive facilities. I'm sure I could persuade Jim to take you off the schedule to accommodate a little vacation." She smiled in a way that said Lara would be a fool to turn the offer down.

Maybe she would be.

Lara felt her stomach tie into knots. She already knew the common man didn't qualify to walk through the doors of the Demimonde Ranch. Only VIPs, the very wealthy, were granted access to the rarefied atmosphere of debauchery. Threesomes. Foursomes. Orgies. Nothing was considered taboo. A twenty-minute drive from Reno was all it took to reach heaven on earth. All private—and legal—in the great state of Nevada.

Tempting. *Very tempting.*

The girls working at the ranch were independent contractors. They set their own prices. But even if she were to consider the idea, one problem loomed. "I'm not licensed."

Eyes crinkling around the edges, Miss Helen subtly closed the folder and slid it under her day planner. "For now let's just say I'm making an introduction of consenting adults. The gentlemen in Parlor 3 have already made arrangements to rent our Presidential Suite for the week. It would be nobody's business if you were to join them there."

Lara thought a moment. Nobody's business sounded pretty good to her.

The parlor looked and felt more like a sports bar than a place where sexual negotiations regularly took place. Two men sat on stools in front of a small wet bar, drinks in hand, making small talk, and ignoring the wide-screen TV stretched across the wall.

Seeing her, the man on the right lowered the bottle he was about to drink from. Gaze skimming, a small smile turned up one corner of his mouth. "Well, who have we here?"

Lara couldn't resist the smile tugging at one corner of her mouth. "I believe you requested my, ah, company."

The man's grin grew wider in appreciation. "I did. I'm Nick Conway." He indicated his buddy. "This is Jared Montgomery."

Jared Montgomery smiled. "God, you're perfect in every way."

At least they appreciated her. "Thanks."

Nick Conway slid off his stool. He walked over, circling around to see her from every angle.

Lara eyed him back. He had the look she liked; tall and broad shouldered with narrow hips and long legs. Dressed casually in faded jeans and a torn T-shirt, he didn't look like he had a dime to his name. He obviously had time to work out and keep those abs rippling, though. Raw energy radiated around him. He had the look of a young male tiger that had its prey squarely in sight. He didn't look very old, maybe twenty-six or somewhere close to that age.

Nick came around in front of her and stood. One hand casually brushed through his long sandy blond hair as his gaze dropped to her mouth, then her breasts. "I've seen you dance," he said. "You're hotter than hell."

An unexpected thrill buzzed her senses. Electricity crackled and popped in the air around them. The energy pouring off him all but zapped her senseless. "Is that why you asked for me?"

"Yes." His grin grew wider. "I'd sure like to find out."

"I'm sure you would." A rise of delicious heat set to simmering between Lara's legs. Heat drenched her thin panties. The mesmerizing glitter of his green eyes seemed to enchant. And, oh, his lips. They were perfectly formed. Nick Conway had one of the most sensual mouths she'd ever seen.

Unbidden erotic thoughts swirled in her mind. Lust coalesced into a hard knot deep inside, the beginning of an ache that refused to be easily satisfied. It didn't take much imagination to guess what Nick Conway's lips would feel like pressed against hers. She could picture their tongues dancing together while his cock stuffed every last inch of her sex.

Lara fanned a hand in front of her face. *Man, oh man.* She hadn't expected to be blindsided by this hunk. If she had her druthers, she'd lead him off to the nearest bedroom and give him everything she had, and more. No charge.

She shook her head to clear it, trying to ignore the signals her body sent her brain. This wasn't a date. It was business. "I'm not easy and I don't come cheap."

Nick Conway gave her a slow smile. "Somehow I had a feeling you'd say that." He turned to his partner. "So what do you think? Is she the one we want?"

Jared Montgomery's eyebrows shot straight up. A glimmer of unholy amusement lit his intense gaze. "Oh, definitely. She's got the look."

"The votes are all in," Nick said. "You're the one, babe."

"They said you wanted a—" The words suddenly clogged her throat. "A sex slave for a week."

Nick Conway nodded. "Right."

Her knees trembled. Things were getting a little bit harder now. She'd never bartered sex for cold hard cash. Strange, yet oddly exhilarating. She was actually considering going through with this. "What exactly would I be expected to do?"

Jared Montgomery chuckled as he slid off the stool. Nothing ugly about him, either. Though he was just as tall as his friend, his build was leaner, more sinewy. A body definitely made for speed, long-term endurance. Icy blue eyes ruled under a mane of short, fashionably spiked black hair. His T-shirt went past radical into mind-bending. Demons tortured a half-naked woman in some sort of medieval dungeon. His own arms were ringed with something tribal.

Jared crossed the parlor, circling behind her. His hands settled on her hips, warm and intimate. "You'd be our very own sex toy, expected to fuck me and my partner in any way we want, anytime we want." Warm breath tickled the back of her neck. "Think you'd like that?"

Temptation surged. Lara gulped and swallowed hard. His statement suggested multiple possibilities, every damn one deliciously carnal. A new vision flashed across her mind's screen. Two wet tongues flicking against her skin, and two cocks eager to fill every cranny and crevice possible. A shiver took hold. Every nerve ending tingled.

Lara eased her ass back against Jared's hips. His body reacted instantly. Yes, he was definitely attracted.

A subtle power play began. The men had the money. She had the warm, luscious pussy. They all wanted something from the other. Kinky sex, a wild ride, and no commitments all of a sudden sounded too damn good to pass up.

She stepped out of Jared's hold. "Hands off the merchandise, honey."

Jared shrugged good-naturedly. "You get to squeeze the bread before you buy," he pointed out.

Lara winked. "What you're squeezing doesn't go stale, babe. It's going to cost to get what you want."

Nick Conway's eyes glinted in challenge. "Name your price."

His eyes spoke volumes. Pure need radiated in their depths. By the tone of his voice, he wasn't interested in negotiation.

Lara tossed her head, enjoying the feel of long hair tumbling around her shoulders. Control belonged to her. She liked it. A lot. It made her feel incredibly sexy. Invincible. "Sex slaves don't come cheap."

Jared Montgomery stared at her through narrowing eyes. Hard knowledge filled his gaze. His body was coiled tightly, a bundle of sparking sexual nerves. "How much?"

A nice round figure popped into her head.

One million dollars.

2

_____

With a man on each arm, Lara walked toward the waiting limo in a daze. She hardly believed the surreal turn her night had taken, like stepping into the Twilight Zone. She felt like Cinderella. Only there were two Prince Charmings to sweep her off her feet.

She'd gotten the million. Cynic that she was, Lara still found that impossible to fathom. A quick phone call to Helen DiMarco's office had revealed that, yes, the guys were good for that sum. Their check would certainly cash.

Holy shit.

Her body was worth a cool million dollars.

Except that she hadn't collected yet. That would come later. After she'd given them one full week of control over her. Whatever they wanted to do, they could. Without restraint.

Lara shivered despite the heat of the desert climate. She had been so hot a moment ago that perspiration soaked her skin, dotting her forehead. She now felt stone cold. The leather halter and skirt clung uncomfortably. She felt like she'd faint if she didn't sit down soon.

Jared helped her inside the car, reminding her to duck her head. "Careful, babe."

Unable to speak, Lara slid onto the seat. The interior of the car was dim and cool, shielding her from the outside world but not from her thoughts. For a moment she wished she could simply close her eyes and go on to no particular destination, just exist in quiet limbo forever.

What were these guys going to think when they found out she wasn't really a sex goddess? Appearances aside, Lara had to admit she could still count her ex-lovers on one hand. One of those had been her husband. That didn't exactly add up to a lot of carnal experience, especially considering that most of her lovers had been straight vanilla in their sexual tastes.

Lara supposed she'd have to wing it, go with the flow. Relax and try to enjoy herself. She'd always followed the rise and fall of her wild and inexplicable impulses. Maybe this time she'd have better luck.

With Jared taking one side, Nick slid in. Sandwiched between two good-looking men couldn't be a bad way to start.

"Are you okay?" Nick asked.

She smiled. "Terrific." If only the unease churning in her stomach would cease.

Up front, separated from them by a pane of tinted glass, the driver waited for instructions.

"Drive around and show us the sights," Jared instructed through the intercom. He turned to Lara and grinned. "You don't mind, do you?"

She shook her head. The car shifted into motion, riding so smoothly it didn't even seem to be moving. "I've never gotten to ride in a limousine before." Hell, she didn't even have a car anymore. Donnie had taken off in it. Nice of the bastard to leave her to get around on foot. Public transportation definitely sucked.

"Oh, you'll enjoy it." Nick snagged a bottle of champagne

from the built-in bar. "Let the party begin." He poured three glasses, handing them around. Probably real crystal. Clients of the Demimonde Ranch were spared no luxury.

Lara accepted hers, sipping the bubbly wine from a fluted glass. The slightly tart vintage tingled, rolling over her tongue and down her throat. It tasted really good. Excellent, in fact. Sure beat the hell out of the buck ninety-eight wine coolers she usually purchased. She took a full swallow. "So what do you guys do?"

Jared held a finger in front of his lips. "No business talk. We're here not to think about work, but play."

"Our work is play," Nick cracked back. "I think this week will certainly inspire our—" He eyed Lara. "Project." He patted her leg. "I think this is definitely the model we want."

Every bit of their conversation flew right over Lara's head. None of it made sense. "Don't guess you're going to fill me in," she sighed, sipping her drink. The bubbles tickled her nose.

Jared refilled her glass. "Nope."

Nick grinned appreciatively. "All you need to know is that we have a shitload of money and we're willing to spend it on you. Satisfied?"

"Still in a daze, actually. I expected you to laugh your ass off when I said that much." She was almost afraid to mention the figure out loud. Didn't want to jinx it.

Nick pinned her under a laser-beam stare, searching the depths of her eyes. His hand cupped her face, his thumb stroking her cheek. "I wanted you the moment I saw you, Lara. If you had asked for the moon, I'd have found a way to get it for you."

Flattering words, indeed. "I don't think you'd have had to go that far."

He chuckled. "You might say you've been a little obsession of mine for a long time."

An obsession? Whoa. Heavy stuff. "I *am*?"

Nick nodded and leaned in closer. "You don't know how

long I've waited for this." His mouth came down on hers with a deliberate and calculated slowness. Strong lips quickly mastered hers, the beginning of a kiss that snatched her breath away.

Tingling to her toes, Lara felt her insides turn to molten silver. An all-consuming ache of pure need seeped through her limbs. Unsatisfied arousal suddenly gnawed, demanding to be fed. Sated.

She gasped with pleasure when Nick's mouth left hers, his lips invading the soft hollow between neck and shoulder. At the same time he popped open one of her snaps baring her right breast. His fingers traced slow circles around the erect tip.

"That feels so good," she breathed, her voice frankly conveying her desire. She groaned when he tugged the tender nubbin, rolling it between thumb and forefinger.

"Glad you like it," he murmured. "Because everything we're going to do to you is wickedly graphic and intense."

On the other side of her, Jared's hand found her left knee.

"We're going to take real good care of you."

Undoing the three snaps holding her skirt closed, Jared tugged the leather aside until her legs were bared to him. He grinned. "I think we're going to have to stretch out here."

Nick scooted to the end of the long seat. Angling his body, he pulled Lara between his legs so that her back rested against his chest.

She willingly molded against him, enjoying the feel of his hard body pressed against hers. Her legs were splayed across the seat. His hands tugged at her halter, pushing the leather bindings away.

He cupped both, weighing them in his hands. "Mmm, now I can play with your tits and watch Jared go down on you."

It was impossible not to sense the static in the air around them, the energy of heated bodies generating lust. The intensity of their need almost stole her breath away.

Jared shifted at his end, arranging her legs the way he wanted, splayed open to reveal everything she had. All she wore underneath was a very skimpy pair of thong panties. He whistled. "Nice." By the glint in his eyes and the smile on his lips, he was more than pleased.

Lara looked across at him, very aware that one man was fiddling with her tits while another planned to munch some snatch. At the same time. Wow. The change from plain vanilla to banana split complete with a cherry on top was a complete change of pace in her sexual world. Not that she hadn't wondered what it would be like to be with two men at one time. *Every* woman thought about that. She'd never had the nerve to try it.

When you're free, single, and getting paid to fuck, no holds are barred.

A little grin crossed Lara's lips. If this is what the guys wanted, well, let them have at it.

Remembering she still held her glass, she tipped it. Champagne drizzled between her breasts, slipping down her abdomen to pool in her navel. "So what are you waiting for?"

Jared leaned forward until his face was just inches from her belly. Hot breath tickled her skin. His tongue stabbed into her belly button.

Lara gasped as if she'd been fully penetrated. Shafts of wonderful torment sped through her.

"Shall I stop?" he teased, his voice dropping to a low husky register.

A mammoth lump formed in her throat, threatening to steal away her breath. "Definitely not," she gasped.

Nick teased her breasts, pinching and rolling her nipples. The touch of his fingers blazed a delicious trail over her sensitive skin. "Does having your tits played with make you wet?"

Shivers of delight shimmied up her spine. "Yes," she breathed. Her nipples were so sensitive that each roll and tug sent a jolt of electricity straight to her clit. The pulse between her legs was excruciating.

Jared's hands slid up her bare thighs. "Let's find out how wet you are." He unhooked her panties and skimmed them over her hips and down her legs. That sensual movement alone threatened to send her straight over the precipice.

Untangling the thong from around her feet, he lifted the small scrap to his face and sniffed. "Mmm, I love the smell of panties fresh off the twat."

"It doesn't get any hotter than that," Lara bit out.

"Let's make sure." Jared skimmed a single finger lightly into her warmth. "Ah, slick."

The slide of flesh on flesh almost did her in. She gasped, her hips lifting slightly off the seat. Her breath came in ragged bursts as she responded helplessly to the overwhelming needs of her body. A carnal waltz swirled through her veins, each move of the sensual rhythm driving her closer to the peak of absolute bliss.

Jared eased his finger between the silken folds of her labia, penetrating her sex. "Warm and smooth, like silk." He stroked the moist sensitive center of her, wringing more soft moans from her lips. Her strong muscles clenched around his finger, and she shuddered all over again as sensations of pure ecstasy unfurled through her.

Lara was close to exploding with the need for a deeper, more complete fulfillment. Her empty glass dropped out of her hand, rolling on the floorboard. The thoughts tumbling through her mind turned her senses upside down, leaving her incapable of coherent speech.

"Ah, oh, damn it . . ." she gasped through a groan. Vision blurred through a haze of sensuality, her hands itched to grab his head and drag his mouth to her pussy.

Nick seemed to be reading her mind. "I want to see some real action, you two." Rather than really participating, he seemed content to be choreographing the action, putting everyone in their place to perform. Of the two men, he was definitely the alpha. And by the erection pressing against the small of her back, he was all man.

Jared's head dipped. Stubble-covered cheeks gently scraped her inner thighs. His lips closed around her pulsing clit. Using just the tip of his tongue, he flicked at the hooded organ in a slow, steady motion.

Barely able to bite back a raw groan of pleasure, Lara almost shot through the roof. Between the masterful motions of Nick twiddling her nipples and Jared's talented mouth on her sex, incredibly fierce sensations were beginning to whip her into a frenzy.

Nick's tongue painted the curl of one ear. His hands continued to control her breasts, pinching and pulling at her nipples in a way that made the pain most pleasurable. His hips rocked in a slow and steady motion, as though he were masturbating himself using her body. "I knew you'd enjoy this."

While Nick denied his cock, Jared certainly wasn't neglecting his own. His hands slipped to his jeans, unbuttoning and unzipping. Palming his erection, his hand jacked up and down.

"That's nice," she heard Nick say. "I want to see you make her come before you do."

"Damn hard to hold back," Jared gritted before his mouth recaptured Lara's clit.

She whimpered. "If he keeps that up it won't be long."

Nick boldly squeezed her breasts. "Good."

Lara thrust her hips upward as Jared's fingers joined his mouth, sliding deep into her sex. Strong inner muscles immediately tightened, clenching him hard. Biting back another moan, Lara swallowed hard against the climax threatening to uncoil in her belly.

Both men continued their control over her body. Nick ruled her breasts while Jared simultaneously fingered her cunt. He followed the deep thrusts inside her sex with slow arousing withdrawals.

"God, she's tight," Jared groaned. "Pussy like this just devours cock."

"It'll have its chance." Nick tweaked her nipples, both tight little buds of bundled nerves. He twisted just enough to deliver a spear of pain. The pinch enhanced the sensations ten-fold. "We're just warming her up."

Lara's own answer was an anguished moan. Trembling, she groaned with frustrated need. She took in a sharp light breath and held it, wanting the sensations to last just a few minutes more. Her entire body throbbed with the need for release.

Nick Conway's gravelly voice brushed her ear. "You think you'll like being a sex slave?" Trapped by his skintight jeans, his erection pressed against her back; the promise of his cock soon stuffing her cunt was almost more than Lara could stand.

"I—I, oh God, d-do." Didn't make sense, but at this point she didn't care. She gyrated her hips to meet the plunge of Jared's thick fingers. Sensing her ache, he lanced even deeper, as far as he could. His free hand stroked his cock with the same steady motion.

Another moan slipped from her throat. "Please, don't stop."

Jared's fingers retreated, then surged back up into her. "Come for us, Lara," he grated. "Now."

Her heat clenched Jared's fingers more tightly than Lara had ever imagined possible. Her entire body throbbed with the tremors of release. Just when she'd thought she could reach no higher plane, the heaving strength of climax picked her up and hurled her toward the stratosphere. Squeezing her eyes tight, she embraced the rapture pouring through her veins—so intense and so exquisite that she nearly lost consciousness.

Slowly the waves of pleasure receded.

Lara returned to earth, sucking in air like she'd just done a hundred-yard dash. Her body was damp and hot, coated in sweat. Her limbs trembled and she had not an ounce of strength left.

She could lie there forever, just savoring the moment. Damn, but she hadn't expected these guys would get her off like that.

Her eyelids fluttered open and she glanced down in dazed wonder. The show wasn't quite over.

Jared intensified his motion, stroking his cock until his body grew taut, shuddering when release claimed him. Warm semen splattered between her spread legs. He collapsed on the seat, exhausted, his breath whistling in and out of his lungs.

"Shit," he panted out a shaky laugh. "I haven't come that hard in a long time."

Nick laughed. "Oh, man. You two just came all over the upholstery."

Jared grinned back. "Guess we'll be getting a bill for cleaning that."

Nick gave her breasts a final squeeze. "This was just the beginning, babe. Do you think you can handle more?"

Lara ran her parched tongue over her equally dry lips. These guys apparently hadn't been kidding when they'd said they planned to fuck her every which way but loose. She hadn't been with them an hour and she already felt like she'd run a marathon.

A whole week of nonstop sex still stretched ahead of her.

Heaven help me survive.

3

The Presidential Suite. Magnificent.

Lara's insides felt as though a ball of snakes writhed inside her guts. She pressed a hand to her stomach to calm her nerves.

Watching her closely, Nick smiled warmly. "You like it?"

A light shiver slipped down her sides. People like her didn't get into places like this unless they were doing the cleaning or repairs. "It's beautiful," she whispered, low, almost afraid the sound of her voice might somehow shatter the splendor.

She'd heard about the luxuries the Ranch offered its clients, but had never had the occasion to see for herself. Now she would be staying there, pampered with sumptuousness the average person only dreamed of.

"Take a look around," Jared invited.

Lara smiled. "I'm dying to," she admitted. Like a kid in a candy store, she did. The living room featured a huge high-definition flat-panel television and a gas log fireplace; the bedroom sported a queen bed and adjoining bathroom. An enormous tiled shower seemed to take up half the bathroom.

"Think we'll be comfortable here?" Nick asked. His hand

rested lightly on her arm as they walked through the place, strolling together as if they'd done it for years. The easy intimacy helped calm Lara's nerves.

She glanced up at him and electricity rippled through her all over again. God, he was gorgeous! He was so tall that her head barely came up to his shoulders. She couldn't help but examine his face now that they had a moment alone. His nose was straight and sharp, his jawline square and strong. Light pocks and scars from teenage acne still marked his skin, but did little to detract from the overall picture.

Just perfect for her.

More than his looks, though, there seemed to be something oddly familiar about Nick Conway. It almost felt like she'd met him before, but couldn't exactly remember where. He'd mentioned seeing her dance, the most logical answer. When she was on stage, she never noticed faces in the audience. Not even when men were cramming bills into her G-string and garter. Dancing was her business. She never got flirty or familiar with the customers. That line wasn't to be crossed.

So why break that inviolable rule now?

Was it because she needed the money so desperately? Or because the attraction she'd felt for Nick when they'd first met had put her hormones on red alert? No doubt about it. There'd been something between them—she'd sensed it just looking at him.

Lara shook her head, clearing away her thoughts. She didn't believe in love at first sight. Love took time to grow, mature. She'd already had a few flings that hadn't worked out, relationships that started with infatuation and the idea of being in love when all they were really in was lust. Too bad she'd married one of her flings. Might have saved herself a lot of trouble if she'd just admitted she didn't like sleeping alone and gotten herself a dog.

"You ever been here before?" he asked.

She shook her head. "Never. You?"

"No." He tightened his grip on her arm. "Good. I want every-thing we do together to be new for both of us." He sounded like they were on their first date together, rather than being a rich man and the woman he had hired to have sex with him.

Well, let him live his fantasy, Lara thought. *He's paying enough for it.* At the end of the week they'd part company and probably never see each other again. Just the way it needed to be. She had plans for starting over, making a better life for her-self. There'd be plenty left over after she cleared Donnie's debt with DiMarco. She wouldn't owe anyone anything and could walk away and start her life over clean.

"Ready to see the rest of it?" he asked. "Jared and I have a little surprise for you."

She smiled. "I'd love to."

With the grandeur of a king escorting his queen, Nick led her upstairs. If the first floor impressed, the second left her speechless. The master suite featured a beautiful king-size canopy bed and an in-room Jacuzzi. A private deck overlooked the gorgeous view of the mountains looming in the background.

But there was more.

While she'd taken the grand tour, Jared had been upstairs ar-ranging things. Lara's eyes surreptitiously flitted over on the dozen or so packages arranged neatly on the bed, each beauti-fully wrapped in colorful paper and decorated with ribbons.

Jared gave a formal bow and waved an arm over the gifts. "For you, my lady."

Her heart did a neat backflip. Goodness. It looked like Christmas. Lara hadn't seen that many gifts piled in one place since her childhood.

"For me?" she parroted.

Jared laughed, his icy eyes taking on unexpected warmth.

With his messy chin-length hair and fine, almost feminine, features, he looked like one of those Japanese anime characters. Nothing feminine about his body, though. He was lean and almost preternaturally sculpted to perfection. A blatantly sexual glint illuminated his gaze.

Just looking at him caused her senses to hum all over again. The space between the three of them seemed to vibrate with energies generated from their bodies. A scent lingered around them, too, a musky odor, thick, heady, and sensual. It was the smell of desire, of two virile young males circling and readying to mount the female.

Suddenly very aware of the sexuality oozing around them Lara felt heat flush through her veins. Her entire body reacted with a powerful surge, the white-hot craving ushering in a powerful ache between her legs. One orgasm had been nice, but hardly enough to satisfy.

"Yes," Nick affirmed. "All for you. I hope you like what we've picked out for you."

Lara laughed. "I'm already itching to see what's inside."

"You will," Jared promised.

"Just as soon as we get you prepared," Nick said, guiding her toward the bathroom.

Jared clapped and headed behind them. "Oh, this is the part I love."

Lara's heart was thumping over speed bumps, and her tummy did more flips. But in a good way. It didn't take much brains to figure out she'd be pampered like a prize Persian. Truth be told, a good spoiling would be nice. No one had spoiled her rotten since her father had passed away. After that she'd gotten a rude awakening that not everyone prized Daddy's little princess.

The adjoining bathroom had a jetted tub the size of an Olympic pool and a tiled shower. An extra-wide vanity took up one entire wall, ruled by a set of double sinks and plenty of electrical outlets. Razors, shaving cream, washcloths, and towels had all been set out, along with a comb, brush, and other miscellaneous cosmetics a woman would normally use.

A look of surprise flashed across her face, reflected back at her by mirrors sparing no angle.

Jared stepped up. "Can we interest you in our little spa here?"

Nick's hands were reaching for her clothes, already in disarray from the little encounter in the limo. She'd barely managed to get the halter and skirt back into place before getting out of the car. As for her thong, well, the driver would probably find that later on. Somehow they hadn't been able to locate it.

Undoing her halter, Nick gulped at the sight of her female curves. His eyes were practically feasting, knife and fork digging in for the banquet. "God, your breasts are amazing."

Lara already knew that she had a hot body. She laughed, hefting and lifting her breasts, enjoying their firm weight. "You think so?" They were round, not a bit of droop. She regularly worked out to make sure that didn't happen for a long time, too.

Nick nodded. "Definitely. They're perfect." Tossing the halter aside, he fumbled with her skirt. His hands were shaking so hard he barely managed the snaps. The skirt finally dropped to the floor. The mirror revealed legs that were slender and muscular from years of dancing lessons. When she was little, she'd dreamed of being a ballerina. She never would have imagined that those lessons would be best used discarding her clothes onstage.

Lara stood, naked save for thigh-high hose and high heels. She struck a pose, demurely covering her breasts. Her nipples were tight little buds, aching for more caresses, more kisses.

While Nick stood there acting stunned, Jared took control. Strong hands cinched Lara's waist. With the ease of a giant picking up a doll, he settled her on the vanity between the two huge sinks.

"Now, let's see what we can't do to make our girl all pretty," he teased. "Do you mind if I rearrange your hair?"

Lara had to grin. Men just loved her mane of long shiny black hair. Reaching up, she peeled off her wig and handed it over. "Not at all," she said. "Do what you like."

Both men looked at her in shock.

She laughed and ran her hands through her real hair, a short pixie cut almost the color of pure white silk.

Jared looked at the mass of hair in his hands. "Well, this is a surprise," he laughed. "It looked so real."

"My natural hair is so fine that it can't take a lot of styling products," Lara said. She didn't explain that it also allowed for a bit of anonymity when she wasn't working. A lot of men tended to think that provocative persona was real. On the street in regular clothes, no one connected the dull little blonde with the wild ebony-haired bitch.

Jared tossed the wig. "You look better without it." Claiming her left foot, he slid the pump off. "And while these look smoking hot, they also look painful as hell. How you women cram your feet into these instruments of torture is beyond me."

Lara wiggled her toes. "It's an art."

Jared slid off her other shoe. Her hose followed. "Ah, all nice and naked."

"And now that I am all naked, what are we going to do?"

Jared set the sinks to filling around her, adjusting the water temperature to a comfortable degree. "First we need two sinks filled with some water." He picked up one of the disposable razors and a can of shaving cream. "Then we need a pussy to present itself."

Her knees parted wide instinctively. She pulled her shoulders back, bringing her hands to rest on the small of her back.

"This what you want?" She glanced down at her exposed sex. "It's already pretty short. Not much there."

Nick looked. "Enough to shave. Nothing sexier than a nekkid pussy."

Lara felt the heat of his hungry gaze on her, recording every inch, every nook and cranny. She squirmed slightly, the intensity behind his wide-eyed appraisal making her throb. "It's all yours," she said, surprised by the tremble in her voice. "Do what you want." She'd always kept the hair on her mound clipped down because of the revealing costumes. Losing all the hair down there would definitely be an experience.

Nick dipped a washcloth in the water. He pressed it between her legs, wetting the hairs, warming them so her shaving would go smoothly. The rough nubs of the washcloth felt strangely sensual against her labia.

Feeling her netherlips warm, which in turn warmed her clit, Lara took a deep breath and closed her eyes. She was just beginning to feel all tingly when the washcloth vanished and Jared applied the shaving cream. She squealed as the icy blitz doused her warmth.

"Damn, that's wicked cold," she cursed.

Jared gave her a look of apology. "Sorry. Should have gotten the heated kind, huh?"

"Damn straight."

Jared handed the razor to Nick. "Would you like to do the honors?"

Nick hesitated. "I've never shaved a pussy before," he said, suddenly shy. "I mean, I don't want to cut her."

Jared laughed. "Just take it slow and easy, man. Pretend you're shaving that pretty face of yours." He stroked Nick's cheek in a familiar gesture. A look passed between them, as though they were reading each other's minds.

Lara caught the look. No doubt these two guys were tight—close enough to share a woman between them rather than get two girls. God knew they were good looking enough not to have to pay for their sex. She still had no idea why they were spending such an outrageous amount for the pleasure of her company. Surely any girl would willingly hop up on the vanity and spread her legs for either one of them.

Maybe they just like threesomes.

Nick looked at her. "Do you mind if I try?"

Lara shook her head. "Go for it. Just mind the deep parts."

Nick went scarlet. "I, ah, I will."

She laughed. "I was just teasing." By the way he was acting she'd have thought he'd never been up close and personal with a pussy.

Or maybe he was just shy.

"Hold very still, babe," Jared instructed. "We've got a newbie at snatch-shaving."

"I'll be very still," she promised.

Easier said than done.

Bending at the waist, Nick settled one arm against the surface to brace himself. The razor hovered a second over her vulnerable privates. A moment later the cool hard feeling of the blade sliding over her mound threatened to drive her insane.

"You're wiggling," Nick warned.

Lara fought her desire to move. "Trying to be still," she gasped.

Jared grinned. "Feels good, doesn't it?"

"Excellent."

Nick laughed softly. "Does this turn you on?"

She tossed back her head. "Yes," she said boldly. "It does."

"Good." Nick kept shaving. The razor slid smoothly over the short hairs of her pussy lips. A few minutes later her privates were slick as a whistle. He wiped away the excess shaving cream, admiring his handiwork. "Nice."

Jared slapped his friend's shoulder. "It tastes great, man. You should try some."

Lara grinned. Her nipples perked up as she squirmed a little. "Don't worry. It's calorie free."

Nick slid his hands between her thighs and bent. Face barely an inch away, he slowly penetrated the folds of her velvety flesh, giving her a long slow lick.

She shivered when the warmth of his mouth connected with her clit. His saliva mingled with the cream already moistening her labia. Her breath came in ragged bursts as she moved helplessly against his face. With soft gentle bites he gnawed the hard little nub, wringing a series of soft moans from her. God, she was so sensitive down there. One touch practically guaranteed an explosion.

Using the gentlest touch, Nick used his thumb and middle finger to part her labia. Her delicate muscles clenched when he stabbed his tongue deep inside her. Lara shuddered and another moan slipped past her lips.

"Feel good?" Nick managed to force out.

She answered through a sigh. "Better than good."

Nick straightened. He leaned forward to taste her rosy lips, his own damp with the juices of her pleasure.

Her hands speared into his long hair, pulling him closer. They feasted on each other's mouths, relishing the taste of carnal need.

Jared's voice broke into their mutual bliss. "Hey, you two. Don't be greedy here. There's plenty to go around for everyone."

They reluctantly broke apart.

"Man, you have the worst timing," Nick groused good-naturedly.

Lara shivered, wondering what would come next. She felt the gentle stroke of Jared's fingers trace one of her thighs. Her nipples hardened immediately. She swallowed, realizing how aroused and excited she was. He slid a finger easily inside her. Her hips undulated against the vanity.

"I'd say you're ready for a good hot fuck." Her juices wetted his fingers, letting them slide easily over her clit. His fingers knew just the right spot to keep her climbing slowly toward the edge.

Lara groaned softly. "You think?"

Jared nodded again to Nick. He stopped rubbing her clit and stepped back. "Time for the next phase of pleasure," he said with a wink.

She whimpered. "Thanks for getting me all hot and bothered."

Jared tweaked a nipple. "That's the point, my dear. What we're doing is tantric sex practice known as *Imsak*."

She pulled a face. "Never heard of it."

"It's an erotic technique of pleasing your partner while withholding your own sexual pleasure."

She eyed Jared. "Seems to me you weren't withholding very hard."

He grinned. "I am part of your pleasure." He indicated his friend. "Nick here is our lord and master, pulling the strings. I'm but a humble puppet."

"And enjoying every damn minute," Nick snickered.

Lara sighed. "I guess I understand. I think." She glanced down at her naked body; her legs were still splayed open and her privates front and center for anyone to see.

"You guys going to keep me like this all night?"

Nick pretended to think. "If I had my druthers, I would," he teased. He picked up a washcloth and dipped it into the sink, wetting it. "But I've got other things in mind right now."

Jared also picked up a fresh washcloth and wrung it out under hot water. He picked up a bottle of liquid soap and squirted out a healthy amount. "First we strip you down to the bare essentials."

"I'm already bare," Lara pointed out, amused. "Can't get more naked than this."

The guys exchanged a look. "Oh, but you're wrong," Nick said. "You're only just getting naked."

Both men attacked, soaping her skin from the tip of her toes to the top of her head. By time they finished, her skin was clean and pink and felt deliciously soft. The exotic scent of cinnamon and sandalwood clung to her skin.

"Now for the transformation," Jared announced. "We're going to make a new woman out of you."

4

An hour later, they emerged from the bathroom. In that time Lara had been primped and pampered to within an inch of her life.

Not only had she gotten a manicure and a pedicure, her hair and makeup had been redone. Her fingernails, normally bitten to the quick, were now long and beautiful, the press-ons painted fire-engine red, as were her toenails. Hair styled and lightly sprayed, her mouth matched the nail polish—the only lick of makeup she had on.

The guys made her stand in the middle of the room. Still in the buff, she followed instructions, wondering what the hell they had in mind. Must have something to do with the boxes piled on the bed.

Nick flipped on the television. Selecting a DVD, he put it in the player. Porn with French subtitles. "Now it's art."

Jared immediately made a beeline for the presents. "Dress-up-our-babe time," he cracked, reaching for one of the larger boxes.

Lara had pretty much figured that was the purpose, to create their fantasy woman. Well, let them have their fun. Truth be told, she was enjoying the hell out of the attention. If she'd had known this much fun waited for her, hell, she'd have come along for free.

Lifting the lid off his selection, Jared reached inside. Digging through decorative tissue paper, he pulled out a gorgeous silk confection. "Oh, nice."

Nick claimed it. "And I have the honor of putting it on her."

Stepping behind Lara, Nick slipped the lingerie over her head. As he pulled it into place around her, she saw that it was a corset, one of those Edwardian-style designs that pushed a girl's tits sky high and laced down the back. Fire-engine red, of course.

"God, these are so sexy on a woman." Nick tugged the laces tight. "Feel okay?"

Drawing in a breath, Lara glanced down at her breasts. The creamy mounds spilled over the top. Her nipples were hard peaks of excitement. Her waistline, already small to begin with, was a perfect hourglass. "As long as I can breathe is what counts."

"Looks terrific." Jared opened another box, pulling out a pair of silk back-seamed stockings with red tops. "And these will definitely add to the illusion."

Nick claimed them, kneeling down in front of her. "If you would," he said with a shy smile.

One hand on his shoulder for balance, Lara lifted her left leg.

"Easy now." Nick slid the stocking over her foot and up her calf, tugging until it stopped mid-thigh. When the garter snapped into place, he repeated the procedure. "Done."

Jared opened a third box. A sexy pair of Edwardian-style stiletto boots followed, as red as the corset and the lipstick on her mouth. They were certainly designing their own scarlet woman.

Nick claimed them. "Foot up," he ordered.

The boots went on, and were laced into place. A moment later Lara stood fully dressed in her new costume.

"What do you think?" Nick asked.

She glanced into the full-length mirror on the wall. There were a lot of mirrors around the room, including one bolted into the wall over the bed. No angle or activity was spared viewing.

"Gorgeous." Since she seemed to be fully dressed, such as it was, she wondered what the other boxes might hold.

"You are." Nick reached up, possessing and molding her breasts. He circled the erect pink tips with his thumbs. His cock was a steel rod trapped inside his tight jeans.

Lara felt herself go wet between her legs. She shifted, frantic to ease the fire he'd lit inside her all over again. She cupped the back of his head, guiding him down, inviting him to taste her. The desire she felt for him fractured her control. She'd forgotten what it was like to desire a man.

Nick's hands swept down, pausing at her hips. She barely managed to smother her cry when he took her nipple into his mouth. Her fingers clenched at his long hair. The world tilted beneath her feet when his hand connected with the dampness between her thighs. Suckling harder, he separated her slick labia with a single finger and crooked the tip of his finger into the small hooded organ.

Contact with her clit shattered her all over again. Lightning crackled behind her lids, as violent and shocking as a real storm outside.

Jared's voice broke through. "God, that is so hot."

Lara turned her head. Sure enough, Jared sat on the edge of the bed. Cock in hand, he made long slow strokes up his length. Reaching the dark-plum crown, he'd ease back down again.

She blushed, feeling heat creep into her cheeks.

Nick moved around behind her. "Time for part three," he whispered. Stepping closer, his lips were warm and gentle against the back of her neck, stroking her nape with the utmost tenderness.

The slow easy heat of arousal shimmered though Lara's body. All her senses seemed to come to life all over again, ready, eager, and very willing. Her whole body was hyperaware, hypersensitive to the two men who had taken control of her. Moisture seeped between her legs.

A chuckle rumbled against her ear. Nick's hot breath caressed. "Does it make you cream to see a cock like that?"

She moistened dry lips. "Yes."

Nick's fingertips went to work, touching her lightly, skimming her bare shoulders, arms, the rounded cheeks of her ass.

Lara's skin tingled. Her breasts ached. She burned from head to toe. The image of his mouth closing over her most private parts flashed across her mind's screen.

Nick's fingers continued their sensual tease across her skin. Jared pumped his cock, keeping a slow steady rhythm.

She groaned deep in the back of her throat. Her juices dampened the insides of her thighs. They had what she wanted, what she needed. Her sex grew wetter, her heart pounded. "Please," she whispered.

Nick's hand slid around and she felt his hand at her sex, a featherlight touch that made her part her legs in anticipation. Small tremors shook her when his fingers reclaimed her clit. "You want to be fucked?"

She gasped for air around the savage need beginning to devour her. Heat mingled with desperation and fused into something uncharacteristically volatile inside her core. Desire and a hundred other emotions pounded through her with every other beat of her heart. "Yes, please . . ."

Nick's free hand slipped around and cupped her left breast. He brushed his fingers over the erect peaks. "That's what I wanted to hear."

Gasping, Lara arched into him, her own hands flying behind

her to catch at his hips and pull his body against hers. She felt his erection straining.

Nick groaned when she rubbed her ass against him. His fingers squeezed her breast tighter. His other hand stroked her clit.

Lara rotated her hips in slow circles, good for both of them. Fire, damn it. She was on fire and about to explode into a raging inferno if she didn't get some relief. A sensual tease was nice, but there came a time when you needed to get down to the fucking. "Come on, Nick," she half breathed, half purred. "I want to know what that cock of yours feels like."

As if struck by a pail of ice water, Nick pulled back. Fingers like steel clamped around her arm, whirling her around. Pupils dilated, his nostrils flared. "Don't try to control me," he growled, catching her by the shoulders and giving her a shake. "I'm the one in control here."

Stunned by his outburst, Lara slowly nodded. "I understand." Fear trampled through her, threatening to snatch control. It took every ounce of discipline she could muster to keep her cool.

This is his fantasy, she reminded herself. *I'm nothing more than an object to make it come true.* She wanted to please him. Where the notion came from or why it should be so important didn't matter. Somehow there was a connection between them, one going deeper than mere strangers should have.

Jared came to her defense. "Take it easy, man. We're all here to have a good time."

Clenching his teeth, Nick stepped back. He dragged his fingers through his hair in frustration. "I'm sorry. Everything has to be perfect. I've waited too damn long to mess it up now."

Heart racing against her ribs, Lara nodded. "I want it to be perfect for you, too." She pasted on a smile. "I just want to please you, Nick. *Both* of you."

Nick relaxed. "You'll do what I tell you?" he asked, voice

shaking. He stared at her for an interminable minute, the emotions alive inside his gaze loving and hating her at the same time.

Lara stared back, her bare breasts rising and falling with each breath. The corset was suddenly too damn tight, too constricting. She wanted to rip it off.

She nodded a second time. "Of course."

Nick suddenly pulled her to him, kissing her hard on the mouth. It was a kiss born of desperation and the very real fear that she'd somehow defy him.

The violence behind his kiss stunned her, knocking the breath from her lungs. Disoriented, she barely had time to think before he shoved her down. Shaky on the toothpick-thin stilettos, Lara felt her knees connect with the carpet.

Trembling, she stared up at him. Waiting.

Nick looked down at her, something akin to disdain and desire mingling on his features. "You'll like what we're going to do. Trust me." He glanced over her head at his friend. "Get it."

Uh, ho. The two words that had ushered a lot of trouble into her life in past time. An involuntary shiver raced down Lara's spine. What the hell was *it*?

She risked a glance over her shoulder.

Jared opened another box, spilling a series of sex toys onto the bed. Another box produced lubes, lotions, jellies, and all sorts of condoms. Judging from the number of toys, Lara knew she was in for one hell of an experience. Jared picked among the items, making his selections. Hands full, he walked over.

"What did you pick?" Nick asked.

"My favorite. A butt plug. I'll fill every orifice she's got and then some."

Nerves feasting on her guts, Lara felt her rear pucker at the mention of the butt plug. She'd never done anal before. Never. She had a feeling her tender little ass was about to take a reaming. "Does that hurt?" she asked, hinting.

Jared settled on his knees behind her. "Only if you want it to," he said cheerily, as if he'd be offering her a delicacy instead of some big rubber thing to be shoved up her anus.

"It's the best experience you'll ever have," Nick breathed softly. Face flushed with longing, his tongue traced his lips.

A vague sense of uneasiness rippled through her. She wondered if *his* ass had ever been a recipient of Jared's butt plug. By the look in his eyes, he certainly enjoyed the idea.

Jared stroked the curves of her rear, slipping his fingers into her velvety crack and tracing its length with a featherlight touch. "Just relax." Ever so gently, his fingers slid up and down, spreading her apart and exposing her.

"Nice and pink," he informed Nick.

"And very virgin," Lara piped in. "Think you can take it easy back there?"

Jared picked up a tube of lubricant. "I'm going to be gentle with you," he promised. "It will feel good once you get over the initial discomfort." He squirted the lube and spread it, making slow circles over and around her anus. "How does that feel?"

A vague sensation of pleasure rippled through her. Mmm. "I think I like that."

"Good. I'm going to use a finger to enter you. Don't fight it. Just let me ease in." The tip of Jared's finger pressed, pushing into the center of her asshole.

Lara automatically puckered.

A little swat stung her rear. "Don't fight it."

She grunted. "Hard not to do."

Jared pushed harder. Another ripple went through her, only stronger this time. A slow rise of heat began to radiate through her as penetration through her anal muscles progressed.

"Feel good?"

Her head bobbed. "Yes, very nice," she breathed.

Jared persisted until his finger was buried to the knuckle.

A sigh shuddered past her lips. She was all too aware that Nick stood in front of her. His gaze burned with unquenched lust. He looked vulnerable and incredibly handsome all at once. Knowing he needed her so badly, yet wouldn't take her, sent a rush of hot blood to her groin, making her clit throb uncomfortably. Her fingers dug into the short nap of the carpeting.

As if aware of her thoughts, Nick slowly unbuttoned the top of his jeans. Unzipped, but just a little.

"More," he mouthed. "Show me more and I'll show you more."

Jared took the cue. His finger slipped out of her rear. A moment later something thicker and harder pressed for entry.

Lara relaxed and let it in. The plug ground into her ass, sending a ripple through her insides. "Oh, God," she cried out. "Damn, that's deep!"

"Right where it's supposed to be," Jared whispered. "And it'll feel even better with my dick up that delicious pussy of yours." He gave one cheek a friendly pinch. "And maybe Nick will let you taste that nice cock of his."

Lara stared up at Nick, trying hard to ignore the hollow beat of her heart and the sexual frustration spreading through her. Her breaths came in short gasps, each undulation of her anal muscles around the plug creating new sparks of desire. She ached. Ached for his touch, for release.

"Please," she murmured.

Nick unzipped his jeans all the way, releasing his engorged cock. His shaft more than impressed. At least eight inches greeted her eager gaze. Long and thickly veined, it had a cherry-purple crown, round and inviting enough to take a bite out of. A few drops of clear semen glistened on the tip.

Her mouth watered. "Looks delicious." She leaned forward. Her tongue flicked out, wiping the droplets away. "Tastes pretty good, too."

Nick guided the tip to her waiting mouth. "Suck it."

Lara opened. He slid in. She engulfed the straining head with a single gulp and automatically tightened her lips, creating suction inside her mouth around his glans. At the same time she traced the corona with the tip of her tongue, making slow circles.

Something primal seemed to break free inside him. "I want you," she heard him stutter out. "I've never stopped wanting you." He closed his eyes against the hot burst of emotion. A violent shiver ran through the length of his body.

Breaking her mouth-lock, Lara pulled back slightly to meet his gaze and waited.

"She's all yours," Jared prompted from behind. "Enjoy her."

"Don't. Stop. Now." Nick's voice broke, but he somehow struggled through the words. His fingers tangled in her hair, guiding her back to his waiting erection.

Lara opened, taking him almost to the back of her throat. Using one hand to hold him steady, she worked the length of his shaft, alternating slow long licks with nips and gnaws around his meatus. She marveled at the silky feel of his cock, the taste of musk and masculine sweat mingling into the sweetest of aphrodisiacs.

It amazed her something so simple as sex—and as complex—kept this man from enjoying himself. It was obvious he wanted it, wanted to enjoy it. But some unnamed compulsion seemed to hold him back from the edge of bliss. He clearly wanted to fuck her. Instead of doing that, he preferred to use Jared as a substitute cock.

The sound of a foil packet tearing grated through her mind. Good. The boys practiced safe sex. She'd wondered how to broach the subject. Not that right this second would be a good time to talk about it. Butt full of plug and mouth full of cock, she wasn't in any position to talk.

Nick moaned, shifting his hips closer. "Go deeper."

Lara obliged by taking the whole of his stalk into her

mouth. Her teeth scraped down at his sensitive skin—not heavily, but just enough pressure to make sure he felt every sensation.

Nick's breathing grew harsh, labored. "That mouth of yours is a fucking wonder," he grated.

No time to think about what Nick said, though.

Jared's cock pushed against her slit, sliding between her soaked lips. With a single thrust, he sheathed himself.

Lara's grip involuntarily tightened on Nick's cock.

"Don't rip it off," Nick cautioned through a low growl.

Jared's hips undulated. "She's really tight," he informed his friend. "God, I've never felt a pussy like this around me. You'll love it, man. Just love it."

So there she was. Nick's cock ravaged her mouth while Jared drilled her from behind, with a butt plug thrown in for good measure. If she hadn't been experienced before, she had a feeling that she'd soon know every position and then some by time these two got finished with her. Thank God they only had her for a week. More than that and she'd die of exhaustion.

Lara closed her eyes against the starburst of sensations. Arousal boiled in her groin, threatening a total explosion at any moment. Every searing thrust shoved her closer to the precipice of total abandon. Even as the sensations flowed through her body, she wondered how being with these two men could feel so right. She knew where such dangerous thoughts could lead, but wasn't strong enough to put a stop to them.

Lara cried out when Jared shifted their position, pulling her off her knees and up onto his lap. She had no choice but to move her knees under her body to keep her balance, not to mention her hold on Nick's cock. Somehow instinct moved their bodies in perfect tandem, kept their rhythm unbroken.

Every thrust of Jared's hips forced the butt plug even deeper than it already was. His cock throbbed inside her with animalistic need. All the while Nick's cock worked its wicked black magic with her mouth.

Ass, cunt, mouth. Every bit of her was stuffed to overflowing. Her clit throbbed with the pain of unreleased arousal. Her inner muscles contracted from the combination of perceptions overwhelming her senses. She finally let herself feel all the things she'd refused to feel before, things she wanted but that scared her too badly for her to admit.

Reaching around, Jared stroked her clit. His touch buzzed with electric power. "Let yourself go, baby."

Lara felt her body go rigid, as if a lightning bolt had stabbed through her mouth and run the length of her. Long-denied needs were finally unleashed to coil and snap throughout her body without any restraint. Pure unadulterated lust seared her veins, and she was lost. To reason. To sanity.

All she wanted to do was come.

The spasm began in her belly like a ferocious explosion of molten lava and spread clear to her toes. White lightning sizzled behind her eyes. Waves of pleasure built inside her, a relentless tide rushing toward a distant and jagged shore.

Lara rose above the peaks, riding them, letting their power drive her higher toward the single profound ache shimmering deep inside her. At the last moment she let go of her control and shattered. Orgasm rocked her from the inside out. Every inch of her shook as nerve endings in her body sizzled with pure rapturous heat.

At the same time, Nick's cock spasmed once in her mouth, then twice. He moaned loudly, pressing himself deep into her throat, holding her head in his hands when he came. His semen jetted down her throat, a hot rush of liquid ecstasy.

The shock of tasting his pleasure stole her breath.

Lara barely had time to gulp and swallow before the next explosion arrived. Behind her, Jared's body tensed. He quivered and then came, the force of his climax seeming to crawl all the way up her spine. A little sob broke from her lips when a third orgasm rocked her system, less intense, but just as pleasurable.

All three of them collapsed onto the carpet, a sweaty but erotic mass of tangled limbs. Somehow Lara found herself pressed between the two men. And while her heart raced against her ribs, the emotions swirling inside fluttered in and out of her mind.

Turning her face to the floor, she quickly blinked back tears she wouldn't be able to explain.

"You're not getting away so fast." Jared immediately spooned their bodies together, moving his hips slowly against hers. He was still deep inside her, his semierect cock throbbing with heat. The lean flex of his muscled body re-created all the wonderful frictions a man and woman could enjoy.

Lara gritted her teeth as need brutally twisted inside her all over again. Her senses flickered. Exhaustion flitted away, along with thoughts she didn't dare examine now that they'd appeared in her mind. "God, you guys don't give a girl a break."

Jared kissed the curve of her shoulder. "Oh, no, honey. We're just getting started. I've got all these wonderful toys I want to try out on you."

She mock-groaned. "You two will be the death of me."

"But what a way to go," Jared laughed. Behind her his lean frame bunched and trembled with restrained power. The flood of her arousal mingled with his urgency.

Nick lay in front of her. Their faces were barely inches apart. Without a word he rolled into her, sandwiching her against Jared with his full weight. Lara felt the hard ridge of him against her belly. Apparently a cocksucking hadn't been enough.

"I want a taste." His mouth claimed, tongue sweeping in to claim and conquer.

The rush of pleasure made her dizzy. The delicious feel of

his mouth over hers reminded her of ripe dark cherries and pure milky cream.

Gentleness was forgotten as Nick gave in to his own desperation and need. The desire to possess what he wanted seemed to overtake him. "I want more," he breathed, his words pushed out by fresh urgency. He brushed his fingertips over her sensitized nipples. "I want to taste every part of you." He scooted down to the level of her breasts.

Lara smothered a cry as he captured one jutting nubbin between his teeth. Her vision blurred in a haze of pleasure when he sucked in the hard peak, drawing small circles around it with his tongue.

Jared murmured something in her ear, but she couldn't make out the words over the rush of blood through her head. To be swept away, lost in the arms of two men, more than fractured her control.

Her body responded to every hard plane, every solid ridge of muscle. Every brush of hard against soft, wet against dry. Suddenly two mouths and four hands were all over her. Two cocks strained to please her all over again.

There was the unspoken promise of more. And the anticipation of knowing she would get it.

Nothing she could do now but hang on for the ride.

5

_____

Consciousness returned slowly.

Lara woke up expecting to find herself pressed between two warm male bodies. Fumbling with the sleeping mask covering her eyes, her lids cracked open to a wide expanse of empty bed. Blinking to clear her blurry vision, she groped to her left. Nothing. Half turning, she groped to her right. No snoozing male lay tangled in the cool white cotton sheets.

Sunshine streamed in through the windows, open to let the warm, dry breeze in. The beginning of another scorching hot desert day. No surprise if temperatures hit 100 or more. She heard the low babble of the television coming from downstairs. Good old-fashioned twenty-four-hour news. She glanced at the bedside digital. Nine-thirty. Someone liked their daily dose of gloom and doom early in the morning. The aroma of freshly made coffee tempted, but not enough to make her get up just yet. She wanted to laze around a little more.

Yawning and rubbing her eyes, she fell back against the pillow in relief. Thank God! She needed a little break from those two wild sex maniacs. A heady rich scent emanated from her sleep-warm skin, the musk of last night's sexual escapades. Sweat, lubricant and semen. She'd not only been fucked, she'd been *claimed*. The guys had branded her skin with their unique scents like wild tomcats.

Closing her eyes, she settled into a light doze. And even though exhaustion swept through her in shimmering waves, she knew she wouldn't go back to sleep. There were too many wonderful sensations to think about. Hitting the rewind button in her mind, she replayed various scenes across her mind's screen, images that would make a porn star blush.

Her eyes still closed, a slow grin spread across her face. She'd loved every damn second of it. She'd never suspected that sex with two men would be so wonderful.

Lara rolled over on her side, hugging a pillow to her body. She slipped a hand under the sheets, teasing one nipple with a gentle stroke until the little peak grew pointed and hard. A shuddery breath slipped between her lips.

Last night Nick and Jared had put her through the paces, bending and tying her like a pretzel in pursuit of the perfect sexual position. Every muscle in her body ached, even a few she didn't even know she had. She'd been creamed and reamed within an inch of her life.

Desire and a thousand other emotions pounded through her. They'd had sex just a few hours ago and she was already wet and wanting all over again. She knew it was crazy, but need hovered in the back of her skull. She was helpless to stop the all-encompassing thoughts. If she had her way, this new and wonderful life would go on forever.

Her hand slipped lower, brushing between her legs. She ached, but in a pleasant, sated way. Fingers brushing her damp labia, she slid a single finger into her creamy sex. Using that as lubrication, she dragged her finger sharply up toward her clit. Static crackled through her.

Gasping, Lara arched against the pillow. A tiny moan escaped her as she worked the sensitive nubbin. Climax exploded, quickly and unexpectedly. Liquid heat trickled through her veins, a deliciously relaxing sensation. God, she could lie there and do that all day. No wonder the girls working at the Demimonde loved their jobs. Getting paid for unlimited pleasure wasn't such a bad idea.

"Two beautiful men making love to me," she swooned dreamily. What more could a girl ask for?

Her brow wrinkled with the memory. Well, kind of sex with two men. Someone always had to throw a monkey wrench into the perfect fantasy.

While Jared hadn't hesitated to plunge in and fuck her three times, Nick had held back from making any penetration. True, he'd kissed and licked every inch of her body, giving her oral sex. And he'd been glad to receive it. However, when it came time to get down to the real dirty deed, he'd pulled away—almost as if he was afraid he'd somehow defile her.

That puzzled her.

Nick wanted her. She knew by the reaction of his body to her touch, the shudder and sigh and longing in his eyes. And she wanted him. God, she'd been attracted to him from the second she'd laid eyes on him. The sudden pang of longing tearing through her chest was so powerful for a moment that she couldn't catch her breath.

Sitting up, she frowned. Nick's short outburst returned full force. A vague sense of uneasiness rippled through her. His angry words reverberated like the echo of a gunshot inside her head. His outburst had shook her more than she cared to admit.

Don't try to control me.

That's what he'd said.

Lara sensed there was more to it than control, though. Something in his psyche went a hell of a lot deeper than that. And until he admitted it to himself, she had a feeling that Nick would continue to hold himself back, hovering on the peripheral edge of unfulfilled pleasure.

Her pulse beat strongly against the lump forming in her throat. Last night she'd been ready to surrender herself to both of them. A voyeur, Nick had watched, touched—but not penetrated.

I'm going to have to do something about that.

Her stomach rumbled, reminding her that almost a day had passed since she'd last bothered to eat. A shower and something to eat would be wonderful right now. She'd think about Nick later.

Sliding out of bed, Lara padded toward the bathroom, shutting the door behind her. She took a hot and steamy shower, letting the water massage every inch. By the time she emerged, she felt like a whole new woman, pink and squeaky clean from head to toe.

Toweled but damp she emerged from the bathroom wrapped in a white robe, one of the complimentary ones. A swirl of her fingers fluffed her pixie cut into place. She liked her hair short and easy to keep. Her wig still lay discarded on the vanity, looking like something coughed up by a sick cat. It belatedly occurred to her that all she had to wear aside from the corset and stockings was the outfit she'd arrived in.

A few boxes from the night before remained unopened. She peeked inside one. A bikini met her eyes. A *very* small bikini.

She lifted it out, holding a piece in each hand. Whoa! It was little more than a few teeny triangles of fabric held together with floss. Her nipples and pubic area would barely be covered—her ass would hang out for everyone to see.

Discarding that as inappropriate so early in the morning, Lara opened the second box. Her eyes widened in surprise. "Holy shit," she muttered. "They expect me to wear this?" Leather bondage gear, the hardcore kind. Studded leather collar, ankle and wrist cuffs, and a few other things that prickled the fine hairs at the nape of her neck.

"Definitely not wearing that," she muttered. She chose the bikini, dressing in the itty-bitty pieces and then sliding the robe back on and belting it around her waist. No reason to incite a riot right away. Apparently these guys intended to keep her as close to naked as possible the entire week.

Hunger gnawed her backbone. The smell of coffee beckoned. She needed a pick-me-up soon or she'd faint dead away.

She found the downstairs area deserted. The television played to no one. Not that the place was totally abandoned. In the adjoining bedroom she detected activity through the half-open door. Grousing, teasing, the general disorientation of living in strange quarters.

She headed toward the kitchenette. Freshly brewed coffee waited. Someone had ordered breakfast, too, a selection of fruit and pastries from the Ranch's restaurant. People having sex worked up an appetite.

Lara poured a cup of coffee, adding a packet of artificial sweetener and loads of cream. She took a small sip, then a larger one. God, it tasted good, fortifying and warming her inside. Didn't quite fill her, though. Picking among the pastries, she selected a doughnut. She bit in, chewing. Mmm. Bavarian cream. Her favorite. Without minding her manners, she wolfed the doughnut down with a few quick bites. A second one tempted, calling her name.

Thinking about her waistline, Lara finished her coffee instead. By time she'd swallowed the last sip, she felt like a new woman. Ah, sugar and caffeine could always be counted on to give her system a quick jolt.

Curious as to what her hosts might be up to, she drifted toward the bedroom and peeked inside.

Though the bed was unused, a couple of suitcases had been laid out and opened. Clothing and other personal items were scattered around; jeans, T-shirts, tennis shoes, and other things guys on vacation would travel with.

Lara's gaze lingered on one of the T-shirts. What she wouldn't give to have a little more to cover herself with. The damp robe wasn't exactly comfortable. The shower still ran, obliterating sound to whoever was inside the bathroom. No one should hear her enter.

She eased into the room with the intention of borrowing one. Creeping like a thief, she tip-toed toward the bed. She stopped dead in her tracks.

Jared stood in front of the bathroom door. His back was to her, his body braced against the door frame.

Lara walked up behind him. The door was angled open in such a way as to allow a liberal view of the shower. Constructed entirely in see-through glass tile, the design gave a clear view of the person standing inside. Despite the steam, the view was spectacular.

The air around her shifted and thickened. For an instant Lara could only stare at Nick, mesmerized, trying not to think of what it would be like to run her hands over his muscular chest, tease his flat nipples. She knew she was spying, but she just couldn't turn away. Completely unaware he had an audience, Nick's soapy hands skimmed over lean hips and slender thighs.

Keenly aware of the heat suffusing her body, she flexed her fingers. Man, oh, man. *Dangerous*, she thought. But, oh, so very tempting.

Unaware of her presence, Jared murmured, "God, he's magnificent." He was shirtless, and his jeans hugged muscular thighs. His dark hair was still wet from his shower. Lowering his head, he let out a long slow groan. "I'd give my soul to have him."

His words connected like a slap. The pain was so sharp that Lara had to blink her eyes and take a deep calming breath. Dear

God, his words had felt like he'd torn a hole through her heart. Well, hell. It wasn't like *she* was in love with Nick.

Realizing she'd stumbled into something very intimate, Lara slowly put one foot behind the other and started to ease backward. Maybe she could escape without letting Jared know what she'd seen and heard.

Feeling her presence, Jared glanced back. Their gazes instantly connected. High tension zinged between them like a bolt of pure electricity. As his darkened gaze met hers, the emotions written across his face said everything: He was in love with Nick.

Jared slowly pivoted, stepping away from the door and leaning back against the wall. The barest hint of a smile flitted across his lips. "Busted."

"I'm sorry," she said. "I didn't mean to stumble in. I—I just wanted a T-shirt."

He shrugged. "It's not like it's any secret."

"So are you two, uh, together?"

He blinked, obviously startled by her question. "Together as in partners, yeah." A whisper of a smile touched his lips. "Together as in lovers, no." His smile was at odds with his words. "Nick doesn't know I'm crazy about him because he's obsessed with you."

Obsessed? Her brows rose. "He's obsessed with me?"

Jared nodded. "He's so freaking in love with you that he can't even see I want him."

"Nick can't be," she spluttered. "We've just met."

He narrowed his eyes. "It's true. He wants you, I want him." He hesitated a beat. "Kind of a strange little triangle we've got going on here."

One nobody had bothered to fill her in on.

Lara shook her head, confused. "He wants me, but doesn't have a problem sharing with you. Having your gay friend doing the fucking for you is a strange way to love a girl, isn't it?"

Jared gave her a little wink. "I'm not gay, hon. I'm bi, and perfectly happy to bat for both teams. Enjoy the pleasures of both worlds, is my motto."

Lara wasn't sure if what he told her was good or bad. She shook her head and raised her chin a notch. "So you two have never made love?"

His reply came back, negative. "No, we haven't. We've fooled around, so I think the desire's there. But he's very damn conflicted about it. I probably shouldn't say this, but Nick's not experienced, with men or women."

Her hand flew to her mouth. Nick had the classic all-American looks most women wouldn't have hesitated to snatch up. How had he remained untouched at his age? "Oh, don't tell me he's a virgin."

Jared raised a knowing brow. "That wick of his has never dipped into cunt or asshole, my dear. The pressure's building inside him, though. Just a matter of time till it blows." His blue eyes sparkled with sudden mischief. "And I hope I have a hand on his cock when it does."

Unbidden, a blush rose to her cheeks. "Cut that out before you embarrass me."

His grin turned wicked. "You've just been fucked and sucked all over and you're turning all Miss Priss?"

Lara crossed her arms across her breasts. "I'm not Miss Priss," she protested in her defense. "I'm just discreet."

Jared smiled, pleased. "And worth every dime, babe." He tweaked the tip of her nose. "Now why don't you get take that little robe off and get your ass into that shower?"

"I just had one."

"I know, but I'm not thinking about getting all squeaky clean. I'm thinking about getting all down and dirty with you pressed between us." He grinned and rubbed a hand against the front of his jeans. "I'm a hungry man, honey."

Rolling her eyes, Lara slipped off the robe. "Your libido is a psycho." The floss bikini followed.

Jared eyed her from head to toe. "You impress me, Ms. Green. I think I might be in love with you, too. Wouldn't that be the perfect trio?"

The sexy image of being trapped between two very naked and willing men wanting to please her in every way filled her mind. Her breath caught in a hitch. Be with both of them? Permanently? That was crazy thinking. Life's harsher realities had drilled into not to put her trust in men.

A subtle tremor rippled through her as unforeseen emotions warred inside her. Pleasure that both men desired her fought with the wariness of letting her heart rule her head. The line between work and play was beginning to blur dangerously. Hard to remind herself that she wasn't here to get involved with either.

For the moment, however, she had to keep the fantasy alive. Didn't mean she had to believe it. Just perform to orders.

"Thank you, Mister Montgomery. You're not so bad yourself."

Jared's grin widened. "Thanks. Now get your ass in that shower and give my friend a nice hand job." He paused a beat. "I'll join you momentarily."

She nodded. "Okay."

Lara slipped through the bathroom door, heading toward the shower and the naked, steamy man inside. Taking a deep breath, she opened the door. "Hi."

Dark eyes met hers. "What are you doing here?" Nick made no attempt to cover his nudity. He wasn't tall, barely six feet, but he seemed to tower over her like a god stepped down from some mystical mountain.

Lara just stood, looking at the beautiful man standing naked in all his glory. Blond hair plastered around his face, the water sluiced around his shoulders, trickling down the thatch of hair covering his chest. She visually traced the line, fascinated by the way the water caressed his groin, the length of his penis—an impressive sight even when flaccid.

She stared, hardly aware of her breath rushing raggedly through her lips. He was so good-looking she couldn't think. The single coherent thought her mind managed to form centered around his gorgeous cock and the desire to feel it stuffing every last inch of her sex. The visualization of his hips sinking between her thighs broadsided her like a Mack truck.

Aware he waited for an answer, Lara swallowed over the lump in her throat. "I thought you could use a little help washing your back," she said, winging it.

Nick's gaze glittered like diamonds. A mischievous little-boy look stole across his chiseled features. "I think I could." His deep voice vibrated.

Gulping as though she were about to jump out of the frying pan and into a bonfire, Lara stepped into the shower. She grinned up at him, very aware that she had to tilt her head to maintain eye contact. "Hand me the soap and turn around."

He complied.

Lara flipped the bar between her fingers until thick foam formed. Slowly she lifted her hands. Her palms settled on his shoulders, her fingers automatically beginning to work his tight muscles.

A groan escaped him. "That feels good."

Her hands skimmed lower, inching toward his lean hips and full buttocks. "Oh, it's about to feel better." Exploring every inch, she lovingly caressed his sinuous planes.

"Babe," he grated. "I think you're giving me a hard-on."

"Guess I'll have to take care of that," she answered, all innocence.

Pressing her body against his, she slid her left hand around his waist. Searching fingers circled his cock. A surge of purely female appreciation swept through her. He wasn't lying. A magnificently hard shaft pulsed under her grip. The muscles and tendons in his neck formed tense cords when her hands slid upward. His erection surged against her palm, and she reveled in the shudder rippling through him.

"Oh, God," he breathed. "I've dreamed of this so many times."

The motion of her arm moved her breasts back and forth against his back, chafing her sensitized nipples against his acquiescent strength. She gasped at the sensations, galvanized by the quiver of lust traveling through her fingertips and coiling in her belly. It was absolutely delightful to masturbate a man like this. Brazen and shameless, but totally delectable.

"Dream no more." Lara was in danger of begging him to lift her onto the shower seat and cram that cock right up her when Jared arrived. His erection pressed into her slippery crack and his arm slipped around her body.

"Don't mind if I do." His fingers closed around hers. Suddenly there were two hands jacking Nick off.

Tension rolled off Nick in thick waves as he recognized the change. He leaned forward, palms pressing against the shower wall to catch his weight. "Just do it," he grated. What he meant by that was debatable.

Lara took a wild guess. The possibilities spun in her skull until she could barely think straight. Abruptly she knew. With utter certainty. The three of them would create a passion so hot and so overwhelming that they'd be forever fused as one.

Confused by the thought that seemed so perfect, but too impossible to even entertain, she released her grip. Wriggling out from between the two men, she pushed her way out of the shower. She needed time to think. Alone.

She took a couple of deep breaths. "I think you two can handle things from here."

Jared's slow-as-molasses grin unfolded. "Thanks, Sugar."

Hand stroking Nick's cock, he dropped a kiss on his friend's shoulder. "We'll be just fine."

Heart filling with jealousy, Lara's eyes abruptly brimmed with tears, swimming with misery, jealousy, and desire.

Aw, hell. A sinking feeling settled in her stomach. *This isn't good at all.*

Turning, Lara fled the bathroom. Once again she was in danger of giving her heart away to someone who might hurt her.

This time the danger was doubly intense because two men were involved.

6

Relief at escaping Nick and Jared's sexual escapade warred with the steady beat of desire pounding inside her. For a moment she thought about turning around and getting back into the shower with those two beautiful men, letting them make love to her all over again.

Lara shook her head. No, she needed a moment to herself, a little space and distance to gather her erratic thoughts. There were too many things to think about, and her mind insisted on going into overtime.

Feeling conflicted, confused, and more than a little jealous, Lara decided the best thing to do would be get out and get some fresh air. It had been ages since she'd gotten to bask outside. The suite had a big patio outside with a set of matching deck chairs. She could stretch out and just breathe. She'd think about her feelings later.

Slipping through the sliding door, Lara walked out onto the patio. The Southwest style Saltillo tile felt warm under her bare feet, almost uncomfortably hot. Another few hours under the unrelenting Nevada sun and the tile would be blistering enough to fry an egg on. Barely ten in the morning and the day promised to be a scorcher.

Discarding her robe, Lara lowered herself on one of the chairs. She hadn't put the bikini back on, not that it afforded much protection or cover.

Stretching out on her stomach, she sighed and closed her eyes. Sunlight caressed her bare skin, the rays sinking in to ease her sore muscles. The warmth felt so good she groaned in relief.

Ah, this was just what I needed. A good dose of natural illumination to ease her tension and quiet her troubled mind.

Years had passed since she'd even spent time outside. In her world, mornings didn't exist. She rarely rose before noon, and was lucky if she managed to make it out of bed by two. When working late evenings and nights, a person tended to fall into a sort of twilight zone of nonexistence. Time felt suspended; the days seeming like they never changed or varied. The only things that seemed to stay the same were the pain and disappointment that dogged her.

Changes. If nothing else, this experience could be used as a wake-up call that things needed readjustment in her life. She didn't want to spend her life stripping, that was for sure. And she damn sure wasn't going to put her body up for sale once this week was over. No, this had been a one-time thing—something she'd done because she was desperate for cold hard cash.

Never again. No one would ever catch her with her back against the wall again. Even after she settled with DiMarco, there'd be plenty of money left over to start a new life. The money—still too mind-boggling of an amount to really fathom—was hers. No strings attached. She could take it, walk away, and never look behind her again. Starting over sounded pretty damn good, no matter what she had to do to earn her ticket to freedom.

Busy arranging the life she planned to change just as soon as she had money in hand, Lara didn't hear the soft pad of bare feet creeping closer.

Nick's voice broke the silence. "Not good to be out here basking without suntan lotion."

Aware that her heart had begun to pound hard against her ribs, Lara didn't raise her head. "I don't think a few minutes will do any harm."

Nick settled beside her on the lounge, which was plenty wide enough to accommodate an extra body. A popping sound followed. Cool lotion drizzled across her back and shoulders. Big hands settled on her skin, rubbed. "Better to be safe than sorry," he commented. "Nothing hurts worse than sunburn. On a day like this, you'll fry fast."

Lara raised her head, glancing at him. She blinked as her eyes readjusted to the bright light. He wore a pair of jeans and nothing else. The muscles in his arms and chest rippled with strength. Aw, damn. She'd love to devour him in a single bite.

Very aware her arousal was heating up all over again, and not because of the sun, she lowered her head back to the pillow of her arms. "Thanks." A pause. "Where's Jared?"

Nick shrugged. His damp and disheveled long hair created a rumpled appearance, making him look even sexier. "Still jacking himself off in the shower, I think."

"He seems to really like sex," she commented.

Nick burst out laughing. "That isn't saying half of it. Jared would fuck a hole in the ground if it'd suck him off."

"You two been together long?" Good. A nice safe topic. That way she wouldn't have to think about the way her clit ached. Not that it'd stay safe very long if he kept rubbing that lotion on. The feel of his hands on her bare skin was about to drive her wild with lust.

Another laugh. "Since freshman year in college. Jared was my roommate. We started our business right out of our dorm room."

"Oh? What did you guys do?"

A slight grin tugged at his lips. "Aw, we just created this little networking site. Kind of a place to meet and hang out online."

"Sounds cool." Well, at least she thought it did. She was an original technotard when it came to computers. Logging in and checking e-mail was about all she could manage.

"Yeah—big-time. We sold a stake in it last year for two hundred and fifty million dollars." He mentioned a name that even a computer dummy like her recognized.

Her eyebrows shot up. "Holy shit."

"Holy shit is right, babe. Who the hell would have thought it would grow into anything? Sitting in front of our computers all those years made us too damn rich too damn young. We've been kicking around, sitting on our laurels for the last year or so. Talk about a wasted life."

She shook her head, still boggled by the figure he'd named. "Doesn't sound like you wasted your life half as much as I did. I didn't even get to graduate from high school. All I've ever done is wait tables or take off my clothes."

"Dropped out, huh?"

She shrugged. "Sort of. I did manage to get my GED, though. I'd planned to get a better education, but things got in the way."

"Oh? Like what?"

Ignoring the steady thump of her heart, she refused to meet his gaze. The conversation was beginning to take a turn into personal territory, mainly her undesirable past. "Just shit, you know. Stuff that happened." She might have had sex with him, but that was just something physical, easy to leave behind. It'd be better if a lot of personal details weren't exchanged. Easier to make the break when the time came.

Keep going this way and she was going to trip up for sure. Though she'd tried to keep her feelings at arm's length, she'd already discovered that she liked these two guys. Really liked them. She wished lust was all she felt for the men, but both had appealing qualities that went past sex—Nick with his shyness and Jared with his brash take-it-or-leave-it attitude. Apart they would have been boring and trying on the patience. Together they were perfectly paired, each complementing the other's strengths and downplaying the other's weaknesses.

She shook her head. Sexual arousal had to be short-circuiting her brain cells.

Knowing there was only one way this could end, Lara found the truth that chilled her deep inside unappealing. Later, when her week was over, she'd have time to think about the unfairness of providence throwing two stellar hunks into her less-than-stellar life.

Later.

When she was far, far away from Nevada and the Demi-monde Ranch. If she had her druthers, she'd never set foot in the entire state ever again. This was definitely a place she intended to leave behind. Waving good-bye would be a relief.

Her world started to blur dangerously. Lara blinked her eyes, forcing back the tears. Damn it, now wasn't the time to start bawling. "Anyway, it's all old history now," she said, feigning a lightness she definitely didn't feel. "Water under the bridge."

"I see." Nick's hands skimmed over her shoulders and down her spine, rubbing the silky lotion into her skin. "Nice tattoos."

Liquid heat rose inside her all over again. Just when she was sure she'd gotten a handle on her desire, he had to go and light the fuse again. Amazing how fast he could drag her out from under her cloud of doom and gloom.

She'd been fucked within an inch of her life just a few hours ago, but she was already wet and pulsing and wanting the sex to start all over again.

Suppressing a little moan, Lara eased her hips into the cushion, trying to stop the ache a little. It didn't work. Between the stress and sexual tension throbbing inside her, she was wound tighter than a cheap yo-yo.

Nick noticed. "You okay?" The sound of his voice held a smile.

Licking dry lips, Lara quickly shook her head. "Just itchy."

"I can take care of that." He squirted more lotion on. His hands resettled at the small of her back, massaging her skin with long slow strokes. "So why the dark death-themed tattoos?" he asked conversationally.

Lara shrugged. "They suited my mood."

"You must really be into pain to have this many," he commented.

Ah, not exactly. She had enough mental pain to contend with. She didn't get off on physical pain at all.

She hurried to explain. "They're not real, just henna. I have a friend who does the work for practice. That way when I want to change the style, I can. They last about three or four weeks before they fade off."

Nick traced the lines of the Reaper dominating her back. "Ah, a woman's prerogative to change her mind. Makes sense." He chuckled. "Damn, you must have been thinking brutal thoughts when you got this bitch."

Her brow wrinkled. "I always think ugly thoughts," she countered. "But somehow they seem less bad if I put them on my skin, you know. Having them on the outside of me means that I don't have to keep them inside, where they fester. Does that make sense?"

Nick stared hard at her. "Yeah. That makes sense. I'm glad they won't be there forever, though. By them look of them you must have had some pretty bad shit come down in your life."

Her throat unexpectedly tightened. She suddenly felt like he'd shoved a dull knife between her ribs. "Some."

"Care to share?" he asked gently.

Lara took a breath. The pain was so sharp it felt real, like blood seeping from wounds that would never heal. "Not really."

Nick leaned forward until his lips were just inches away from her ear. "I've got big shoulders if you want to cry."

Nerves all of a sudden gnawing at her guts, she pursed her lips. She was already in over her head because of her feelings for him.

His hand traveled down her spine, brushing over the round curve of one buttock. "I can handle anything you'd tell me." His palm settled there, warm, heavy. Somehow reassuring.

Stomach doing a backflip over his intimate caress, her nerves coiled tighter. As a general rule, Lara didn't choose to remember the last seven years. 2001. That's when her perfect life had taken a turn for the worse.

"My dad died when I was fifteen," she confessed, choosing each word carefully. "When I was seventeen, my mom married some fuck named Al. He was a psycho, a real creep. Always looking at me, telling me how pretty I was, touching me. One night when my mom was gone to play bingo he got drunk and came into my bedroom..." Goosebumps flashed over her skin, stopping her mid-sentence.

Nick's hand lifted away. "Oh, God. I'm so damn sorry."

Rolling over onto her back, Lara faced him. "Don't be. He passed out before he could do the deed."

"What did your mother say?" he asked. "I hope she kicked the bastard out."

She shrugged. "Mom never would believe me when I said Al put the moves on me. It's like she had blinders on when it came to him. She said I was leading him on. I ran away a few months later. Just couldn't handle Al's touchy-feely ways."

"I don't blame you."

Lara shrugged again. "It's probably twisted, but sometimes I enjoyed his attention. It was like my body gave me some special power over men." Despite the heat of the day, a tremor rippled though her as she realized the implications of what she'd just said.

Visually devouring every naked inch, Nick raised an eyebrow. "I'd be inclined to agree," he said, voice more than a bit strained. Breathing ragged, his expression mirrored pure lust. His erection pressed against the hard confines of his jeans.

Looking at him, she felt a rush of liquid desire. Just thinking about that thick cock of his made her feel all twisted inside. She'd tasted it. Now it was time to feel it, really feel it, inside her. Taking his virginity would be a treat.

Licking her lips, she circled the tip of one erect nipple with a single finger. "Did I tell you it wasn't the first time I'd ever seen a cock? This guy used to live next door to us, you know, and his bedroom faced mine. He used to jack off all the time. He thought I couldn't see him, but I did." Her finger continued its slow sensuous circle. "Maybe he wanted me to see. I liked watching him."

Turning beet red, Nick gulped back his moan. His eyes never left her breasts. "Did you two ever hook up?"

She laughed. "I was only fourteen and he was a lot older. My dad almost shit a brick when he found out."

"No doubt." Nick swallowed thickly. "What happened to the perv?"

Lara subtly shifted to give him the best view of her naked body. Perspiration and suntan lotion created a silky sheen on her skin. Her nipples jutted, hard, and flushed rosy pink. She flicked one sharp nail across the tip. "He moved away a few weeks later. Too bad, too. He was cute in a dorky kind of way."

"Oh, yeah?"

She eyed him. "Well, cute. But not the drop-dead gorgeous

hunk I've got sitting right here beside me." Hand on his thigh, she slid her palm toward the crux of his legs. "I've been dying to get you alone and take advantage of your *fucklicious* body."

He moaned and closed his eyes. "Oh, God," he murmured. "This is every dream I've ever had come true."

Hearing his response sent a surge through her. That heady, powerful feeling of knowing that she was able to incite a riot in his body thrilled her. "Long time to wait to lose your virginity, Nick," she teased.

"It was worth it to have you."

Nick leaned forward, bringing his lips down hard on hers, tasting her, drinking her, needing to consume every last drop of her. Their kiss broke long enough for him to stretch out beside her on the deck chair, then started all over again, magnificently sensuous as their need drove them together. She felt his sweet breath against her face before his mouth claimed hers. Ravaging her like a starving man, his teeth clicked against hers as if his urgency were more powerful than any need for restraint.

Opening her mouth, she returned his kiss with an enthusiasm born of pure lust. The hard tips of her nipples grazed his bare chest. This time the tempest of desire simmering between them wouldn't be denied.

Nick drew in an unsteady breath, cupping one breast and brushing his thumb over the erect peak. "God, you feel good," he breathed.

Lara gasped, arching into him when he rolled her nipple between thumb and forefinger. The knot of desire in her stomach tightened.

"So do you." Her hand settled on the front of his jeans, slowly rubbing the length where his cock strained inside tight denim. He groaned from the friction she created.

He traced the delicate line of her jaw with his lips, mouth caressing her throat with teasing nips before his tongue tickled the small hollow at the base of her neck.

Close to turning into a puddle, Lara felt the violent surge of blood through her veins, the hot burn of lust in her core. A shiver ran the length of her when his head dipped, his mouth capturing one distended pink tip. Dazzling sensations drenched her senses with each pull on the silken nub. Her breath came shallow and fast as he suckled. Every searing pull on her sensitive nipple traveled all the way to her clit.

"I want you," she heard him murmur against her skin. "I've never stopped wanting you."

Lara's earlier indecision about the situation she found herself in evaporated under the enjoyable sensation of his mouth on her. She'd never felt so swept away. The lean flex of his rock-hard muscles felt wonderful under her exploring hands. She wanted to touch every inch of him. "I want you, too." She'd forgotten how powerful desire could be when true attraction was involved. Nick's kisses, his touch, intoxicated her as thoroughly as any drug. His hands were warm and possessive against her skin, every caress stealing her breath away.

She drank him in, enjoying the way he fed something insatiable and ravenous deep inside her soul. The fact that they'd just barely met didn't make a difference at all. She felt as if she'd known him all her life.

Nick's hand slid down the plane of her flat belly to cup her bare mound. Her body reacted instinctively, her thighs automatically parting for him. Thick fingers probed her, slipping in between slick inner lips. Her hands delved into the curve of his shoulders, holding on tight. He dipped into her slowly, caressing and suckling, sending her into a spasm of glorious erotic insanity.

Lara closed her eyes, preparing to be launched into the stratosphere. Moaning, her fingers tangled through his long blond hair, holding his head as he sucked and licked her taut nipples. Instinct rolled her hips against his hand, a silent plea to go deeper, harder.

Heaven was just a sin away and she was ready to enter the Pearly Gates. The surge for completion screamed out from every cell inside her body.

It didn't quite happen that way.

Jared flounced out onto the patio at full speed. "You two keep fucking in that sun and the only thing you'll get is a chapped ass."

The mood vanished.

Lara's senses clenched involuntarily at the interruption. Damn, she was just getting turned on when the interruption rudely arrived. Teeth grinding in frustration, she opened her eyes. Naked except for a towel draped around his shoulders, Jared stood over them. She was only too aware that Nick's hand still rested on her mound.

Nick blew out a short breath and chuckled. As he gave her a quick wink, the tip of his index finger wriggled lightly against her clit. She gasped when an electrical shock zinged through her. "He's right, babe. Fuck outside and we'll both end up with a hell of a burn."

Jared's gaze, intense and focused, raked them both. "And did you think you were going to leave me out of Nick's deflowering?" He grinned. "You and I are going to see to our little virgin's complete pleasure. I'll tell you now that his perfect fantasy had his dick in your cunt, and my dick up his ass. The perfect threesome."

Lara looked to Nick. "Is that your fantasy or his?" She jerked a thumb at Jared. "You know he lusts after your body."

Both men laughed.

"Oh, I know he lusts," Nick explained with a grin. "And he's offered to drill my tender little butt repeatedly. But he's not getting up my ass with his dick until my dick is buried to the hilt in that sweet twat of yours. That's how I plan to lose my virginity." He crooked his finger up against her clit and burrowed. Just a little. Just enough to make a sizzling connection. *"Capice?"*

Lara gasped in surprise. A strangled sound choked up in her throat. "Oh, yes," she squeaked. "I understand."

Perfectly.

The seduction had been carefully prepared.

Unwilling to settle for a predictable round of bedroom action, Jared had arranged the living room as the scene of complete sexual abandon. He'd lit scented candles and scattered rose petals all over the place, specifically around the Tantra chair he'd moved into the middle of the living room. Every other piece of furniture sat against the wall, well out of the way of interference.

Locking the sliding glass door behind them, Jared drew the curtains shut. Dark and heavy, they obscured all sunlight. Strange filtered shadows danced against the walls around them, the darkness broken only by the flicker of candlelight.

Intimate. Romantic. Perfect. Guaranteed to make anyone's fantasy come true.

Lara eyed the chair. With its high arc, lower curving middle and second, lower arc, it was a marvelous blending of angle, curve, and dimension. Condoms and lubricant lay within comfortable reach.

"You're not going to use this on me, are you?"

Jared grinned. "No, we're going to use you on it."

Nick reached for Lara's hand. "Allow us to demonstrate, my unimaginative little lady." He led her toward it. "Step over, please."

Lara stepped. The high arc of the chair was behind her, the low one behind Nick. "Now what?"

Flashing a pirate's grin, he pressed her back against the high arc, guiding her down until her body curved over and around it. Her head lay back at a comfortable, if upside-down, angle, and her pelvis thrust upward, knees bent and feet braced against the cushion. The soft curves of her body were completely his for the taking.

Jared grinned and stepped up, giving her a nice view of his balls. "My cock is already starting to swell at the sight of that. And that mouth of yours is just at the perfect angle for a little cocksucking." He guided his swollen erection toward her mouth.

"Let's have a lick." She opened wide.

As Jared pushed his cock past her waiting lips, Nick's hands settled on her knees. His palms slid higher, parting her legs. "I'm betting you're soaked already."

Mouth too full to speak, Lara managed an incoherent mumble. All rational thought fled at the touch of his fingers caressing her moist slit. The glide of thick fingers though her most sensitive flesh caused goosebumps to rise on her skin.

"Nice and wet," Nick breathed. "Ready for the slide of a nice big penis." He leaned his pelvis into hers, bracing his weight on his outstretched arms as he lowed his body over hers.

The velvet length of his penis settled against her abdomen.

Without her consent, Lara felt her hips shift in an attempt to guide him into entering her.

Nick caught her move. A smoldering intensity had come to light in his eyes, sending a ripple of desire straight to the pit of her stomach. "Mmm. Naughty girl." His head dipped, tongue slowly laving one erect nipple. "But I'm not going to give you my cock right away. First, I'm going to make love to your beautiful body."

The pressure of his mouth increased. It was no longer tentative or unsure. It was demanding, confident. His tongue made damp circles around the tip, causing her breath to catch in the back of her throat. Unconsciously, she imitated his movements around the crown of Jared's cock.

Closing his eyes, Jared moaned, a low keening of pure pleasure working its way up from the back of his throat. "Oh, God, babe. Your mouth is almost better than your pussy."

Lara popped the tip out of her mouth. "Glad you think so."

Nick slowly teased each nipple in turn. Her skin burned where he incited fires with his expert touch. She was bombarded with so many sensations, each one more pleasurable and body-shaking than the last. The Tantra chair was so wonderful that she wondered why every home didn't have one.

"You like this?" he asked

"Oh, hell, yes."

"It's about to get better." Nick's mouth came down just below her rib cage. The magical sensation of his lips brushed her belly, tongue circling in her navel, then below. It was a purely erotic action, one that inspired even deeper need and desire in her. He kissed and touched and tasted the rise of her bare mound until she was literally mad from the sensations emanating from her hungry clit.

A small moan escaped. The knots in her stomach wound tighter. Desperate for him to take more, she spread herself wider.

Just when she was sure she'd scream from frustration, Nick knelt between her legs, kissing the insides of her thighs. Whiskers tickled her sensitive skin. His tongue poked, followed by the soft gnaw of teeth.

"Oh, Nick," she gasped through a strangled moan. "Don't keep me on the edge." The sensations delivered red-hot darts of pure sizzling power, like she was being buzzed with a cattle prod.

Nick lifted his head, looking up at her with a burning gaze. "Don't come yet," he commanded. "We're not ready."

Her laugh was strained. "Keep that up and I don't think I can last much longer."

"You mean this?" He passed his tongue over her clit, then stabbed deep into her creamy slit.

Lara's answer came out as a rough growl of approval, her hips bucking upward, desperate to satisfy the ache clawing inside her. Gripping the edges of the cushion, she hovered on the brink of delicious climax. Tremors began in small waves, then totally swallowed her up in an intense convulsion of pure pleasure. She gasped when the first detonation of sizzling delight landed on her with the intensity of an atomic bomb. A pulsing, devouring frenzied fire consumed her.

"Oh, wow . . . !" A cry of surprise burst out of her throat. Hips bucking, she closed her legs against the sides of his head. Beads of perspiration covered her body. She gasped, half-laughing, drawing air into burning lungs.

Untangling himself before she smothered him, Nick bent over her. "Good?"

A shaky laugh escaped. "The best, the freaking best." Her hands slipped over his shoulders, down his back. She looked up at him. "But it's not enough." She still felt the tremble in his body.

"I'll try not to hurt you." He kissed her lips, then her chin, tracing the softness of her neck to the valley between her breasts.

"It's time," Jared murmured. He passed his friend a condom.

Tearing the foil packet with his teeth, Nick slicked the protection down his shaft. Hands on Lara's hips, he repositioned his body into alignment with hers. The swell of his erection pressed, but he didn't enter.

His gaze searched hers. "I want you, Lara." He hesitated. "But only if you want me."

She looked back, keeping her own gaze steady. "I want you," she murmured with a smile.

Nick's lean hips rolled forward, slowly easing into her sex. He fought to keep from impaling her with one hard thrust, clearly savoring the way her tight, wet flesh rippled around his shaft. By the look of intense concentration on his face, he was fighting to keep a leash on his own needs. "Oh, hell, you're so tight . . ." The rest of his sentence vanished in the complete wonder of full penetration.

Jared clapped his hands. "Houston, we have achieved lift-off."

"Join us," Nick invited. "All three of us, together."

His grin a mile wide, Jared stepped behind Nick. A shiver went up Lara's spine when he slid his hands over Nick's shoulders, then down his sides, palms coming to rest on Nick's narrow hips.

"I've waited so long to get my hands on your ass," Jared murmured, dropping a soft kiss on Nick's left shoulder.

Lara's body reacted instinctively to the sight of one beautiful man making love to another. The sight mesmerized. She'd never witnessed anything so erotic, or anything that made her clit pulse so hard. She heard Nick's name on Jared's lips when their bodies finally made contact in the most intimate of ways.

A grunt broke from Nick's lips as Jared penetrated from behind. He leaned forward, supporting his weight on his outstretched arms. Pushed by Jared's thrusts into his ass, Nick's hips slammed into hers, driving his cock deeper. There wasn't just one man making love to her. There were two.

Looking up into Nick's eyes, she watched his pleasure build with every slow thrust. His cock slid into her sex, even as Jared's cock slid into his anus. Perfect synchronicity. Lara whimpered as his thick shaft slid out of her in a long silken glide, only to jack inside again.

Three bodies. United as one.

The three of them commenced a sweet rhythm, one that grew steadily more frenzied and more eager with each undulation of flesh against flesh.

Just when she thought Nick could go no deeper, he pulled out. Flipping her legs up, he pressed her knees against her shoulders and drilled back in without missing a stroke. If she'd thought his cock big before, it felt three times as huge now. Her second climax built like a hurricane about to make landfall, the pressure inside her escalating with each body-shuddering lunge.

Melting and contracting around Nick's length, Lara heard herself cry out for longer, harder strokes. With every lunge of his hips, Jared drove Nick further inside her. The waves built, a relentless tide threatening to sweep them away into a dark and devouring sea. She fought the current, determined not to sink alone. They would, must, all go under together.

The sensations built, surging higher and higher with each hard stroke of Nick's cock. He bent over her, his face just inches from hers. "I never stopped wanting you," he whispered.

Too far gone to hear or understand the meaning behind his words, Lara was beyond responding. Rapture had turned every muscle in her body to liquid. The control she'd fought so desperately to hold on to slipped through her fingers.

The crescendo of climax came without warning, sweeping the trio away all at once.

Orgasm roared through her, shaking her from the inside out. Every nerve ending in her body screamed with satisfaction. A sob broke from her lips, a cry wrenched from somewhere deep inside her soul. Strong inner muscles rippled, clamping around Nick's cock like an iron fist clad in a silk glove.

Nick groaned. His fingers dug into her thighs. His cock

pulsed and surged, spilling hot semen into the safety of the condom. Behind him, Jared roared out his own completion.

Nobody moved for the longest time.

Lara's body trembled with the aftershocks. She doubted she would ever breathe normally again. Their bodies still coupled, Nick and Jared grinned down at her. It seemed the most natural thing in the world for them to be together.

"That was incredible," Nick said through a sigh.

"The best fuck I've ever had," Jared agreed.

She gasped in surprise when the two men broke apart and swept her up between them. "Where are we going?"

No need for them to answer. They carried her to the bedroom, unceremoniously depositing her on the bed. Nick stretched out on one side of her, Jared on the other. Two muscular bodies snuggled close. Four hands caressed her skin, which glittered with perspiration. She became acutely aware of every aspect of them, including the fact that two hard cocks were pressing against her bare thighs.

She lay between them, unsure what to do or say. She'd made love to both men with a wild and complete abandon. The experience had been primitive. Her heart rate hadn't yet even begun to return to normal. "I've barely had a moment to catch my breath."

"If you think we're done, Nick said with a grin. "Think again."

Jared palmed a breast, teasing a nipple. "Oh, we've only just begun," he warbled in a bad imitation of an oldies song. "There's so much more we need to explore together." He winked toward Nick. "This ex-virgin of ours has a lot of catching up to do."

"I hope you don't mind," Nick chimed in.

"Am I supposed to?" she countered, unable to get her thoughts straight.

"I hope not."

Nick kissed her. His lips were hot, the stubble of his morning beard slightly abrasive. For a virgin he'd proven a skilled and amazing partner. And why shouldn't he be? He'd been tutored by Jared, one of the horniest—and hottest—guys she'd ever met.

A shiver went through her when he slid his hand down her pelvis to cup her sex. He separated her labia and caressed her clit. Lara dropped back against the pillow. A long slow moan slid through her moist lips. "I've thought about it," she said, gasping when Jared's lips settled over one distended pink bud. "I don't think I mind a bit."

The duo never stopped kissing her, never stopped touching her. There were so many sensations for her mind to process that her brain threatened to overload, short out completely. All she knew was that two men were holding her, stroking her, and the sensations they created streaked through her veins like white lightning.

This time she didn't fight the currents dragging her helplessly toward orgasm. She wanted to embrace it. Enjoy it.

Lara closed her eyes against the starburst of emotions. Before her memories slipped away and faded, she vowed to commit every nuance of her experience to a special place in her mind. She wanted to enjoy Nick and Jared while she had them. Too soon their time together would come to an end.

Nothing this perfect lasts forever.

She sighed and nestled deeper into their embrace. Forever didn't matter right now. She'd finally grasped that one perfect moment in her life when everything felt right.

8

Lara looked at the check in her hand. Her name and an amount had been filled in. One million dollars. A hell of a lot of zeros. More than she'd imagined.

Blinking, she shook her head. The numbers all stayed in place. It wasn't an illusion. She'd been paid in full for one week of sexual services. Now it was over and the time to go had arrived.

She stood, dressed in the same leather halter, corset, and stilettos that she'd arrived in only a week earlier. Her wig—well, that had gotten tossed away due to obscene sexual abuse. That vision alone would make her grin for many years to come.

As she fingered the thin piece of paper, a sigh escaped her lips. Something just didn't feel right. She'd leave as she arrived, with nothing more than the clothes on her back. Once she walked away, well, the whole world stretched in front of her like a piece of ripe fruit to be plucked. The limo idled outside the suite, ready to whisk her away.

Anything she wanted to do, anyplace she wanted to go. No limitations held her back.

Nick and Jared stood, watching her. Nobody was saying a word. Nobody wanted to be the first to say good-bye.

Heart pounding hard against her ribs, Lara tore up the check. "I don't want your money."

Jared's eyes bulged in disbelief. "You just tore up a million-dollar check. Are you fucking crazy, woman? That sucker would have cleared, no questions asked."

Lara snorted. "Maybe I'm not that impressed by money." She scattered the pieces with a flippant hand, sending them flying. Fuck Angelino DiMarco. Fuck Donnie, that asshole who'd run out and left his shit on her plate. Somehow she'd find the money to settle the debt.

Not this way. Not selling herself as a whore. She wasn't a piece of merchandise to be passed around to the highest bidder. If she'd enjoyed the experience—reveled in it—it would be as a woman in touch with her own sexuality.

Nick blinked as if her move surprised him, then a slow smile pulled at his fine mouth. "Why did you do that?"

Trying to pull her scattered thoughts together, Lara scrubbed both hands over her face, curiously numb now that the feeling seemed to have drained away. She had no idea what she was doing, only that it needed to be done.

"This has been the best time of my life. Cashing that check would only cheapen my memories of you two." Feeling desperate, scared and a little out of control, she hurried to add, "This week meant everything to me. For the first time since my dad died, I've felt cherished. He used to call me his princess. I'm so lucky to have two men who treated me like a queen."

The two guys exchanged a glance.

"What do you think?" Nick asked.

Jared rubbed his chin, nodding slowly. "I think she's fucking crazy to toss a million dollars."

Nick nudged his friend in the ribs. "Yeah, me too . . ." His words trailed off. The two fell silent, as though sharing some sort of unspoken communication.

Breath catching in her throat, Lara felt the oxygen disappearing from her lungs. Watching them, a vague sense of uneasiness rippled through her. Had she done the wrong thing?

A hot flash of embarrassment burned her cheeks. *Oh, God! I've totally insulted the hell out of them.* She pressed her fingers against her aching forehead. Damn. This wasn't going the way she'd planned, the way she'd rehearsed in her mind. These guys had had their fun, and were ready to kiss her good-bye so they could return to their lives.

Party time had ended, not with a bang, but a disheartening thud. If the floor opened up and swallowed her down into oblivion it wouldn't be fast enough. *Business is business,* she reminded herself. Cutting the ties and walking away clean was the best way to go.

Jared stared at his friend intently. "This won't work," he suddenly blurted. "Unless you tell her the truth."

Nick blushed, dipping his head and brushing his fingers through his long hair. He was dressed in one of Jared's Goth T-shirts; his faded jeans fit him snugly. There was no denying the sinew of his long legs or the bulge of his cock beneath. "You think I should?" he asked.

Jared smacked his arm. "Do it."

Catching the gist of their conversation, Lara looked at them both. "Tell me what?"

Nick sighed. "The truth," he mumbled. His steady gaze never veered from hers when he reached into the back pocket of his jeans and extracted his wallet. "I guess you don't remember me," he said softly.

She noted his serious expression, not sure what to say in return. "I'm sure I've never met you before, Nick."

He winced. "I didn't expect you would remember." Flipping through his wallet's contents, he pulled out a picture and handed it over. "I looked different back then."

Lara glanced at the photo, a snapshot from high school photo day. The image of a pale-skinned, rail-thin teenager with thick black-rimmed glasses and braces met her eyes. His face was eaten up by the scabs of acne, and his hair was styled in an unflattering mullet.

Dismay flooded her. Her hand flew to her mouth. "Oh my God! *You're* the one we used to call 'Freaky Nicky'?" She looked closer. It didn't seem possible. Seven years had certainly changed things. A lot. The braces were gone, showing a set of straight white teeth. His hair was fashionably styled and contact lenses had replaced the Coke-bottle glasses. Working out with weights had turned his noodle-thin body into a strong and sleekly muscled machine.

Nick grimaced at the use of his teenaged moniker. "Guilty as charged. Remember me now?"

Dismay flooded her. "You used to jack off an awful lot," she mumbled.

Nick laughed, shaky and unsure. "That was your fault, neighbor. You were so damn hot, even if you were only fourteen. God, I wanted you. I lusted after you, but a nerd like me wasn't your style."

She handed back the photo. He'd obviously worked very hard to get in shape. He had every right to be proud of his accomplishment. She chose to ignore his self-deprecating comments. "My dad wanted to kick the shit out of you for ruining his little girl's virgin eyes."

Nick tucked the picture away. "I went to college, but I meant to come back, Lara. I always swore that I was going to come back and get you, make you mine." He toyed with his wallet. "I did make it home, but you'd gone. Your mom didn't know where you were. She said all she knew was that you married some guy named Donnie Green and moved to Nevada." Raw pain simmered beneath his words. "I'd almost given up finding you again."

His words warmed her, but Lara didn't let herself react. Her mind still spun from his revelation. Something about him had always niggled in the back of her mind; he was familiar, but not recognizable. Now she understood why.

"You really came to Nevada just to find me?" she asked.

"Don't be mad, but yes, I did." Nick paused, then rushed on. "All these years I've had a fantasy that you and I would be together, you know, in a relationship. I've never had sex with another woman. I've always wanted you."

"I—I don't know what to say," she stammered. She stared at him, trying desperately to sort through the myriad emotions running riot through her skull. It seemed a dream she'd soon have to wake up from, a fairy tale too damn twisted to be real.

Vision suddenly blurring, Lara felt the sting of unbidden tears brim in her eyes. The seven years they'd been apart melted away like plastic under hot flames. The urge to fly back into his arms pulled at her like a dangerous undertow.

Crossing to her, Nick pulled her into his embrace. "Will you stay?"

Her gaze met his. Looking up at him, she felt tenderness tug deep inside her heart. At the same time she imagined him spreading her thighs and sinking his cock deep. She didn't have to be asked twice. "Yes."

Jared's voice broke through. "There's a problem here, you two."

They both looked his way. "What?" Lara asked.

Jared acidly arched an eye-brow. "Don't forget I'm part of this deal." He nudged in between Nick, pushing him out and capturing her in a tight hug. "You don't get Nick without me."

Clapping Jared on the shoulder, Nick gazed fondly at his

two lovers. "And you don't get her without me, bud." He winked at her. "Think you could love us both?"

Lara closed her eyes, feeling her answer solidify. And she knew. She'd always known. "I don't think it." She smiled even though tears blurred her vision. "I know it."

Somehow they all came together, all three of them embracing, touching, enjoying. Clothing slipped off, naked skin making contact with naked skin. Two sets of searching hands explored her body. Jared stood behind her, brushing her hair away from her nape, and then nibbling her neck. His hands found and kneaded the cheeks of her ass.

Cupping her breasts, Nick teased her sensitized nipples with his thumbs. "This is how it should be." He leaned forward and kissed her on the forehead. "The three of us together."

Lara let out a long shuddery breath. Desire swept through her in shimmering waves. She'd never felt so swept away. For the first time in her life she needed not one, but two men. Their touch, the feel of two hard bodies pressed against hers. She needed both of them as much as she needed oxygen to breathe. As much as her heart needed to beat.

"I agree completely," she said, tilting back her head for his kiss. The circumstances that had brought the guys into her life didn't matter anymore. Somehow the three of them had found each other. It only seemed right that they belonged together.

Forever.

BRING IT ON

JANE LEDGER

1

Another ticket. Nancy Roman didn't want to believe what she was seeing, but she had to. A rookie was making her quota with new-girl-on-the-job zeal. The chick lifted up the windshield wiper of Nancy's dented Toyota and stuck the damn thing under it. She would have banged the window down but it was already stuck in that position. Then Steve Karan showed up.

Save me, Stevie.

He talked to the rookie while he removed the ticket and inspected it. Then he jabbed a finger at the paper.

"Looks like you made a mistake, honey," he said cheerfully. The rookie shrugged and ripped it up when Steve handed it back.

Oh, yeah. My hero. Gotta love those shoulders. And that thick, dark brown hair. Even from three stories up, Steve Karan looked good. He wore his usual off-duty Average Joe jeans, linen shirt, and scuffed sneakers. Perfect fade on the jeans over the quads. The muscle in those legs just didn't quit. Nancy watched him slap the rookie on the back, then swing around to the parking meter.

She owed him. Big time.

He walked down to another car that was so nondescript it screamed undercover cop car. He opened the door and placed a white cardboard box in his arms that was almost as long as he was, carrying it lightly. A mystery package. Long-stemmed roses?

Interesting. Maybe he was her secret admirer. Ha ha. She had known him since high school.

She tried to lift the window so she could call to him but it was stuck shut. Humidity. Everything swelled in June.

Steve took the stairs two at a time and disappeared into the vestibule of her apartment building. Nancy buzzed him through the downstairs door before he pressed her button, knowing he'd come all the way up without waiting for an OK. Working at home meant you got to know your local cops. Of course, she already knew him.

Her publicity business was doing all right. Her clients, creative types and minor celebrities who had gigantic egos and ambitions to match, had not one clue about how to manage their careers, let alone their seriously screwed-up lives. Rather than maintain an office, she had them send in their publicity materials in bulk: head shots, glowing reviews of productions that their mothers hadn't even seen, and highlighted clippings about their pathetic lives.

None of which arrived in pristine white boxes. Not what Steve was bringing up. She went to the door when she heard him thunder up the last flight of stairs and opened it before he knocked.

"Hiya, Nancy. Package for you." He held it out, holding it at either end with strong, long-fingered hands, but she didn't take it, only looked at the shipping label.

"From Racks, huh?" She knew the name from one of her clients, who liked to give his girlfriend ultraexpensive, super-sexy evening gowns, which she, a temperamental Russian model, liked to rip up, just to show him who was boss. "That's a dress company. I didn't order a dress." She hitched up her baggy gray sweatpants.

Steve winked. "I know that. This was a gift from the store. We just broke a big shoplifting ring for them."

"So they gave you a dress. What does that say about your sexuality, Steve?"

"That I'm good at my job. Seriously, Nancy, they sell dresses, not suits. The store manager said I should give it to my best girl."

"I'm not your girl."

"So? Bet you'd look good in this dress."

"Aw, shucks. Bet you say that to all the slobs."

"Only the beautiful slobs like you."

"Thanks a lot," Nancy said. She cast a glance into the hallway mirror by the apartment door, just in case there was a grain of truth in his friendly compliment. No surprises there: blond hair with thick bangs that needed trimming. Round eyes, greenish. Full lips, glossed, but otherwise no makeup. Pretty good boobs and small waist, concealed under a beige sweatshirt with a peeling logo that said *Almost Famous*.

A relic of her brilliant career at Frieder & Ripkin, publicists to the stars. Former publicists. Playing switcheroo games with a couple of celebrity clients' wives got Eddie Frieder beaten up and his office trashed. Bob Ripkin got off a little easier, being totally ignored by *Variety* and *Entertainment Tonight*.

Kudos for the uninvolved: Nancy Roman got a pat on the head from a famous columnist who praised her integrity.

"I'm being honest," Steve said nonchalantly. "We're friends, right?"

"Sure are," Nancy said. "Since forever. Especially since I started working at home." How long had it been since Frieder & Ripkin had gone under and she'd struck out on her own? "Which is why you've never seen me in anything but sweats. Take me as I am."

Steve looked her up and down with an amiable leer. "I like to be comfortable myself."

Nancy glanced down at his mighty, jeans-clad legs. Amen to that. And how good it felt to be looked up and down in sweatpants that didn't do anything to advertise her curves. She could count on Steve to cheer her up.

"At least you get to run around all day," she pointed out as she walked with him into the kitchen. "I get to sit and mail out head shots for the hopelessly untalented."

He slid the long box onto her kitchen table, bumping a big wooden bowl that usually held bananas, occupied at the moment by a comatose cat.

"Sorry, Frisky."

"His name is Lump. For obvious reasons."

"Oh, yeah. I forgot." He scratched lightly between the cat's ears. The Lump raised his head and gave a huge, tongue-curling yawn, then went back to kitty dreamland.

"So c'mon," Steve said. "Open the box. Your name's on it."

Nancy shook her head. "Is this your way of living vicariously?"

"Yeah, I wanna see you naked."

"Fuck off."

He grinned at her wolfishly. "Me and Jack hung on the gym wall like ivy during senior year, trying to."

Jack Ginnis. Steve's best friend and fellow cop. "I'm still curious," he added.

"But I can't fit into anything from Racks."

"You could be wrong, Nancy," he said patiently. "Anyway, it's a gift. Is it your birthday?"

Birthdays. Nancy loathed birthdays. Annual reminders of the march of time and the downward pull of gravity. She didn't celebrate hers and no one outside of her immediate family knew when her birthday was. And it was weeks away. Anyway, no one in her family would ever give her something from Racks.

"No," she said finally. "But I'll open the box if it'll make you happy. You'll probably have to take it back, though."

He patted the box with a proprietary air. "Nah. I'll give it to the rookie who was giving you the ticket."

"I wouldn't dream of it." Nancy stuck a fingernail into the thin tape that sealed the box and ran it lengthwise. "Wouldn't want to use a box cutter. Don't have one anyway, come to think of it."

The top flaps separated and she could see tissue paper underneath, folded neatly over a black something adorned with a gold Racks label.

Steve looked inside the box, interested.

"Drum roll, please," she intoned. He obliged, beating the table on the side. The cat, startled into offended life, uncurled himself from the banana bowl and jumped off the table onto the floor with a thud, waving his tail.

Nancy lifted a big piece of the tissue paper, crumpled it into a ball, and tossed it on the floor in front of her cat. Lump ignored her attempt to placate him and stalked off.

She parted the rest, revealing a voluptuous heap of what appeared to be shirred black velvet.

"Wow," said Steve. "Nicer than I thought."

Nancy stopped what she was doing and looked at him. "You haven't seen it yet. Did you know what was in here?"

He held up his hands. "I confess. There was a Racks catalog with it. I compared the product code on the shipping label and so—yeah, I did know."

Nancy touched the velvet without removing the dress. "I've seen that catalog. The parent company is unreal. Kinda like Neiman Marcus. For people who can drop $10,000 on an impulse buy. You know, gem-encrusted pet dishes and stuff."

Her cat sauntered back into the kitchen with a now-you're-talking look on his face. He jumped up on the table again and stuck a paw into the box, patting the velvet.

"Quit it, Lumpkin," Nancy said, shooing him away. "This is not your new nest. Don't get cat hair all over it."

"Hold it up," Steve said eagerly. "Let's see what it looks like."

Nancy only shrugged. "Not as if I'm going to wear it." But she reached into the box, found the straps, and lifted the dress out of the enfolding tissue. She held it against herself, striking a glamorous pose. Steve's eyes lit up.

"Wow. Fantastic. You have to try it on. Black has got to be a great color on you."

"Ya think? Better than boring old beige?" She looked down, taking in the details of the dress. Spaghetti straps. A fitted, very low-cut bodice carefully designed to give boobs a lift without the wearer needing a bra. Subtle shirring down the front seam and bias-cut side panels that flared over the hips without clinging. It really was a movie star's dress, like nothing Nancy had ever seen. She didn't want to let go of it.

"You know, I think you're right about the black. To hell with beige. My sofa is beige. My life is beige."

"You need some excitement," was all he said. His voice was lower and a little rough around the edges.

Still holding the dress against her body, she walked over to the hallway mirror and inspected herself, blowing her bangs out of her eyes with an upward puff. She caught Steve looking at her pouted lips and smiled at him.

"You said it all, Steve. Wow is right."

He kept his distance but his gaze was riveted to her, almost as if she were really wearing the dress.

Nancy turned this way and that, marveling silently at how alive the dress seemed and feeling a flash of chagrin at how shabby her sweats looked. She didn't have to wear them every day—they were just there in the morning, easy to pull on without a second thought. Undemanding. Able to accommodate a few extra pounds without her even knowing she'd gained a little weight.

She looked in the mirror once more. And she looked at the man standing behind her. Keeping his hands on his hips made Steve's shoulders look larger and his waist leaner. His wide-apart stance was totally male and his long, strong legs were well worth a sneaky look at what was between them, barely restrained by the soft denim.

"Okay," Nancy said offhandedly. "I'll try it on. Labels and all. Prepare to be dazzled, o humble law enforcement professional."

"I'm a cop. A fucking cop."

"Whatever. Have a seat."

Steve nodded, and pulled a chair out with a hasty scrape against the floor, sitting down and leaning back against the table, gently scratching Lump's head again. The cat got into it, rubbing its whiskery cheeks against Steve's fingers for an added-value petting experience. "Ready for the show, pal? I am. Even if she did call me humble."

Nancy laughed and headed down the hall to the bathroom, shutting the door behind her. She hung the dress on a high hook and stripped quickly, kicking the ugly beige and gray sweats and the balled-up socks she'd had on into a corner. Her practical white briefs joined the pile next.

Naked, fluffing her pubic curls, she looked at the dress one last time. Then she took it off the hook, positioned it over her head, and let it slide down her body. Just putting it on was erotic. It fit like a . . . body glove. And speaking of, wouldn't it be nice if she had a pair of long gloves to accessorize it with? Diamond earrings, too. Mink eyelashes. And a couple of gigolos. Or a matching set of hunky cops. Her favorite fantasy was two men, when she had time to fantasize, which was hardly ever.

She stepped up onto the edge of the bathtub to see more of herself in the mirror over the sink. Wow wow wow. What it did for her boobs and her butt was nothing short of amazing.

Nancy stepped down carefully, inspecting her face critically.

A little eye pencil wouldn't hurt. Just a dab of powder blush—but only a dab. The black velvet made her fair skin glow. When she got done with the makeup, she grabbed a brush and did a major fluff on the hair. Good to go. Then she scrabbled in a little basket of cosmetics that she hadn't used in way too long, finding a lipstick in a come-hither shade of red.

Nancy uncapped the tube, parted her lips, and put it on with precision. The result was overwhelmingly sensual. She blew herself a kiss, gave her bangs a final fluff with the brush, and opened the bathroom door.

"Don't be shy," Steve called.

"It doesn't fit," she called back, smiling to herself. Might as well play him.

"Awww." He sounded utterly disappointed.

Barefoot, Nancy walked down the hall. Under the flared sides, her thighs brushed together in a way that was erotically stimulating. And the dress cupped her ass almost like . . . a man's hands. She thought of Steve's strong hands holding the box and the eager look on his face when he'd asked her to open it. Nancy took a deep breath and stepped into the kitchen.

Steve almost fell off his chair. He rocked back, righted himself, and stood up. "You look—so beautiful."

"Think so?" Nancy asked innocently. She strolled around the kitchen, flipping the skirt with one hand and running the other through her hair. That lifted her bosom even higher, and Steve looked hungrily at her breasts.

"Yeah. I do."

"So . . ." she breathed. "How much time do you have left on the meter?"

"What?" Steve just gaped at her.

Nancy threw him a flirty look designed to melt belts. Maybe it was the magic of the dazzling dress, maybe it was the months she'd gone without a date, maybe it was Steve's friendly but totally male vibe and all that healthy energy he radiated . . . but she had suddenly decided to seduce him.

No second-guessing herself. No filling out *Glamour* quizzes on whether he was Mr. Right or just Mr. Right Now. No calling a girlfriend and discussing it in advance. Her inner vixen was in charge, and inner vixens did not think twice, especially when she was pretty sure there were condoms in the nightstand drawer.

He could always go and get some if not.

Steve was just so fucking cute. The sudden admiration that glowed in his brown, dark-lashed eyes was enough to turn her on, big-time, but it wasn't as if she had never noticed how gorgeous Steve Karan was. She had just been too busy to do anything about it, what with getting a home-based business off to a solid start and donning baggy sweats every damn day to work nonstop.

But opening that white box with a flick of her fingernail changed everything. The shoplifters were behind bars and it was meant to be. If a magic dress got dropped on your doorstep, you couldn't say no. Nancy ran her hands over her velvety hips. "I said, is there time on the meter?" She ran her hands up her torso and lightly cupped her breasts. Steve clenched the back of the chair for support.

"Guh," was all he said. "Go. I mean, I'll go see." He thrust a hand into his pocket, not taking his eyes off her as he rushed for the door, jingling the coins in his pocket and, she suspected, forcing his erection down.

Nancy nodded, giving him a glistening red come-back-soon smile. Steve focused on that for a split second, stopped, then grinned in response. "I don't believe this."

Nancy murmured a barely audible, "Believe it," then picked up the cat and tickled him under the chin. Lump stretched out his neck, purring blissfully as she rubbed the sensitive spot with long strokes in one direction, completely focused on the animal's pleasure. Steve took in the sight, then ran through the open door, not shutting it behind him.

"Guess what, Lumpkin," she cooed. "I'm going to get laid. And you're going to get locked in the living room. Is that okay with you?"

The uncomprehending cat seemed to agree. He was a fool for a good chin rub. Nancy carried him down the hall to the living room, grateful for once that the rooms in her ancient apartment building had doors that opened into the halls, awkward as the arrangement was. She didn't want Lump pouncing on Steve's ass once he got naked and got on top of her.

Cooing to the cat, giving him one last head scratch, she set him down inside the living room and closed the door. Then she walked back to the kitchen, hearing Steve thunder up the stairs and almost colliding with him when he burst back in.

"Easy. Calm down," she said, patting his chest. He was breathing hard.

"Fed the meter. So—this is for real, right? You want me to jump you—believe me, I want to—oh, Jesus, Nancy. I thought you'd like the dress, but not this much."

She looked at him wide-eyed. "Don't tell me you bought it for me. Was that story about the shoplifters for real?"

"Yeah." Unable to resist touching her, he ran his hands over her shoulders and down her bare arms. "It's kind of a long story, though. Tell you later, okay?"

"Tell me now."

His hands moved around her waist. "I just wanted to give you something. But I didn't know if you'd like the dress."

"I like the dress." She put her arms around his neck, not quite believing what he was saying but loving his confusion and his arousal.

"You're so sexy, Nancy. Even in those goddamn sweats. Last few months, I couldn't stop thinking about you."

"That's sweet," she said softly. Feeling wanton and womanly, she pressed her body ever so subtly against his, as if the dress had possessed her. Until she'd slid it on over her bare body, Nancy did not do wanton, did not think of herself as a temptress, and did not, as a rule, coo. Steve's hands held her tighter, keeping her exactly where she was and not letting her get a millimeter closer.

"So, uh, anyway, I was talking to the manager, Mr. Grateful—"

Nancy looked at him sideways. "Is that really his name?"

"No. But it'll do for now. Anyway, I was talking to him at Racks after we broke the ring, and his assistant happened to have the catalog at the page with the dress and I—"

Nancy put a finger over his lips. "I get the idea. You don't want to be accused of graft. Municipal corruption marches on. Kiss me."

His sensual mouth opened and then . . . he didn't do anything. "Good as you look," he began nervously, still holding her around the waist, "and I do mean good enough to eat—can you lose the lipstick? I can't show up at the precinct with smooch marks all over my face, grinning like a fool."

"I like that picture," Nancy said, smiling and letting her hips move a little from side to side. Steve drew in his breath and let it out very slowly. His body reacted. If she wanted to, she could reach out a hand and touch his jeans-cupped balls. Did he wear boxers? Or briefs? Or nothing? There was only one way to find out.

She kept one arm around his neck and moved the other one, stroking the soft denim that covered his thigh and sliding up. She was pretty sure he wore boxers. Light and soft.

Imagining pulling them down and seeing his big cock jut out made her instantly hot. But she withdrew her hand and patted his face. "Sure. No problem." Nancy went to the sink and got a paper towel, getting most of the lipstick off, then ran another paper towel under the hot water and blotted her mouth with it. Between the removed lipstick and the rubbing, her mouth was tender. She turned to him but Steve covered the distance between them in two big steps, pulling her into his arms and kissing her with a raw, turbocharged hunger. His hands ran over her hips and behind, feeling her there with passionate intensity. "No panties, huh? All right."

He backed her up against the kitchen counter and kissed her again, a little more gently this time, exploring her mouth with his tongue and nipping her lower lip. One big hand pushed her blond hair out of the way and he moved to her neck, planting small kisses on the sensitive skin there, going down and then up again to take a sexy little munch on her earlobe.

Good thing she didn't have diamond earrings on, Nancy thought dreamily. God, he could do this to her forever and she wouldn't mind.

He pulled back, looking down at her with fierce desire. "Okay, hot stuff. There's another part of you I want to taste. Ready for it?"

Without waiting for an answer, Steve lifted her up and set her on the counter, settling her butt on the black velvet so her skin didn't touch the counter but pushing the front of the dress up. He clasped her ankles and spread her bare legs. Nancy braced herself on her hands and leaned back, watching him grab a chair and set it where he wanted it, right in front of her. He sat down and looked at her pussy for a long, satisfying moment. Not touching. Just looking.

Nancy relaxed, feeling giddy, happy to be so shameless, so in the moment. She knew from the way he kissed that he would treat her pussy with just the same delicious mix of mostly tenderness and a bit of roughness. Looking at his mouth, the slight smile that curved it, and the sensuality of his downcast look heightened the anticipation of the sexual pleasure to come.

When he began to stroke the soft skin on the inside of her

thighs, still enjoying his intimate look at her, not glancing up, Nancy closed her eyes. She could just feel his breath on her pussy, warm and soft, but not that close. She knew he was observing her body's involuntary arousal, getting off on looking at her labia, swollen and slick, turning a deep pink. His strong, caressing hands warmed her thighs and kept her from trembling.

But Steve still didn't touch or lick her pussy, just kept stroking. Then he moved his hand to the skin under her navel, stroking her there in a sensual semicircle that made her arch and push her pussy closer to his face. He dropped a kiss on the springy curls but kept his hand where it was, pushing against her womanly belly with a rhythm that she knew instinctively was natural to him—and how he would fuck her when he got around to that.

For now, she was too into what he was doing to move. The waiting between his caresses only intensified the sensation of his hands moving over her flesh—then watching him look at his fill at the succulent pussy he'd wanted for so long—both were erotic to the max.

Steve took his sweet time about loving her, and he did it right.

He scooted forward in the chair and rested his head on her thigh. Just close enough to dart out his tongue and flick it over her swollen little clit.

Nancy dropped her head back and moaned, wriggling her buttocks an inch or so closer. Steve grabbed her thighs and buried his face in her pussy, licking her labia and sucking her clit into his mouth as gently as if it were a nipple. Bingo, she thought. Oh, Jesus. This was better than anything.

Except maybe two guys. Jack Ginnis came to mind. Don't be greedy, she told herself.

Steve slid a finger into her juicy pussy and held it there while he kept sucking her clit. She could feel herself begin to pulse around his finger. A few seconds later, Steve took his mouth away. He rested his head on her thigh again, just breathing on her clit, letting her sexual excitement subside. A move, Nancy knew, that would only make her come harder.

That seemed to be something he wanted to have happen. He didn't say a word but the skillful way he handled her made her smile inwardly, wondering without jealousy what woman had taught him that.

Probably an older one. He must have been a willing student and he had obviously paid worshipful attention to his much more experienced lover.

The thought of Steve as a strapping eighteen-year-old, naked and stiff-cocked, spurting a little cum that he couldn't control, made Nancy shiver with sexual excitement. She could imagine him kneeling between the legs of a woman who was as wild for him then as Nancy was right now, licking his first lover tentatively, then with sensual boldness.

Sitting in front of her as he was, fully dressed, only made the fantasy that much more vivid. Nancy moaned and messed up his thick hair with rough strokes, supporting herself with just one hand as he began to push his tongue between her labia, spreading them open to get deeper inside. His tongue was as long and as strong as the rest of him, and it felt a lot like a cock.

She imagined him again as a neophyte, and what he had looked like from behind, ass up and muscular thighs tensed as he went down between a woman's legs, his balls tight to his lean body and his buttocks shaking from trying to control his imminent ejaculation. Another woman floated into Nancy's fantasy, also older than the youthful Steve, one who reached between his legs to stroke his balls and reached around to clasp his hugely erect young cock with an oiled hand, pumping him until he sprayed helplessly, moaning against the pussy of the woman he was pleasuring with his mouth.

Nancy gasped and pushed Steve's head away. Even though

he was staying away from her clit while he licked, her visualizing a trio like that was just too intense.

"What?" he said softly, wiping his mouth. He stood up and put his hands on either side of her, kissing the creamy skin of her breasts, pleasurably compressed by the fitted bodice of the black velvet dress. "Hmm," he murmured. "I've been neglecting these." He pulled out one breast and then the other, resting them on the soft upper edge of the bodice so they overflowed it and the nipples stuck out. "Hot. I love the way your tits look like that. Really stacked. Ready to be sucked, too."

But he kissed her mouth first, fondling her breasts and pinching her nipples. He tugged a little harder at them when he broke the kiss, pushing her tits together and getting his tongue into her cleavage.

Nancy began to sweat. He licked up every drop. "Sexy. You taste so good. Sweet here—" he stuck a finger into her pussy "—and salty here." He licked between her breasts again but he didn't take his finger out.

She shifted on the counter, pressing her thighs around his chest. With one swift move, Steve picked her up, getting an arm under her ass and supporting her upper body with the other one.

She clung to him, not caring about the tangled dress, not caring about anything but enjoying herself with a hot guy in this abandoned way. His clean shirt was going to smell like pussy but she couldn't help that. He'd wanted to pick her up, let her squeeze him with her thighs to help him carry her—for a guy like Steve, a pussy print was probably a badge of honor.

With her arms twined around his neck, he toted her down the hall. "Which way to heaven?" He kicked open the partially closed door to the bedroom when she breathed, "That way," in his ear.

Steve set her down on the bed with a bounce and didn't waste any time getting his sneakers off. "Gotta love speed laces." He grinned at her and tossed the sneakers aside. Then he flicked his belt open and shoved down his jeans and boxers all in one go. Just as she'd imagined it, his cock sprang out from thick, dark, curling hair. He got his balls where he wanted them with a fast motion but he was too aroused for them to hang down.

Later for that, Nancy thought with pleasure. She planned to cup them after he shot his load, enjoy their spent softness—but by the looks of him now, the condom tip was going to be full to bursting with his cum.

"Dress on or off?" she asked softly.

He stood by the bed, towering over her, one hand just brushing the outside of his thigh and one resting loosely on his lean hip. The pose made him look like an incredibly sexy Greek statue of an athlete in his physical prime.

But oh God, was he alive. The veins in his cock pulsed as he looked at her sprawled on the bed, and it bobbed a little, then got stiffer, rising smack up against his tautly muscled belly. He took himself in hand, stroking his cock to the tip, watching her watch him do it. Nancy couldn't take her eyes off that mesmerizing sight. Watching men masturbate in front of her was a really strong turn-on.

She knew she could never handle a cock quite the way a man did his own—they were often a little rougher than she would be, paused to rest when she wouldn't know they had to, and could squeeze the shaft just right to hold back on ejaculating— or to make it spurt in long streams, showing off, coming with fierce male pride. And the way a man touched his own balls, strong fingers cradling both while the other hand jacked off his hot cock—that just did her in.

And wouldn't it be nice to watch two guys do that just for her viewing pleasure? Not gay guys, just super-horny straight ones who were willing to set aside their natural male competitiveness and, uh, worship her simultaneously.

Nancy loved to have a man come on her body: on her breasts,

or straddling her waist to give her a pearly necklace, or on top of her, rubbing on her belly until he ejaculated; or even thrusting between her clasped thighs while she lay on her back or on her front, pounding her until he exploded wetly all over the sheets beneath.

But right now . . . she didn't know what Steve wanted her to do. He had amazing self-control, that was clear.

"Dress on," he said at last. "Tits out and on display. And get on all fours."

"Yes, sir," she said mockingly, but she was willing to play along. Steve going alpha was intriguing. Her pussy began to pulse again as she flipped over to get on her hands and knees. The dress slid down over her bare ass and she reached around to lift it up again.

He stopped her with one big hand. "Let me have the pleasure of pulling it up."

Nancy looked up at him through her tousled hair, smiling. "All right."

Before he did that, he sat down on the edge of the bed, fondling her tits, filling his hands with them, even slapping them lightly just for the hell of it. Nancy relished the way he did it, enjoyed the feel of her breasts bumping and swaying, and his hands brushing over the sensitized, sucked nipples as he slapped and fondled them gently. To be on all fours for amorous tit play that was mostly tender and a little rough felt very natural and deeply female. Having her bottom bared while he did it would feel even better—a touch of submissiveness always got her more excited than she wanted to admit.

But he had asked for that pleasure and she wasn't going to deny it to him, not in so many words. All the same, she could use her body to let him know that she was ready for that, too. Nancy wriggled her velvet-draped haunches and pushed against his side.

Steve chuckled a little and increased his stimulating slaps. "Want me to do that to your ass?" he murmured.

"Maybe," she said softly, not looking him in the eye.

"I think you should put on some panties," he said. "Just so I can pull them down after I lift up your dress. Pretty ones."

Nancy rose up and sat back on her haunches. Steve seized the opportunity to suckle her nipples and kiss her breasts. She pulled the black velvet dress down a little and straightened the twisted middle, then got up, so turned on that she stumbled a little. She went to her dresser and opened the bottom drawer, bending way over. "I keep the pretty panties in here. Don't wear them often. Hey, these even match." She pulled out a pair made of black stretch lace. "Skimpy enough for you?" She waved them at Steve.

His hard-on got harder. "Put 'em on," he growled.

Nancy flipped up the skirt of the dress and swathed the material around her middle, leaning back against the dresser to hold it there and balance herself. She leaned forward, letting her breasts spill out, stepping a little awkwardly into the stretchy panties she held spread between her fingers, pulling them up over her calves and thighs with deliberate slowness. He watched her intently. She let the dress fall back down and walked to him.

Steve grabbed her hips when she reached the bed and pressed kiss after kiss against her pussy, hidden by the dress. "I don't know which is more sexy," he said in a low voice. "Seeing it or not seeing it."

"Up to you, lover. I think I need to have you take charge for a little while. You know what I want." She stroked his hair as he looked up at her for a few seconds, then rested his cheek on the beautiful dress that made her feel so feminine and so desired.

"All fours is what I want." He gave her a slap on the butt. "Do it. But keep yourself covered."

Nancy eased down, giving in to his unspoken request for a long, hot kiss on the way to the next stage. Then he put her away from him, letting her get on hands and knees, waiting for him to lift her dress.

He kneeled behind her, sliding the sensuously soft fabric over the backs of her thighs, lifting the dress inch by inch until she felt the material slide up and over her lace-clad buttocks. Steve draped it around her waist, then began to pull down her panties.

She could hear him breathing hard and his stiff cock bumped against the back of her legs now and then. He stopped when the stretchy panties were rolled down to just below her ass cheeks and her behind was bared.

He touched the lace in between her legs. "Nice and slow gets you hot. Your panties are wet. Good girl. Now get your legs farther apart but keep your ass up."

She moved her knees and did exactly what he said. Steve pulled her panties down to the middle of her thighs. The stretchy lace was taut and she got her knees even farther apart, until the elastic strained to the snapping point. She could imagine how the sight turned him on. Dress up, panties down, her round ass, big and bare, and a very, very hot pussy completely available to his fingers, his tongue, and his huge cock.

She'd had the first two . . . she craved the last.

"I think you need your pussy pounded," he said. His voice was harder now. "No more foreplay. Time for rock-solid fucking."

"Yes," she breathed. She felt him behind her, heard the rip of a condom packet and the slight sound of him rolling it on. Then he kneeled behind her, placing the head of his sheathed cock directly against her labia.

Nancy wriggled, wanting to thrust backward. But she reminded herself, dazed with lust though she was, that he was in charge.

He reminded her too . . . by bringing both of his hands down on her buttocks for a double smack. Nancy moaned with pleasure. "Uh-huh. You like to bare your ass and be disciplined a little, don't you?"

"Yes," she whispered. The feeling of being just barely penetrated by the tip of his huge cock made her want to cry out for more. Allowing him to spank her while he maintained his strong self-control was unbelievably exciting.

"Reach around," he told her. "I want you to keep your panties pulled down and your face in the pillows."

Again Nancy did as he said, going deeper into the sensual excitement of the moment, aware that her half-dressed, half-naked show was making him crazy with desire. She grabbed the rolled-down elastic that kept the panties stretched between her thighs and held it with her thumbs, knowing that he was going to spank her some more.

He did. She moaned and shoved her ass up, wanting still more. He gave her that too, then rested his big hands on her tingling behind, gasping for breath, pushing his cock tip in just a little further.

"Fuck me now," she begged. She was imagining sucking Jack Ginnis's big rod while Steve did her pussy. Oh yeah.

With a ragged breath, he rammed his big rod all the way up her pussy and grabbed her around her hips, pulling her back to him. His balls brushed her pulled-down panties, which she pulled up tight around the bottom of her ass before letting go, freeing her hands so she could brace herself against Steve's vigorous thrusts.

He slammed into her, crying out softly. "Feels so good—so good. Deep inside you—so hot. Make me come with your tight pussy, Nancy—oh—yeah! Make me come!"

They rocked together on the bed, aware of nothing more than the heat of each other's bodies and an excitement that went so deep they truly did become one. He curved his powerful body over hers, keeping himself up on one arm and reaching between her legs to do her clit. She screamed with pleasure, writhing uncontrollably at the moment of climax as his body shook and he came, too, shouting out her name.

2

Nancy awoke naked, feeling a very gentle breeze move over her skin. She vaguely remembered Steve unzipping the dress and easing her out of it, letting the folds of black velvet fall into a puddle on the floor. Where was it now?

She looked around drowsily and saw it on the back of her bedroom door, on a hanger. The rich material caught the golden light of early afternoon coming through the blinds and the dress almost glowed, even though it was black and every other color in the room was on the bland side. Steve had been right about her needing some excitement and he had sure as hell provided it.

But never mind the dress. Where was he?

She listened and heard him moving around in the bathroom down the hall, and also heard the plaintive meow of Lump, hoping to be let out of the living room so he could get a snack and go back to sleep in the banana bowl.

Steve must have heard him, too. She heard him walk softly down the hall barefoot and turn the creaky knob of the living room door. The Lump shot out, stopped, and wound himself around Steve's ankles, judging by the nice-kitty murmurs Steve was making. Very faintly, she heard the cat purr and then Steve headed back to her. He came through the bedroom door, a towel knotted around his lean hips, freshly showered, his hair wet and spiky. Nancy felt a rush of affection for him and reached out a hand to draw him down to her.

"And how are you?" Steve grinned and sat on the edge of the bed, the towel coming apart to show his cock and balls, nice and clean and damp, and smelling like her soap. She cupped it all, liking the resting softness of male flesh, and looked up at him, still a little sleepy.

"Just fine, thank you. That was fun. Sure beat looking at Photoshopped head shots. I have to let you interrupt me more often."

He rose for a second to pull off the towel, and sat back down next to her. Nancy looked him over, feeling awfully lucky. Bareassed and gorgeous, Steve Karan was just all-around amazing. He scruffed the towel over his wet hair. "I had a good excuse, remember?" He pointed to the dress hanging on the back of the door. "Or maybe I should call it a bribe."

Nancy sat up too, feeling very comfortable being naked with him. "Steve, you didn't buy that dress, did you? Racks is a really expensive store."

"Um, no. I tried to explain that, but your mind was on other things. I sorta borrowed it. On a trial basis. To see if you would like it."

She patted his cheek, feeling a slight scratch of stubble and liking that too. No way would any man in his right mind use a razor a woman had used on her legs. "I did like it. But I'd guess it cost, what, five thousand?"

He shrugged and let the damp towel fall into his lap. "In that neighborhood, yeah."

Nancy planted a big smooch on his cheek. "You're totally sweet. But you have to return it." She looked at the black dress again, feeling a flash of guilt that she hadn't asked that question before she'd let him make love to her while she was wearing it.

She bounded up from the bed and went to the bedroom door, carefully inspecting the dress for any signs of wild sex.

"What are you doing?"

Nancy raised the skirt, looking inside for stains and finding none. "A Monica Lewinsky check."

"I already did. The dress is like new. I was careful. I mean, we could have it dry-cleaned but then I'd have to take the tag off."

She looked for the discreet little tag that she'd tucked down the side before she'd strutted her stuff. There it was. The price wasn't on it but they couldn't return it without that.

"You could keep it," he offered. "I'll find a way to pay for it."

"Nothing doing," she said. "That's, what, two month's salary for you? We could get something like it at a discount store and do whatever we wanted in it."

"I liked the idea of giving you the real thing," he said, a stubborn set to his chin.

She shook her head and let the dress fall from her hands into voluptuous folds. "You're my friend. Friends don't give friends designer dresses." She stroked the material almost lovingly, though, noticing that the June humidity had taken care of every possible wrinkle. It did indeed look like new.

"You're way too practical. And I think we just graduated from friendship to lustship."

Nancy took the few steps between her and the bed and pushed her great, big, naked, gorgeous pal flat on his back. "Yeah." She straddled him, then caught a whiff of her unwashed body, waving it away with one hand. "Whew! I have to shower. You're too clean to mess up."

Steve grabbed her ass. "I like that smell. You and me. Male and female. Hot and juicy."

She laughed. "A little too juicy at the moment." She got off him awkwardly and swabbed his belly with the damp towel. "You don't want to go around smelling like a happy pussy the rest of the day, do you? Don't you have to show up at the precinct?" Another thought occurred to her. "Oh, Jesus—your car. The rookie might get mad and have you towed. What about the meter?"

"Took care of it. I didn't sleep very long. You were out cold, though."

She put her hands on her hips and glared at him. "Were you watching me sleep? Did I drool on the pillow?"

Steve grinned in a lopsided way. "Yes and no."

"I know I drooled."

"Not on me."

She picked up a pillow and looked at it. Nothing on that either. "Hmm. Guess you're telling the truth. I won't have to hit you with this." She did anyway, connecting with a soft whomp. Steve grabbed the pillow, pulling it out of her hand as he rose to enfold her in a hug.

"Not going to say uncle. And I do have to show up but not at the precinct. I have another shoplifting case I'm working on with Jack. Wanna ride along?"

Nancy pondered that. Whatever she had been doing before he showed up with the dress in a box, she couldn't remember. So it could wait. But her practical side reasserted itself. "Isn't that against police rules or something? I don't want to get you in trouble."

He hugged her again. "I won't tell if you won't. Not like I'm going to strap you down in the back like a perp. Sit up front and wear your seatbelt, that's good enough for me." With his hands on her shoulders, he set her back from him. "Hey, you know what? I have a uniform in the back somewhere. Wanna dress up again? That way, if another undercover guy sees me, he'll think you're just out of the academy or something."

"Nancy Roman, rookie cop?" She thought it over for a few seconds, then nodded. "Sure. Why not."

He slapped her bare butt. "Into the shower. Let's get going."

* * *

Two hours later, the day was winding down. The sticky weather made her sweat but the uniform, which was way too small for Steve, was loose on her and that helped. Nancy leaned forward a little in the seat to turn up the air-conditioning, for what it was worth. Steve had to get in and out of the car now and then to talk to his fellow officers. She was getting good at spotting them.

Fred in the homeless-dude overcoat. Marie in the hooker shoes and matching handbag, her gun under the candy-colored condoms. Hank in tourist garb: argyle sweater and plaid pants.

She got to be in charge of the clipboard, making neat notations on crime fighters all over town, doing a fair job of faking his handwriting. He made a left turn into a service road, letting the wheel spin back between his big hands, then wrestling the freaky automatic transmission to get up to speed again.

Nancy didn't have much to do but look at him, and think about . . . well, wow. He'd gone from friendly cop to lover man in the space of a few short hours. She wasn't quite sure how the hell that had happened, but she was more than happy to stay on the ride, however long it lasted.

Just looking at him turned her on—and made her heart beat faster too. As in r-o-ma-n-c-e fast. Steve Karan seemed to be pretty much everything she'd ever wanted in a man, she thought uneasily.

So either he would screw up or she would, sooner or later, she told herself. Nancy didn't trust the word romance, something she felt compelled to spell just to take the emotional charge out of it, let alone the experience of romance.

Love didn't add up. It was an illusion, like other dangerous illusions, such as the pursuit of celebrity. She decided to do elementary math in her head to distract herself from dangerous thought processes that led to overindulgence in premium ice cream and fantasies of happily-ever-afters. Just watching his muscular thighs as he braked, one big hand on the gearshift like he was driving a sportscar instead of a Nondescript, was enough to make her want to watch forever.

An unsecured box of stale doughnuts—was that standard issue, even in an undercover cop car?—shot forward into the well between the front seats. "I'll get 'em when you stop," she said. Steve went through a green light and pulled over, patting her butt as she bent over toward the back. A nice old grandpa shuffling by saw him do it and gave Steve a bespectacled wink and a thumbs-up. Steve grinned back, looking a little sheepish.

"Straighten up, Nancy," he said out of the side of his mouth. "Don't get the senior citizens too excited."

"Then get your hand off my ass." Nancy stuck the spilled doughnuts back in the box with care and fastened a webbed strap around them. "How am I doing?"

"You're doing great. We can give those to the birds, give a few pigeons indigestion, maybe. Want a new job?"

"Nothing gives pigeons indigestion. And I actually like working at home. But I'm having fun today. Thanks for bringing me along."

Steve was preoccupied, having declared his intention to check in with all of his colleagues in the neighborhood before the end of his run. He hummed along to a heavy-metal CD—Nancy didn't know it was possible to hum to heavy metal but he seemed to be doing it—and he looked at her now and then with a smile that got to her emotions in a big, big way.

She smiled back—her best businesslike one—and tucked a fresh sheet of paper under the metal clip, about to mentally list the good things about him and assign each a percent value to write down. Steve didn't have to know what she was doing.

First and foremost he was a nice guy, she thought. A really, really nice guy. She wrote down 50 percent at the top of the page. Hot in bed. Another 50 percent. Nancy sighed. He was already up to 100 percent on her improvised man-o-meter ranking and she had barely begun.

Okay. She would bend the math.

He liked animals, was kind to the Lump. 25 percent. Looked out for his coworkers and buddies even when he was bending the rules a little. 50 percent. Looked good wet, 30 percent. Nancy couldn't say why that was important to her, but it was. She tapped the point of her pencil on the paper, absorbed in what she was doing.

She thought some more. Able to unzip a sleepy woman and get an expensive dress off her without ripping it. 25 percent. Then it occurred to her that he might have practiced that smooth move on someone else, maybe more than one someone else, and she downgraded that rank to 5 percent.

Funny. Smart. Sweet. 35 percent. 35 percent. 35 percent. Healthy. Athletic. 25 percent. 25 percent. Took stairs two at a time. 15 percent. Tall. Nancy hesitated. That was genetic and not something he'd done. But even so. 10 percent. Majorly hung. She smiled inwardly and gave him a solid 25 percent on that.

Sexy. Outrageously sexy. 50 percent.

"What are you doing?"

"Um, crunching numbers."

He patted her thigh and slid his hand higher, giving her an affectionate crotch squeeze. "Crunch on. We're almost there."

"Where?"

"Racks. Want another dress?"

"Now wait a minute—"

Nancy looked around. The tall buildings radiated the heat of the long summer day and shafts of sunlight thrust between them. She could see the converted loft with the Racks sign and got a look at the new window displays. Racks set trends and their bizarre windows usually got reviewed on the arts page.

Blue mannequins, unclothed except for fetish underwear, were doing unspeakable things to each other. A group of fanny-packed, chino-pantsed suburbanites, refugees from a double-decker bus tour of the city, were giggling and taking pictures of each other in front of the windows.

Steve laughed at the sight and turned in to the alley behind the loft. Nancy looked into the back of the car for the long white box. She'd rewrapped the dress in the tissue before they'd left her apartment, checking it carefully for stains one last time. None. More magic? She couldn't say, but the dress was pristine, as if she had never worn it.

When he parked, she reached for the box, waiting until he got down to hand it to him. "What are you going to say?"

He grinned wolfishly. "That I fucked you silly in it."

"No, really."

"That it didn't fit. No biggie. I think it was a sample, actually. They're not going to sell it if it was."

"Oh. Well, then, I don't feel guilty."

He slid the driver's side door open and got out, turning to put his foot up on the running board and take the box from her. He balanced it on his knee. "Nothing to feel guilty about. You in this dress, being as wicked as you wanted to be—I'll never forget it. Although you look just as good in that uniform."

"Aw, shucks. Thanks."

He gave her a serious look. "I mean it. The dress made you look like a goddess, but that's because you are a goddess."

"Not in sweatpants, I'm not. You're totally sweet, but get real." She pointed a pencil at the box. "Bring it back."

He picked the box up again in one swing, and disappeared into the loading-dock area, leaving her alone in the car. Nancy leaned back and looked down at the column of meaningless numbers. So far, Steve Karan had captured about—um—465% of something. The popular vote. As in the instant attention of every woman who walked by him and appreciated the easy way he hoisted heavy boxes and his long strides and—lots of things.

She'd seen him getting not-so-subtle once-overs all day long. What else had he captured? *Your heart*, a little voice said.

Uh-oh. She started a separate column for his bad qualities but couldn't think of any. Of course, their relationship until now had been casually friendly, everybody on their best behavior and so forth. Cops didn't have to be friendly, it wasn't part of their job. Whatever. She bet Steve got hit on all the time. Nancy chewed absently on the eraser end of the pencil, not caring that it tasted terrible.

He came back, hopped into his seat, and slammed the sliding door shut. "Nice girl. All she said was no problem, happy to help, blah blah. It's back on the sample rack and no one even knows it was gone."

Nancy felt a small pang of regret. Not like she could ever wear the black velvet dress anywhere but it would be a great souvenir of sex that had rocked her world. For all she knew, she might never have sex that good without it.

Do not obsess, she told herself sternly. Do not assign magical powers to an inanimate object. If Steve Karan wants you, he wants you. Didn't he just say you look great in a baggy uniform?

He reached toward her. Feeling the first waves of Postcoital Nervous Second-Guessing Syndrome hit her and hit hard, she looked down at her bare thighs and pressed his knees together before he could slide his hand between her legs.

But Steve only wanted to turn her face to him and he did, touching his lips to hers in a tender kiss that was nonetheless passionate. Purely, physically passionate.

Do not interpret this to mean more than it means, she told herself, parting her lips and yielding to the sensual mouth on hers. Tongue tango is a lot of fun. But tonight you'll be sleeping with the Lump. Steve will be heading home to—she wondered where he lived and what his place looked like and whether he had a cat or a roommate or what. She kept right on kissing him. Nancy was expert at multitasking.

Steve pulled back. "Hm. Why do I have the feeling you just weren't into that?"

She scrubbed at her mouth with the back of her hand. "It was nice. I'm tired, I guess."

"Want to go home? I'm done for the day." He looked at her expectantly.

Was he waiting for an invitation? Nancy hesitated before answering.

"Yeah. Gotta feed the cat, do some laundry." She realized how dreary that sounded and put a smile on her face. "Early bedtime for me. I'll make a cup of cocoa and catch a couple of cartoons on Adult Swim." Not exactly sophisticated, but then she didn't have to impress a really, really nice guy like Steve. Which was all part of his incredible charm, goddamn it. How had she missed it in high school? Maybe between him and Jack Ginnis, who was, if anything, cuter, her mind had just shut down.

Nancy wondered what had gotten into her. Just wearing a movie-star dress and being a raunchy sex goddess, demanding and receiving the ultimate in pleasure, hadn't ruined her for ordinary life, had it? Nah. She shouldn't be thinking about doing two guys.

She looked into Steve's soulful brown eyes, trying to read his mind. Despite his average-Joe job, he was anything but ordinary. Something about him made her weak inside. Made her crave more. Her ever-present common sense warned her to take it slow.

"Home," she repeated. Where she could think.

Five months later . . .

I am a woman in love, Nancy thought miserably. Which totally sucks. She tossed and turned in bed, annoying Lump into jumping down and stalking off.

"Tough luck," she said to the tip of his tail before it vanished around the doorjamb with the rest of the cat. She sprawled out on the bed and punched a pillow into the right shape to hide her face and indulge in teenager-style sobs of self-pity. Feeling suffocated, she gave up on that and rolled over on her back, sprawled out even wider.

Being alone sucked even more than being in love. Steve had been assigned to a night shift and he couldn't swing by. He was working extra hours as it was, saving up for Christmas, or so he said.

His mother wanted this, his father needed that. The nieces and nephews in his big Polish American family adored their Uncle Steve, and he was already thinking about a small but good gift for each and every Karan brat, as he called them. He had to be about the most generous guy she'd ever known. And he didn't have all that much to be generous with either, not on an honest cop's salary. Her clients contributed to charities but only because they needed the deductions.

And as far as Nancy was concerned, he gave her everything she wanted. She craved his company, his easygoing sense of humor, his anything-goes attitude in the bedroom—all of him.

Her pussy throbbed with longing. Nancy pressed her thighs closed. Didn't help. She thought about her latest client's disastrous foray onto MySpace. Someone had outed Frank Fabulous as not the college guy he pretended to be and posted his real age. forty-five, not twenty-nine. No new friends for Frank.

As distractions went, it didn't work. She still wanted Steve, right here, in her bed, in her arms. If she could figure out a way to clone him, that would be even better. Two Steves. Or, her bad self whispered, one Steve and one Jack. Shut up, her good self whispered back. You don't even know what he's like now.

The phone rang and she rolled on her belly to answer it, crabbily. "Hello?"

"Hello yourself." A thrill shot through her at the sound of Steve's amused low voice.

"Hi!"

She could hear him grin. "That's better. A little enthusiasm is always nice."

"I wasn't expecting it to be you, Steve."

"Who were you expecting?"

"At this hour—I don't know. Just didn't think it would be you. How's work?"

He chuckled. "Got about an hour here between shifts, went out to my car. Just thought I'd call you. I know you haven't been fucked silly for way too long, so I was thinking . . . how about a little phone sex?"

She drew in her breath. "You're not going to, like, do yourself in the parking lot, right?"

"No. This is just for you."

Nancy unstuck her thighs. Trying to control her horniness by pressing them together wasn't a good idea. "Wow. Okay. But—um—I wouldn't know where to begin."

He laughed. "Just tell me what you want me to do to you. I'll take it from there."

"What is this, Steve Karan's Bedtime Story Hour?"

"Something like that."

Nancy relaxed and wriggled her hips into a comfortable position. Just listening to his low voice in the dark made her hot. "I want you to . . ."

"Don't be shy. Nobody's listening. You know you can tell me anything."

"I want you to come in the bedroom when I'm half asleep," she began, "and I'm naked under the covers. And . . . you're not alone."

"Oh, yeah?"

"Yeah."

"Is this like a threesome fantasy?"

Nancy sucked in her breath. "Yes."

"Huh." He sounded amused. "Anyone I know?"

Should she tell him? Nancy took a deep breath.

"Don't get mad, okay? Or jealous."

"I won't. Just tell me."

"You come in with . . . Jack."

"Jack Ginnis?"

"Didn't you say you two used to hang in the ivy on the gym wall to try to get a glimpse of me?"

"Uh, yeah. Until he broke his ankle."

Nancy giggled. "You never told me that."

"I wrote your initials on his cast with black marker."

"You two were that into me?"

Steve harrumphed. "Well, yeah."

"Then I picked the right guy for a fantasy threesome."

"I see your reasoning."

"Okay. You two come in. Then you sit down by me and put your hand on top of the covers to rub my back and my butt. I move a little but don't wake up. The smooth warm sheet slides over my skin, and it's your hand that's making it happen."

"Mm-hm."

If only he was doing that to her right now, Nancy thought wistfully. Well, in a way he was, so there was no point in wishing he was actually here. Emotionally he was. He understood that she was lonely and frustrated without her having to whine about it.

"And then . . ."

"Go on."

"You concentrate on my behind. Stroking and squeezing each cheek. Using both hands. But I'm still under the covers. What you're doing is getting me hot. I wake up a little more and you push the blankets down to my waist, keeping me cuddled up. You show off my naked ass to Jack."

"You're getting me hot," he said softly, a heavy longing in his voice.

Nancy smiled into the receiver. "Good."

"Now what?"

"I push up on my elbows so you can reach around and feel my tits. They're super-warm because I've been lying on my front and having you fondle them feels really good. You start tugging on my nipples and I arch up to let you. Then you start rubbing my ass with your other hand, sliding the blanket and sheets around. I love having my breasts and behind stroked at the same time. Jack says you are a dirty dog and a lucky duck, and he laughs a little. His voice is kinda growly—and just knowing he's watching you handle me makes me kinda shameless."

Steve gave a long sigh and didn't say anything.

"You bend over to start kissing my bare back and push my hair aside to kiss the nape of my neck. I'm still arched up, loving what you're doing to me. Loving you."

"Do you, Nancy?" he said softly.

"You know I do."

She heard him smile again. "Go on."

"Then you pull the covers all the way down and bare my ass. Tell me how soft it is and how much you want to look at me on all fours. Let your best friend admire me. You take your time. You're good at that, Steve."

"Maybe too good."

"You roll me over on my back and treat me to a long session of nipple-sucking. I try to touch my pussy because I'm getting hot but you won't let me. You grab my wrists and keep my hands together above my head, and really do my nipples, until I almost can't stand it. Jack's looking on. He's got his zipper down and his cock out, and he's stroking it, tight and hard."

"Do the same, angel. Touch yourself. I can't stop you."

Nancy's voice dropped to a whisper. "I don't want to. I'm not ready yet. I want to wait. I want you to make me wait and not rush anything. It gets really intense that way."

"Yeah."

His disembodied voice, saying that single word so softly,

made her dripping wet. Nancy could feel the moisture on her thighs but she kept her hands away from her swollen labia.

"You roll me back over my belly and tell me to put a pillow between my legs."

"Do it."

She shook her head, even though she knew he couldn't see her. "Not yet."

"Okay, talk about it some more."

"You want me to confide in you, tell you a really wild fantasy while you stare down at me riding that firm pillow, holding it between my thighs. I talk and talk . . . about wanting you . . . and wanting Jack to watch us fuck. And I get into what I do in private to satisfy myself sexually when you're not around. You tell me to go ahead and rub and lay your hands on my soft asscheeks so you can feel me clench them . . . as I begin to lose control. Up and down. Around and down. I get to work my hot pussy and you get to watch."

"Yeah. Oh, yeah."

She breathed into the phone, imagining the size of his erection. He had to be about to break a zipper.

"Then you pull out the pillow, really fast, and take it away. I turn over, about to object, but you're ready. Your cock is out and you put it near my lips, because you know I'll open right up and suck you hard."

Steve moaned. She had him with that bit. Nancy grinned and licked her lips. "So I do."

"Most of the way in. So you're comfortable."

"I press my tongue against the front of the shaft and swirl it around to under the head. And repeat that, until you have to get your fingers tightly around your cock to keep from ramming it into my mouth, you're so turned on.

"I lick your fingers, too, and suck you like a porn star. Hard and pulsing. You gasp and pull out, go for a condom. I lie back, pleased with myself for getting you that hot."

He didn't answer.

"Steve?"

"Still here. Losing my mind. Not touching myself. But I hope you are."

She slid a hand between her legs and kept the receiver cradled between her ear and her shoulder. "Yeah, I am. And I am so slick and tight, you wouldn't believe it. So swollen, Steve. Waiting for you. I have my legs spread really, really wide. And I'm watching you struggle to slide a condom over your huge, stiff cock. That one breaks and you swear. I don't care, because I get to watch you do it a second time. I love to watch a man handle his cock and balls, absolutely love it."

He didn't reply.

"What are you doing right now, Steve?"

"Making a list. One item. Condoms."

"All right. You get the second one and get over me on the bed, pushing my legs even farther apart. Then you kneel and put your hot tongue where it feels best, penetrating my pussy with it. I lift my thighs up and hold myself open to get more and more. You're making me cry, it feels so good. Jack is groaning, still stroking himself."

"Then you move your mouth a little higher and suck my clit. It's a weird feeling, almost too intense. I get my hands in your hair and make you stop. Pull you up to me so you can kiss me. So I can taste my pussy all over your mouth."

"Oh, God," he murmured.

"You can't stop now—"

"Get that thing," he interrupted her.

"What thing?"

"That dildo we had so much fun with. Put it in. I want to know that your pussy is totally filled when you start coming so you're completely satisfied. I have to go without but you don't."

"Okay. Hang on." She put down the phone receiver and

looked in two of the nightstand drawers before she found it. He'd bought it in a sex shop when she dared him to go in, and like he said, they'd had a lot of fun with it, even given it a name. The Boyfriend. No matter what, he believed a woman should be pleasured in every possible place and he only had one cock.

Nancy picked up the receiver. "Got it."

"Good. Lube it."

"Don't need to, Steve."

"Okay. Lie back in the pillows and hold it right outside your pussy, so you can feel the head but don't put it in. I'm over you and you're waiting to feel the first thrust."

"I want you so much, Steve. I wish you were here."

"I know. You ready, angel?"

"Uh-huh," she whimpered.

"Now. Do it."

Nancy thrust the dildo she was clutching deep inside her, moaning, wishing his mouth was covering hers and moaning, too.

"Yeah. I'm in you, fucking you hard but not fast. A slow thrust in with clit pressure at the end. And slow reverse while you writhe. I keep on doing it. Use the dildo just like that. And now . . . I want you to take Jack's cock in your mouth. "

Nancy lost the receiver in the sheets for a few lust-crazed minutes but she figured he would understand. She thrust the sex toy into herself, extremely stimulated knowing that he was listening to her very real moans, and had a huge hard-on he couldn't do anything about. She rolled over onto the phone and heard it beep, then grabbed it. "You still there?" she whispered.

"Yeah. Figured you lost the phone. Good. Still have that thing rammed up you?"

"Mm-hm." Her voice sounded far away to her own ears, shaky with unfulfilled desire.

"Hold it in and sit up on your thighs. Use the bed to keep it in. Like we changed places and I'm on the bottom and you're riding me."

Nancy obeyed.

"Now rub your clit. Get the Boyfriend exactly as deep as you want it. Imagine Jack in your mouth and me in your pussy, giving it to you good. You're so hot you need two men to satisfy you. Now put the goddamn phone down."

She did but carefully, wanting him to hear her orgasm. Nancy got her clit between her fingers and stroked it, increasing the pressure and speed until she was moaning again. With the big dildo deep inside her, with the sensation of Steve's presence in the dark, quiet room, she knew it wouldn't be long before she came.

Aching with longing, she touched herself just as lovingly and expertly as he did, and curled over when a powerful climax rocked her body. She pushed her pussy down on the dildo, crying out again and again, calling his name. Then she collapsed and fumbled for the phone, leaving the boyfriend he'd bought for her inside her throbbing flesh.

"Nice," he said softly.

"Oh, Steve. That was amazing. No matter what, you do it to me. You don't even have to be in the room."

"I wouldn't take it that far. I think I can get out of here before dawn."

"Mmm," she murmured drowsily. "I hope so."

"Go to sleep, beautiful. And when I come in, I'm going to do exactly what you just told me. Step by step. I remember every word you said." He blew a soft kiss into her ear and hung up.

For a little while, Nancy slept. And when Steve finally did come in, Jack was with him.

"Still want to do two guys?" Steve asked softly.

She stared at him, then looked at Jack. Then she nodded.

"Dreams do come true," Jack said.

"On all fours," Steve said. And they took her to heaven two times over.

3

Christmas was three weeks away and Nancy was already tired. Her clients regifted her with weird sweaters that didn't fit and Sausage-N-Cheese Combo Pax that had circled the globe more often than fruitcake. For some reason, creative types, when flush with cash, tended to squander it on dubious investments: shares in Patagonian llama ranches and chicken-nugget-restaurant stocks and things like that, and there wasn't a penny left over for their hardworking publicist. Not even a tax-deductible, business-expense-type penny.

After years of scraping by, Nancy had a feeling that the best way to save money was not to spend it in the first place, especially around the holidays. But she knew that Steve—sweet, generous Steve, her own personal sex god—loved Christmas and would go all out. He had dragged himself out of bed by noon, the equivalent of dawn for a night-shift worker, and gone out to find the perfect tree.

Therefore, she had to find him a truly great present. But what did you give a guy who truly didn't care a whole hell of a lot about material things? Who was so unselfish that he'd fulfilled her wickedest fantasy, even if it meant letting his best friend see her naked? Steve hadn't seemed to mind when Jack Ginnis decided to move to Florida. Nancy got the idea.

Once was enough.

The question of what to give him wasn't easily answered. She finally decided to trust fate and follow whatever called to her. So far she had been called to a deluxe athletic-wear store, where she had contemplated buying state-of-the-art footwear with space-spring soles to replace his beloved but very scuffed sneakers.

But he loved those sneakers.

Next, she'd gone into an audio equipment store with the interesting name of Bang & Olufsen. Apparently buying their high-end goods was supposed to be akin to a religious experience, not retail. Nancy decided that God didn't want her to spend a month's salary on speakers for a guy who'd blow them out listening to heavy metal anyway.

That left something sexy. She wasn't going to wrap herself up with a bow and a tag that said ho-ho-ho, although he probably wouldn't mind. He could have her anytime, without the wrapping paper, and she didn't want him to think she was too cheap to buy an actual gift.

As to what he was giving her, Steve wasn't saying. Not dropping the most infinitesimal hint.

Nancy closed the spreadsheet file on her computer when her cat strolled in front of the monitor. "Hello. You hungry again?"

He meowed. The Lump was always hungry. She had an irrational notion that he was capable of eating the bananas, peel and all, just so he could fill his furry belly and go to sleep in the bowl.

Leaving him sitting on her desk, she got up and went into the kitchen, rattling the box of cat food to get him to follow. He appeared a few seconds later, and she dropped a few crunchy bites into his dish, just for form's sake.

Then she made herself a cup of tea, cinnamon apple something that smelled vaguely Christmassy, and sat down to think. The black velvet dress came to mind. But she couldn't buy that for him when it really was for her.

And besides, he'd said it wasn't really for sale. Nancy sipped her tea, letting the warmth and spicy smell clear her mind. Actually, he had been a little vague about that dress from the beginning and some of the things he'd said about it hadn't made much sense. A pricey store like Racks wouldn't hand an expensive dress to an honest cop, even if it was a sample, even if he had brought shoplifters to justice.

Jeez, maybe she should have been brave enough to buy it, even though she hadn't wanted him to blow that much on it, back when they hardly knew each other. As grown-ups, that is.

She finished her tea, feeling refreshed but well aware that she still didn't know what to get him for Christmas.

The sound of thundering feet in boots coming up the stairs snapped her out of her reverie. Steve was back. There was a rustly sound—pine branches—in the hall, followed by a thump as he set down the sawed-off trunk. Nancy opened the door. The tree was taller than he was. Steve peered around the side, grinning. "Just got back from the frozen North." There were pine needles in his hair and pine needles stuck in the wool of his plaid jacket. "Whaddya think? Not big enough?"

"Bring it in. With the star and the base, it's going to touch the ceiling."

"All right," he said with evident satisfaction. He pinched the needles to release their cold, sharp fragrance. "Nice and fresh. Hope you like it."

"I love it. Our first Christmas. Jeez. Hang on while I get the camera." She went down the hall, trying to remember where she put it.

He dragged the tree in, holding onto the trunk with a leather-gloved hand. "What for? It isn't decorated."

"I want to get a picture of you with it," she called from the living room. "All lumberjacked up and looking cute."

He stood it up when she came back, looking brawny and sexy and sweet enough to make her swallow the sentimental tears that made her a little misty. She squinted at the little digital screen and tried to get him and the tree into the frame. "Smile," was all she said.

Christmas Eve . . .

They'd visited his parents. Her parents. His brothers. Her college friends. They'd wrapped and shopped and wrapped and shopped. Nancy had given in at last and gone to Racks to see if she could find the black velvet dress. No one there even knew what she was talking about. She'd resigned herself to getting him a big, fat gift certificate to an electronics store so he could pick out the laptop he'd been talking about.

Not very imaginative, but what else could she do? A really good laptop was the best present she could come up with at the last minute, and she knew he would love it. She'd tucked a black velvet thong for herself and for him into his stocking, along with a Matchbox car and candy canes.

They collapsed on the sofa and looked at the Christmas tree they'd decorated together. Steve had found about a million ornaments in the basement of his parents' house and brought them over, carefully hanging every single one once they'd got the tree to stand up straight. She almost couldn't see the needles under the decorations. The tree sparkled richly and the big colored lights made her think of childhood Christmases, before everything got so damn tasteful and into white wicker reindeer that nodded electronically.

Steve poured himself a shot of single malt from the very expensive bottle his brother had solemnly presented to him. Nancy had been pleased to see that Steve had given Stanislaus the same thing. They did it every year. So maybe he wouldn't mind that her present for him wasn't so imaginative.

He sipped it, savoring the flavor. The Lump jumped up on the coffee table and sniffed the glass in Steve's hand, widening his golden eyes when the fumes went up his nose.

"It's whiskey, Lump. Have some. Good for your whiskers." The cat shook his head, not liking the fumes, and Steve laughed. "Look at that. He's a teetotaler." He scratched the cat between the ears and got him purring. The Lump settled down next to him as he sipped and watched Nancy put back an ornament that had fallen off. "Ahh. Doesn't get any cozier than this."

"Nope." She was feeling wonderful, absolutely wonderful. Being alone with him at last and looking forward to sharing breakfast in bed with him on Christmas morning was bliss, pure and simple.

"When do you want to open presents? Now or in the morning?" He didn't wait for an answer. "I'm a now kind of guy myself."

"And why is that not a surprise?" Nancy's voice was gently teasing.

"Well, I got you something really good."

Her heart sank a little. "Oh, my."

"Go ahead." He leaned back with the shot glass in his hand and gestured to a long white box under the tree. Nancy looked at it with surprise. She could swear it hadn't been there when they'd left earlier in the evening.

"That isn't . . ."

He was humming to himself, trying to look nonchalant. Much as she loved the guy, he couldn't carry a tune. Could be Metallica, could be a Christmas carol, there was no telling.

Nancy crouched under the tree and pulled out the box. "You didn't."

"I did."

"You spent way too much money."

"My sales associate friend gets an employee discount. I'm not completely crazy. Except about you."

Nancy was too blown away to reply. Or meet his loving look. She ran a fingernail down the tape that sealed the box and opened the top flaps. There was the tissue paper, neatly folded, and there was the Racks label, gold and gleaming. And there was the black velvet dress.

"Take it out. Put it on. Christmas comes but once a year."

She left the room and came back wearing it. Steve's eyes lit up. "Yeah," he said with feeling. "Come sit in my lap." He grabbed her hand and pulled her down to him, making her laugh. The cat meowed a faint protest until Steve turned to him. "Hey, kitty, I heard they're serving free mice in the kitchen. And three's a crowd."

Lump stayed put until Steve put a hand under him and scooped him off the sofa. The cat stalked out.

And then the fun began.

Turn the page for a preview of
Delilah Devlin's devilish story,
"The Demon Lord's Cloak,"
in DAMNED, DELICIOUS, AND DANGEROUS!

On sale now!

Prologue

"We'll all be dead by morning." Martin's voice quavered as he emptied another glass of Frau Sophie's precious peach schnapps.

"Who'd have guessed it'd be nigh onto impossible to find a virgin in this valley?" his companion said.

"Pah! Even my own daughter," Martin moaned. "What's the world coming to, Edgard? Young women giving themselves like barmaids . . ."

Edgard's shoulders slumped. "I tell you it was the last May Day celebration. The bürgermeister should never have let Sophie provide the drink."

"We should have locked every last one of the unmarried maidens in a cellar. Well, no use grousing." Martin set down his glass. "We have a problem. Now's the time for clear thinking."

"There's no solution. The village will disappear, swallowed by Hell itself when we fail to provide *his* bride." Edgard's reddened eyes widened. "Couldn't we mount a raid on Fulkenstein down the valley . . . take a girl or two . . ."

"There's no time left. We only had the new moon to give

that devil his due. It ends tomorrow night. We'd never be back in time."

Edgard shook his head, sighing. "We've failed. Daemonberg will be no more. Best get the women packing tonight so we can flee come morning. A thousand years of prosperity and health—gone for the lack of a single maidenhead."

"We're doomed, I tell you." Martin lifted the schnapps bottle and tilted it over his glass. He gave it a shake, and then slammed it down on the table. Turning toward the bar, he shouted, "Sophie, *liebchen*, bring us another bottle, will you?"

As he turned back to his friend, he saw a woman step through the doorway of the inn. Her beauty arrested him: far prettier than any of the strapping blond women of the village, this one was slender and delicate, with deep reddish hair that glinted like fire in the torchlight, reminding him of the bay he'd bid on and lost at an auction in early spring.

He elbowed Edgard beside him. "Look there."

Both men turned to stare at the young woman.

"Where's her escort?" Edgard whispered.

"She looks wary. I'd wager she's on her own."

They shared a charged glance, shoulders straightening.

"What do you suppose the chances are she's a virgin?" Edgard asked softly.

"She's beyond fair. What man would care whether he was her first just so long as he's her last? Besides, what other options have we?"

Sophie slammed another bottle in the center of the table and gave them a scathing glance. "If you go home to your wives legless with drink, I'll not take the blame."

"We'll have just one more glass," Martin assured her, reaching around to pat her rump. "For the road. We've business to attend."

Sophie rolled her eyes and turned, her ample hips rolling as she walked across the room to greet the young woman who waved her away.

"If they only knew the solemn duty we perform," Martin whispered. "They'd call us heroes."

Only, Martin and Edgard could never tell a soul. That, too, was part of their sacred oath, handed down from father to son.

Edgard poured them both another drink, then lifted his glass. "To another hundred years of peace and wealth."

Martin lifted his glass with one hand and crossed himself with the other. "To the fair maiden with the red hair—God rest her soul."

1

Voletta felt faint with alarm; her stomach was in knots. *I can't have lost it. Someone must know where it is!*

But what were the chances anyone here would just give it back to her? She didn't have any gold to offer as a reward for its return. She'd already had to steal the voluminous cloak she wore so she wouldn't walk naked into their midst.

She stepped farther into the entryway.

"Hullo, Miss," an elderly gentleman said as he approached, his avid gaze sliding over her hair.

She clutched the edges of the cloak, only too aware its thick folds hid her nudity. "Good evening, sir."

"You're a stranger here."

Her nose twitched at the sour smell of liquor and unwashed skin that emanated from him. Not many men believed in the value of a thorough cleansing.

If only she hadn't been so fastidious herself, she might never have paused beside the gurgling brook, then noted the thick green curtain of foliage that rendered the glade an irresistible temptation.

"Miss, are you looking for someone?" he asked, his gaze looking beyond her shoulder furtively.

She took a deep breath. How to explain? "I lost something."

"Yes?" he said quickly. "Perhaps we can help you find it. Why don't you come have a seat? Can I take your cloak?"

"No! I'm chilled. And I won't be staying long. I've just come to make an inquiry."

"Come along, now," he cajoled. "You must join my friend, Edgard, and myself. I am Martin, by the way. I promise we are as harmless as we are hospitable. We might even be able to help."

The old fellow seemed a friendly sort, although she didn't feel quite comfortable with the way his gaze kept searching her face.

"Come, come. You seem overset. Have a wee drink with us—just to warm you up. Then we'll help you find whatever you've lost."

Unused to talking to men, to anyone for any length, really, she tried to demur. "I shouldn't. I must keep looking."

A frown drew his thick peppered brows together, then quickly faded as he smiled once again. "What is it you've lost?"

She nibbled her bottom lip, then blurted, "My fur. I've lost my fox fur."

"A fox fur, you say?" His glance slid away, and his gnarled fingers scratched his head. "Was it part of a garment?"

"No . . . not yet. It was . . . a gift. I need it back."

"Come along. Edgard purchases furs. Although one fur is hardly distinguishable from another."

"Oh, mine was unique," she murmured.

She let him lead her to a table at the rear of the establishment. Another man stood, younger than his companion, with a large, round belly and ruddy cheeks. He drew up a chair and indicated that she should sit.

"No," Voletta said, holding out a hand. "I really should be on my way."

"But your fur . . ." the elderly man began.

Each passing moment deepened her unease. "I'm sure I just missed it in the darkness. I'll retrace my steps."

"A fur, did you say?" the fat man said, giving a pointed glare at his companion. "Where did you leave it?"

"Beside a brook. I put it down for only a moment."

"Today?"

"Yes, just before dark."

His gaze sharpened. "A fine fur, was it? Unblemished by any trap's teeth?"

"Of course!" she said, feeling hope at the man's brightening expression.

"And red as your hair, miss?"

"Yes, as a matter of fact, it is."

"I saw just such a fur. The bürgermeister brought it to me. My wife is even now sewing it onto a fine cloak."

"Sewing it?" she asked, pressing her hand to her belly.

"Yes, as part of the dowry for a nobleman's bride."

Voletta reached for the man's arm. "I must have it back."

The heavy man dropped his gaze to her hand, then reached up slowly to pat it. "And you shall. We will go to my shop in a moment. Would you have a drink with us first?"

Relief made her lightheaded, and she nodded. "But quickly, please."

"Of course. Don't fret yourself."

Voletta accepted the beaker the older man handed her and took only a sip, then set her glass on the table. "Sir, I apologize for rushing you, but could we please go retrieve my fur?"

"Of course." He stared expectantly. "How are you feeling?"

Voletta shook her head. "Fine, can we go now?" Only she didn't feel fine. Her head swam. The men before her seemed to teeter and stretch. "How odd," she said, her voice sounding to her own ears as though it rose from the bottom of a deep well.

"Best get her out of here, Edgard, before she topples."

"Come, miss. You wanted to see my shop?"

She tugged at the collar of her cloak. "S'warm."

"Catch her!"

"Seems a shame. A beautiful girl like her."

The voice, Edgard's, she remembered, came from right be-side her.

"Just get the trunk off the cart," Martin whispered harshly.

Voletta tried to lift her head, but the movement made her nauseous. She pried open her eyelids and found herself looking down at a rutted track. Graying daylight stabbed like tiny daggers at the backs of her eyes.

The air around her was damp and cold. Her skin prickled—she was naked! A fog had rolled in, droplets catching on her breasts and cheeks. The bastards had taken her cloak!

She forced up her head and stared after the men riding atop a cart rolling down a long, steep trail. Then she noticed other things: her hands were tied behind her; a rope was wound around her waist to keep her upright against a pole.

She pulled at the ropes around her wrists, to no avail. Should she call out? Naked, she felt terribly vulnerable . . . *human*.

Then she heard a sound . . . soft, measured footfalls.

In front of her a shadowy form appeared beyond a dark iron gate at the end of the trail. The outline of the figure shimmered, then solidified before her widening gaze. She blinked. Maybe the apparition had just been a floating tendril of fog that had given her that impression.

The fog cleared for a moment to reveal the imposing figure of a man.

Voletta's breath caught. The man stood still, only feet away, his hard-edged face devoid of emotion, his lips drawn into a thin line.

He was tall, his shoulders broad, his hair and eyes black as midnight. The cotte and chausses he wore were equally dark, unrelieved by any embroidery or a bright cuff. He lifted his hands, pushed open the gate, and stepped through it.

"Please," she whispered, "untie me."

"I shall," he replied, his voice deep and ragged, as though rusty from disuse.

He stepped behind her, and his fingers glanced against her wrists. The ropes fell away.

Voletta turned, ready to flee down the rough trail, but his hand snagged her wrist. Alarmed, she gazed back.

"You don't understand," he said slowly. "I know you are frightened, but you must come with me. You are mine, now."

She tugged her hand, hard, but his fingers wrapped tighter around her wrist, and he started to walk back through the gate.

Digging her heels into the ground, she said, "You must release me. Those men kidnapped me. I'm not supposed to be here. I can't belong to you."

Silence greeted her outcry, and he forged onward, forcing her to walk behind him or fall to her knees.

"I'm expected. My family will be looking for me," she lied, shortening her steps only to stumble when he walked faster. He was strong; his fingers banded her wrist like steel. She tried to pry them away, but his grip bit into her flesh, and she gasped.

"You only harm yourself," he said, his voice as devoid of softness as his clothing and his face.

"I beg your pardon, but you are the one dragging me, sir," she bit out.

He shot a glance over his shoulder. His eyes peered at her, curiosity easing his dour expression. "Don't you fear me?"

"Of course not," she said automatically, but then realized it was true. She didn't fear him, *exactly*, but she was wary, and growing increasingly so the further into his demesne they went.

The man grunted and turned away, tugging her behind him.

They continued along, lush grass giving way to slick cobblestones. Above her stretched a tall, imposing keep made of large gray stones. Two menacing towers stood watch at the ends of a long wall. A portcullis, its gate raised, loomed like a great, toothed maw.

Voletta shivered, and her alarm caused her heart to thud loudly in her chest the closer they approached. Despite her creeping trepidation, details began to niggle. No heads appeared above the crenellated curtain wall. No gatekeeper greeted them inside the portcullis. In fact, no one appeared to be inside the bailey as they entered.

And yet, everything was perfectly attended. The cobblestones were clear of falling leaves; the grass beyond the cobblestone was perfectly manicured; the iron chain that lifted the portcullis gleamed with oil. As she stared behind her, the gear that lowered the gate began to move and creak, and yet no one stood beside it to work the mechanism.

Again the fog licked in front of her, and, in the mist, she saw the outline of a ghostly figure leaning over the lever he turned.

Cold, afraid now, Voletta quivered, her knees shaking so badly she stumbled behind him and landed on her knees at last.

The dark man halted, his back to her, his hand still clasping her wrist. A sigh escaped him, and he turned. Bending over her, he pushed away her outstretched hands and lifted her into his arms.

Voletta had been close to a man a time or two—had felt the hardness of their muscular bodies pressed to hers, had breathed their hot breath and inhaled the musky scent of them. They'd been pleasant to touch, delicious to kiss.

They'd also been easy to evade when their caresses grew too intimate, too unnerving.

With this one, however, she sensed strength beyond the tensile muscles that held her easily to his chest. His square jaw and straight lips spoke of an inner will that would brook no arguments.

He held her naked, completely vulnerable to his will. That

she wasn't squirming, fighting tooth and nail for her freedom, shocked her—and deepened the shivers that pricked her nipples into tight buds.

She had to find the cloak with her special fur, and quickly. This man tempted her to linger and discover just what belonging to him entailed. Voletta guessed his possession would be a carnal form of enslavement. For what woman wouldn't be drawn by his rugged form and fierce, enigmatic gaze?

However, she'd managed to escape manly lures for a very long time. No matter the fascinating package, she'd just as soon flee before she saw him fully unwrapped!

She'd heard the men talking. Her fox's fur had been sewn onto a cloak for a nobleman. This nobleman, she had no doubt. It must rest in the trunk they'd dropped on the trail outside the gate.

"You've left the trunk behind," she said, in a small voice, not wanting to let him see how much it meant, and certainly not wanting to draw his gaze downward. The thought of him staring closely at her body heated her skin.

"The trunk does not concern you," he murmured, sounding not the least winded by carrying her so far.

"But it contains things that belong to me."

"I will provide all that you need."

Her legs squeezed together. He hadn't purred, hadn't injected a hint of heat into his voice, but his low, growling words still scraped her nerves raw. "That's so arrogant! What if there is something that means the world to me inside that trunk?"

He halted on the steps leading into the keep and stared into her eyes. "From this day, I will be your world, your only companion, your only lover."

A shudder racked her body. He'd said it so intently, as though making her a promise.

A sudden fullness choked her throat. She read steely determination in his eyes, yet at the same time, she detected a hint of vulnerability beneath that hard gaze. The yearning she sensed pulled her, and she drew back. This man could make her question her need to escape.

Voletta knew in that moment he would never willingly let her go—and part of her, the weak and feminine dimension of her being, was grateful he intended to remove the choice.